How to Marry a Duke

The Cinderella Society, Book Two

Alyxandra Harvey

ARE YOU SIGNED UP FOR DRAGONBLADE'S BLOG?

You'll get the latest news and information on exclusive giveaways, exclusive excerpts, coming releases, sales, free books, cover reveals and more.

Check out our complete list of authors, too!

No spam, no junk. That's a promise!

Sign Up Here

www.dragonbladepublishing.com

Dearest Reader;

Thank you for your support of a small press. At Dragonblade Publishing, we strive to bring you the highest quality Historical Romance from some of the best authors in the business. Without your support, there is no 'us', so we sincerely hope you adore these stories and find some new favorite authors along the way.

Happy Reading!

CEO, Dragonblade Publishing

For my mother, who loved romance novels and art.

Chapter One

FOR A VISCOUNT'S daughter, Meg Swift really was quite good at stealing things.

Not the hearts of enamored gentlemen—as the novels would have you believe—but proper things. *Useful* things. What did she want with a heart, after all? Messy business all around. No, she preferred stockings. Ribbons. Soap. And sweets.

So many sweets. Once, an entire tea cake with a lurid orange fondant frosting in the shape of marigolds. She knew to carry a large reticule with her, especially to breakfast where guests were groggy and fully consumed with acquiring a strong cup of tea. She knew to avoid sticky buns as they always left an oily smear on her reticule—a dead giveaway. The main trick was never to take too much at any one time. Rock candies were the easiest, as were bread rolls. Blancmange was impossible. Though she sometimes wanted to test herself and the wobbly decorated jelly pudding would make a decent adversary.

Meg only stole from fancy dining rooms in even fancier houses—never from the shops. Not only did she not have any particular wish to be hanged, but shopkeepers would miss their wares. The Duke of Pendleton wouldn't miss gilded almonds. She could have stolen a mouthful of pudding right off his spoon and he wouldn't have missed it. No one would have.

Until now.

This ought to have been child's play. Her godfather, the very same duke, was hosting a ball for his many goddaughters. Well, his *unmarried* ones, anyway. It wasn't especially subtle. In fact, it had already earned the nickname of "The Cinderella Ball", which was mildly mortifying. But he was a good man who only wanted to see his goddaughters happy and safe and so she agreed to attend. Not to mention that any excuse to get away from her uncle was a good excuse. And she was certain her friends Tamsin and Priya would have hopped into a carriage to fetch her otherwise. By the ear, if needed. As would have Persephone, if she wasn't currently traveling through Egypt on her honeymoon. She had sent the duke an envelope full of sand which he'd promptly put on display in a gold box.

Music swelled from behind a screen which Meg had painted with river nymphs for the duke's last birthday. The friezes she had done more recently for the duke's Festival of Antiquaries watched her from the walls. Romans in their white chitons, Zeus watching from the ceiling, thunderbolts in hand. Across the parquet floor freshly painted with the Pendleton family crest, lay Ancient Egypt: papyrus fields, the pyramids, ladies with kohl around their eyes. Persephone, more than a trifle obsessed with Egypt, had insisted Meg use real kohl.

Tonight, the rest of the decorations were rather restrained for a man with a life-sized statue of the jackal-headed Egyptian death god in his breakfast parlor. Beeswax candles burned in tiered crystal chandeliers, sweetening the air along with a cheerful riot of flowers spilling from vases, balconies, and wall sconces. Dancers whirled like dandelion seeds blown about a summer field. Champagne flowed like the Nile.

It should have been perfect.

It was late enough in the evening that no one paid her any mind as she made her way to the buffet tables. They were piled blue Wedgewood filled with cheeses, tarts, rosewater custards, chocolate truffles, grapefruit ices in delicate teacups. And bowls of gilded almonds. Not just bowls, but veritable troughs. She knew several children who would be thrilled to their toes to eat gold. And best of all, almonds wouldn't spoil. There were days yet before she had to return home, and she hated to go back empty handed.

Despite the abrupt attention of a man at the other end of the table.

He leaned against the wall, more darkly handsome than he had any right to be. He attracted attention. Which was unhelpful.

And he was looking straight at her.

Also unhelpful.

She shifted slightly so that the impressive marzipan peacock sculpture blocked her hands. There was no reason for him to notice her. She looked like every other lady in attendance, with pearl pins in her hair and a white ballgown. Hers was trimmed with a considerable amount of embroidery, to be sure. But she liked to embroider. It was brilliant at hiding worn spots in gowns four years out of fashion.

The man wore the same sort of evening wear as the other gentlemen, only with far less gilt and decoration. Maybe he thought it made him blend in as she did, but it did the exact opposite. There was nothing to detract from the edge of his jaw, the slash of his eyebrows. The kindness to his mouth. Even his waistcoat was plain, no embroidery at all, not even gold buttons. But it was such a beautiful shade of blue that she longed to capture it with her paints. It was the summer sky at twilight, just before everything turned to shadow. He had none of the languid ennui of the others; his was the boredom of someone who wanted to be *doing* things. It sizzled under the stunning lines of his coat and cravat. It sizzled in his eyes, the same blue as his waistcoat.

Several ladies murmured to each other nearby, watching him but not yet approaching. Diamonds flashed around their necks. Good. Let him be distracted. With any luck, he hadn't actually seen her filch the almonds. He could have glanced in her direction for any number of reasons.

His single raised eyebrow said otherwise.

Blast.

"Are you *still* eating?" Tamsin asked, suddenly at her elbow, grinning. "Honestly, I don't know how you're not as round as a hedgehog."

Tamsin was the daughter of a duke and could say pretty much what she liked whenever she liked. Mind you, she would have done the same as the daughter of a fishmonger. Tamsin was Tamsin: beautiful, clever, and with a morbid curiosity she camouflaged with a sunny smile. No one else, lady or gentleman, could have filled a London townhouse with artifacts ranging from tarot cards to a scrying mirror reputed to have belonged to Queen Elizabeth's sorcerer John Dee.

"Why aren't you dancing?" Tamsin asked. She wore a gown of green sarsenet, with emeralds in her hair and around her throat. She spooned up a mouthful of grapefruit ice.

"Because Pendleton is watching," Meg remarked. "And he's likely to make the first gentleman who asks marry me on the spot."

"You only dance with married men who have no interest in you," Tamsin scoffed. She was quite correct. When one had no dowry, there was no sense in playing the game. No offers would come and if she flirted, her reputation might suffer. If her reputation suffered, she wouldn't be able to get the things she needed to get done, done. It was that simple.

"Pendleton is not the only one watching you," Tamsin said, mischievously. "So is the Duke of Thorncroft."

"Is he here? I've never met him."

"He's just there, leaning against the wall while the debutantes circle at a safe distance. Cowards."

Meg turned her head, already knowing who she would see. "*That's* the Duke of Thorncroft?"

Dougal Black, lately from Manchester and only the duke as of three months ago. He was all the gossip papers could talk about. Even *The Times* mentioned him more than once. No one could remember the last time a duchy was inherited by such a distant member of the family, previously living on fifteen pounds per year working at a mill. She couldn't imagine how confusing it must be to move between such conflicting worlds.

Actually, she could.

Best not dwell on that right now.

He was entirely too handsome with his thick brown hair and

lean muscles. She'd paint him as a warrior-king. Arthur, or Perseus, holding the head of Medusa. Actually, she quite liked Medusa. Make it Jason, then.

In short, he didn't look like a duke.

Mind you, she wasn't exactly acting like a viscount's daughter, either.

It served her right for getting overly confident. Still, even if he accused her, no one would believe that Meg Swift, quiet artist with a dab hand in the genteel arts of embroidery, watercolors, and flower arrangement, would steal. She had cultivated an impression of refined politeness for years now. No one knew that she could also scrub an oven clean, polish silver, and make a passable stew. Not even the other Cinderellas knew that.

On the other hand, he was a *duke*.

And she had a reticule filled with gold almonds.

Double blast.

Pendleton would never begrudge her sweets, even if he didn't know what she did with them. But she would hate to embarrass him, and any rumors would enrage her uncle. Not to mention shred the thin veil of secrets she'd spent so long stitching together.

"He's rather delicious, wouldn't you say?" Tamsin asked.

"I suppose." She hoped her voice didn't sound as strange as it did inside her own head. She needed to redirect Tamsin's attention. *Now.* "Is that the waltz?" she asked when the music changed.

"Already?" Tamsin shoved her cup of melted grapefruit ice at Meg, who barely caught it before it toppled to the floor. "Have you seen Henry? He promised to waltz with me to save me from Eaton the Lecher."

Lord Eaton was notorious for his wandering hands on the dance floor and what she could only assume was much worse behavior in private. He was tall and blonde with a blindingly white smile which distracted from his misdeeds. And he was convinced that as a duke's daughter, Tamsin was the best catch of the season. Despite her obvious objections. Or perhaps because of them.

And he was coming this way.

"Do you think I can hide under the table?" Tamsin hissed.

"He's already seen you," Meg hissed back.

"Who has?" Henry asked.

Meg and Tamsin both jumped at his abrupt apparition. As Persephone's oldest friend, they had known him since they were in leading strings. He was sturdy and kind, with brown hair and brown eyes and a new gauntness he'd never had before. And he was a hero now, much written about in the papers after nearly being scapegoated for treason.

"Oh, thank God," Tamsin grabbed his hand. "We're dancing."

"We are?"

"*Now,* Captain Talbot." She tugged on his hand.

"What's the rush? I thought you were saving me from waltzing with debutantes looking to snag themselves a husband. And they seem otherwise engaged at present."

"Bah. As if that's anything. Try dancing with Eaton and fighting his hands off *your* backside."

"What?" For such a friendly, calm gentleman, even after his return from war on the Continent, he certainly had a commendable grasp of the cold, deadly tone. Meg half wondered icicles didn't shiver into being around them.

"I'll explain when I'm safe," Tamsin said as he followed her.

"You're safe *now,*" he said darkly. There was a promise in it.

But Eaton's next target was not safe.

Meg watched his expression as Tamsin took to the floor with Henry: annoyed, surly under that smile. And then he noticed the debutante just a few feet away from Meg: eighteen if she was a day, excited to be at a ball, diamonds glittering in her hair. Her chaperone, her mother most likely, was just as eager, especially when she spotted Eaton. Which meant she'd clearly never met him and did not know to avoid him like the plague he was.

Waltzes were dangerous and not just because the more old-fashioned set was convinced it would make ladies dizzy and delirious. And not because it required partners to stand close enough to whisper secret remarks to each other or that it was often the only chance to touch a member of the opposite sex, beyond a hand offered at the carriage step. You could feel your partner's muscles under his sleeves, the warmth of him, his breath on your cheek if he was very daring.

Or so Meg vaguely recalled. At twenty-seven years old and without a dowry—thank you Uncle Dermot—she was not often asked to waltz. Country dances, certainly, but not waltzes. Not without the duke forcing a gentleman's hand, which was why she usually visited the ladies retiring room during this particular dance. It was easier all around.

But she wasn't about to leave that poor girl in Eaton's clutches.

There wasn't time to warn her. Meg gave serious consideration to smacking the earl in the face with her bag full of almonds. It would make such a satisfying thwack when it hit him in the nose. There might even be blood.

Instead, Meg took a step closer to the girl and then let her spine loosen as she swooned. She kept her eyes slitted open so she wouldn't hit her head when she landed. And so that she was properly aimed. She needed to cause a disruption near enough as to make it awkward for Eaton to ask for a dance. The girl's mother gasped loudly before Meg even touched the floor, her hand artfully outstretched. No use injuring herself with a face plant.

But the ground seemed awfully far away. Shouldn't she have landed by now?

And then it became obvious that she wasn't going to land at all.

Strong arms caught her easily. Her eyes fluttered open of their own accord. She shut them again abruptly.

The Duke of Thorncroft had caught her.

She nearly cursed. His arms were warm and solid as they tightened around her. He smelled of frankincense and cedar soap. The girl's mother fluttered around them, her silk ribbons tickling Meg's ear. "Poor dear. I'll fetch a vinaigrette. I've just the one. Vinegar with lavender and mustard."

"Bollocks to that," Meg muttered before letting her eyes pop open.

The Duke of Thorncroft bit back a chuckle.

"No need," Meg said, a little louder. "It was only a small swoon."

His mouth quirked with amusement. "So I see." He still held her close, draped over one arm. It was disorienting. And oddly thrilling. She licked her lips though she didn't know why. His gaze fell on her mouth. She nearly blushed like a newly-presented debutante. Ridiculous.

"Let me up," she said briskly. There. That was much more in character.

"Oh, you've revived her, Your Grace." The girl's mother sighed as if she might also swoon. Meg might have accidentally started a fashion. Thorncroft would have to grow another set of arms.

And while being caught up in a duke's embrace was all very courteous and romantic, she'd never get free of him now. At least Eaton had stalked away towards the card room, his throat mottled red. He did not like it when plans shifted without his permission.

"If you're faint from hunger," the duke murmured in her ear as he pulled her back into a standing position. "I know where you might find some almonds."

His summer eyes twinkled. Oh no. He was handsome as the devil, *and* he had a sense of humor. She was going to be trampled by a horde of debutantes before she'd gotten her feet properly under her. "Thank you, Your Grace," she said politely. "For your assistance."

"You have been the most entertaining part of this evening, I assure you. Are you quite well?"

"Perfectly."

"I'm relieved to hear it. Because now it's your turn to save me."

"I'm sorry?"

There was something brittle to his smile. Something self-deprecating and faintly horrified. She glanced over her shoulder and as predicted, a disconcerting number of ladies pressed closer and closer, fans fluttering, cheeks fetchingly pink. "I suppose you should have let me hit the floor."

His laugh was strangled. "Help me."

She let herself go limp again, but only slightly. He caught her again. "I don't think that's going to do it."

She sighed. "I expect not." The ladies might be upside down from her current vantage point, but it was obvious they had not been deterred. It would take a cannon to dislodge them now that the new duke had proven himself to be chivalrous as well as handsome. It was almost enough to make up for his dubious background. "I need air," Meg added, loudly.

"You sound far too healthy," he scolded under his breath.

"Loud, you mean."

"That too."

"I'm starting to feel much improved," she shot back warningly. "Sprightly, even."

"I don't know what they do to almond thieves. I shouldn't risk it, were I you."

She wrinkled her nose. Even though she did not know him, she knew perfectly well that he was teasing. "You may escort me to the terrace, if you please."

Chapter Two

THEY TURNED THEIR backs to the approaching horde and made their way, a little too quickly, through the other guests. "There should be others taking the air," Meg continued. "It won't be *too* unseemly. Even if we haven't been properly introduced." And she was nearly thirty years old, hardly a young miss to flutter and fuss.

"Dougal Black," the duke replied. "There. And you are?"

"Someone *else* has to make the introductions," she told him. "The Duke of Pendleton or the majordomo. Otherwise, it doesn't count."

"But we're right here."

She nearly smiled at his expression. "Oh, very well. I suppose you shouldn't be punished further for being chivalrous. Even if you did try to blackmail me. But I should remind you that you are not actually Dougal Black. You are the Duke of Thorncroft. And I suspect also a marquess and an earl of someplace or other." A dukedom usually came with a scatter of other titles.

"Don't remind me," he muttered.

Definitely curious for a duke.

"And you are?"

"Miss Swift."

"Just Miss Swift?" He asked as they stepped out into the cool autumn air. As predicted, other guests milled about, taking a respite from the overheated, over-crowded ballroom. Meg relaxed. She had no wish to court gossip. She just didn't have the time for it. "That doesn't seem likely."

"Whyever not?"

"It's my very limited experience that this lot has some kind of allergy to plain sensible names," Dougal continued. "Surely you are The Splendiferous Miss Swift or the Shining Lady Swift."

"How did you guess?" she returned drily. "My friends call me Splendor for short."

Dougal laughed. It was a wonderful sound. Honest, warm. "I will take note."

She laughed with him, just a little. It probably wouldn't do to encourage him, but he was rather refreshing. He hadn't tried to look down her dress or ascertain the shape of her hips through her gown. And he wasn't talking to her because he wanted Pendleton's attention, or Tamsin's eye. And though her uncle might only be a viscount, his temper was vicious and very few gentlemen wanted *his* attention. All in all, it made for a confusing place in Society.

The Duke of Thorncroft's place was even more confusing, by all accounts. The previous duke had no sons and only one male cousin, who had mostly daughters. Except for one son, who died, but not before having two sons of his own: Dougal being the eldest. Dougal wasn't just a distant relation, he was also nearly the last, except for his younger brother. It had required a team of three lawyers and a historian to find Dougal where he was working as a manager in a mill in Manchester.

To say that the aristocracy did not know what to do with him was an understatement.

He was handsome, which would invariably help. He was also strong and rugged and clearly had yet to muddle through the astronomical number of rules held dear by the *ton*.

"Just Miss Swift?" he asked again, dubiously. "Truly? That seems entirely too sensible."

"Yes, but if you must know my mother was Lady Swift, the Right Honorable Viscountess Henshaw."

"There we go. I knew I wouldn't be disappointed. And you must have a first name, after all that."

"Meg," she told him, even though she shouldn't have.

"Meg," he repeated, tasting her name as if it was a sweet. "I like it."

"Thank you. But you mustn't use it."

He sighed, as if he was suddenly a thousand years old. "I remember this part. Names are too intimate."

"Correct."

"Then these toffs truly don't know the actual meaning of the word."

She didn't know how to respond. He wasn't *trying* to be shocking. He was mostly muttering to himself. Still, the first thought that leapt to her mind was: *You could teach me.*

Something in his glance made her feel far too warm. Not just warm, but *hot*. Her blood may as well have been mulled wine, tingling through her veins.

Goodness.

She cleared her throat. "Even so."

He leaned against a column, crossing his arms. "There are roses in your cheeks."

Was she blushing? Damn it. Best to pretend she wasn't. "Are there?"

"You weren't in any danger of swooning, I reckon."

She pretended great interest in the giant pots of white roses scattered around the terrace, mostly held aloft by marble Roman nymphs. Dougal followed her gaze, at which point she realized they were surrounded by rather a lot of white breasts. The Pendleton terrace was forbidden to many a young lady, and not just this evening. Meg refused to blush further. She was too old to be all aflutter.

"Tell the truth," he said coaxingly, a big, muscled man with a gentle voice that shivered across every inch of bare skin revealed by her ballgown. "You were playacting."

She inclined her head.

"Why?"

She gave a small sigh. "There are gentlemen in that ballroom who do not deserve the title."

"I believe it."

"Lord Eaton was descending upon a young lady, barely out." She used his name because she vaguely recalled that Dougal also had a younger sister. He ought to be armed with the proper information. "I don't believe she or her mother knew of his reputation. His *real* reputation, that is."

His eyes narrowed. "Which is?"

"He has more hands than an octopus. And he is very adept at cornering women."

"You speak from experience?"

"Only once. And never again since."

"*Once?*" He pushed from the column, furious. His voice went hard, she could hear knives and swords in every syllable.

She smiled grimly. "Ask him why he can no longer bend the little finger on his left hand."

"You will point out this man to me."

"He's already abandoned the dancing," she assured him. He looked like a storm cloud, all coiled menace and purpose. She probably shouldn't find it attractive.

She really, *really,* found it attractive.

She was saved by the Horde. Younger debutantes, forbidden from leaving the ballroom by their parents, hovered by the open terrace doors. A few bolder ladies ventured outside, claiming, loudly, to be interested in seeing the stars as they were so seldom visible in London.

"Is it true, then?" Meg asked, watching them. "What the Prince Regent decreed?"

"That son of a—" Dougal broke off with a cough.

Meg smiled a little. "Definitely true then."

It was said that in order to safeguard the vulnerable Thorncroft dukedom, Dougal had been ordered to marry with haste. Should he not be quick enough, the Prince Regent would choose his wife.

He didn't look the sort to be pleased about that sort of thing.

"I must marry by Christmas," Dougal said. "If I have any hope of choosing my own bride."

"So soon?" Meg asked. "Is that even legal?"

"The seven different lawyers I hired assured me it is unusual but legal. More to the point, he is the prince and will be the king one day and he can make my family's life very difficult."

The ladies drifted closer, like swans in their white dresses. Anyone who had ever had to clear a pond of swans, as Meg had, knew there was nothing delicate or gentle about them. They could break your arm with one swipe of their beak. These ladies might be a touch more subtle, but they were every bit as dangerous. "I feel like a plate of dinner at the chop house," Dougal shifted uncomfortably. "Napoleon has nothing on them."

Meg knew she was supposed to agree with him, say something cutting about the desperation of unmarried ladies. They were referred to as being 'on the shelf', called spinsters, old maids, even ape-leaders since the punishment for not marrying was being damned to 'lead apes in hell'. Correction: the punishment for a *woman*.

And she was one herself. Spinster, Old Maid, Ape-Leader. She ought to have new calling cards made. Something tasteful, with a gilt edge. *Miss Splendor, The Ape-Leader.*

And Dougal, feeling the same trap close around him, ought to have a little more compassion.

"Can you blame them?" she asked quietly. "We must marry but we seldom have a say as to who will take control of our fortunes and our very lives. Even less so than you. It's strange for you to be in that position, but we, as women, are meant to take it with good grace and nary a question or complaint. And you retain your rights, Your Grace, after marriage. We do not. Being a duchess would be some consolation, I suppose, when one is not a person in the eyes of the law."

"I suppose so." He glanced down at her. "But not for you?"

She snorted. He looked even more startled. Even he had to know that ladies did not snort.

"I didn't mean to cause offense," he added.

"Of course not." It wasn't his fault. And her struggle with her own lot was not his fault either. This was a ball. It was meant to be dancing and games and light entertainment, despite Pendleton's unsubtle hunt for husbands for his goddaughters. The only way through was to laugh about it. To paint it in her mind's eye with bright yellows and whites for the candlelight, an eerie blue for Dougal's eyes, pretty pastels for the pastries on the table. Gilt for the golden almonds in her reticule.

"Are we friends again?" Dougal asked. He sounded more vulnerable than he looked, especially with that burning gaze, the tension in his shoulders. If Henry still looked the part of a man returning from war, Dougal looked as if he had just entered one. Some battlefields were strewn with bodies, others with roses. Her fingers itched to paint it.

"Of course," she replied. "But we should return to the others."

"So soon?"

"I'm afraid so, Your Grace."

"Don't call me that."

"I must."

He grumbled to himself, and it was strangely endearing. He offered his arm and when she took it, she was not disappointed by the warmth and the strength of him. By the sheer presence and energy of him invading her carefully controlled space. The ballroom, by contrast, was too bright and too crowded and too exposed. "Bugger it," he muttered when ladies began to creep closer, like ivy up a garden wall. Or hunting hounds on the scent. Still, Meg could not stop a startled laugh. He slid her a sidelong glance. "I should apologize for that, I'm sure."

"You should, but there's no need," she assured him. "Although I would not recommend it for drawing room conversations."

He grinned, fleeting, a lightning flash from that storm cloud. "Am I too old for a governess?"

"I should say so."

"Pity. I might have let you instruct me."

Heat liquefied in her thighs. She kept her smile polite. His grin turned positively wicked, as if he could see her reaction. The heat spread, tingled.

Botheration.

"Ah there you are," the Duke of Pendleton's hearty voice boomed in their direction.

Oh, thank God.

She moved to released Dougal's arm and his hand tightened over hers for a moment, as if he did not want her to.

He really was dangerous, this one.

"I see you've met my dearest Meg, Thorncroft." The duke wore his favorite frock coat, a few years out of date but resplendent with embroidery. It was her own work and he never tired of telling anyone who complimented it. It had taken an entire winter to complete the procession of Vestal Virgins to the temple. A thousand, thousand stitches.

His expression was concerned when he turned to her. "I heard you swooned. You're not ill, are you?"

"Fit as a fiddle," she promised.

"Hmph." He eyed her carefully. "You do look flushed."

She absolutely would not comment on that. Nor would she look in Dougal's direction. Not even a glance. She didn't have to. She could already *feel* his quiet smirk.

"And you've lost weight," the duke continued, oblivious. "Thorncroft here is the fellow with the collection I want you to draw for me."

Meg froze, then turned slowly to look at Pendleton. With some accusation, it had to be said. He'd never mentioned the project involved the Duke of Thorncroft. With whom she'd just had a most inappropriate conversation. Pendleton blinked innocently, fooling her not at all.

Dougal's eyebrows raised. "Miss Swift is the artist you are sending to my estate?"

"Indeed."

"Is she?" Meg said mildly. "You might have mentioned."

"Didn't I? Terribly sorry, my dear. You know how an old man's memory can be."

"Yes," she muttered under her breath. "Wily."

"I beg your pardon? You see, my hearing is going too."

What rot.

"The previous Duke of Thorncroft left me his collection of artifacts, on the understanding that I would keep the items that interested me and donate the rest to a museum. And I'm not keen on four hours in a carriage to catalogue it," he added.

That much she could believe. Even with the best newly-sprung carriages the jostling would be murder on his bones. She stifled a sigh. Of course, she would help him. And he knew perfectly well that she would. "You can leave from here," he said cheerfully. "And save yourself some time."

"I will need a chaperone, Your Grace," she reminded him. She couldn't very well traipse across England alone with a man she barely knew. Even as a spinster.

Dougal was watching their exchange with some fascination. "I have inherited two elderly ladies at the estate," he offered. "Might they suffice?"

"The Ladies Marigold and Beatrice, is it?" Pendleton said. "Are they still alive, then?"

"It would seem so."

"Good for them! And does Lady Marigold still insist on wearing yellow?"

Dougal smiled. "She does." He leaned a little closer to Meg, conspiratorially. "She looks a little bit like a pot of lemon jelly most of the time."

She smiled back. "I'm sure she's lovely."

"She is."

"And dotty as a hen," Pendleton added. "But I still like her more than most people I've met to this day. And I'm old, you know. Seventy-two."

Now that was laying it on a bit thick. Next, he would pretend to stoop and call for arthritic cream even though he was hardier than most men half his age. Meg shook her head. "I'll still need a chaperone for the journey."

"Leave it to me!" He promised. "I'll have you sorted by breakfast."

"That's what I'm afraid of."

Pendleton waited until Dougal was distracted before turning towards Meg and lowering his voice. "Come to my study in the morning, if you please. There's more to discuss."

That did not bode well at all.

More guests surrounded them, eager for a moment of attention from two dukes and so Pendleton was unable to elaborate.

It did not bode well, at all.

Chapter Three

A N HOUR LATER, Meg found herself in the supper room, seated across from Dougal. She tried not to worry that he might notice Pendleton was trying to throw them together. He ought to know better. Honestly, she had no dowry, and Dougal had the pick of the peerage.

Beside her was Lord Forsythe and his wife, and next to them Persephone's grandmother, Lady Blackwell, as well as Tamsin and Henry. "Don't we make for a merry party?" Lady Blackwell remarked cheerfully. Her wig was best suited to the drawing rooms of her youth, being at least two feet high, dyed a fanciful pale green, and ornamented with over a dozen silk butterflies.

Meg ate a quail's egg off her plate slowly, trying not to stuff two in her mouth at once. She was famished, but ladies did not eat demonstrably in public. It wouldn't do to appear hungry, even if Meg was *always* hungry. Her uncle restricted all of the food she ate, even tea. She mostly picked mint from the garden, or lemon balm for a tisane. Which was why she could drink a bathtub full of good strong tea when she was visiting Pendleton. Sometimes she lay awake with her blood pulsating with tea until dawn, only to start again with a pot of breakfast chocolate. If she told her friends, they would clamor to get her away from Henshaw Hall. Already, she knew Priya suspected. And if Priya suspected, it meant she was already digging for dirt.

Meg had considered confessing, to be honest. More than

once. But traveling from friend to friend and being dependent on their goodwill, with no money of her own gave her pause. And more importantly, how could she help her family's tenants if she wasn't there? There was already so little she could do. She could barely protect herself from her uncle's dodgy dealings, never mind the tenant farmers, but she could at least *try*. If nothing else, she knew of one little boy who would go mad for gold almonds.

She must have glanced at her reticule reflexively because Dougal smiled. "Care for a slice of almond cake, Miss Swift?"

She narrowed her eyes. "No, thank you, Your Grace," she returned. "I don't care for almonds."

Tamsin leaned close, looking mischievous and delighted, as usual. "Meg Swift," she said under her breath. "Are you flirting?"

"Of course not. I'm discussing almonds."

Maybe also flirting a little bit.

The smallest bit.

Barely the size of an almond crumb.

Tamsin nearly crowed. "I knew it."

Meg turned pointedly towards her friend. "You think everyone is flirting because *you* are flirting so hard with Henry that I'm afraid you might do yourself permanent injury," she teased.

"I wouldn't have to work so hard if he wasn't so hardheaded," she grumbled. "Captain Talbot, indeed."

"I have every faith in you," Meg assured her. Tamsin was a force to be reckoned with, from her bright curls to her collection of questionable severed body parts from folkloric history. She had no doubt Henry would see her shining like a torch in a dark room—just as soon as he remembered to open his eyes.

"Give him time," Meg murmured. "I've yet to hear of a man back from the war who isn't changed in some way."

"True," Tamsin grimaced. "But he was always hardheaded. He just used to be less obvious about it."

She was right. They all knew Henry well, having visited the Pendleton estate every summer since infancy. He lived with his grandmother, the dowager countess Culpepper, just outside the village, near Persephone's family. It was always a lively, troublesome reunion. Meg missed it in many ways, but there was no use looking back. Her parents had taught her that. Not on purpose, it had to be said. But a lesson was a lesson. It definitely made Meg stand out in their circle of history-obsessed antiquarians.

She ate another quail egg when she was certain no one was looking.

Fairly certain.

Had Dougal just winked at her?

Surely not. Dukes did not wink. Even newly-made dukes with no experience with the title.

The tiny, tiny smile fighting at the edge of her mouth told her differently.

"Miss Swift," Lord Forsythe said from her right side. "I so enjoyed our conversation about turnips last time we met. I've been curious to know if you were successful."

Turnips might have sounded like a tiresome subject to the rest of the company, in fact Lady Forsythe rolled her eyes, albeit fondly, behind her husband's shoulder. But Meg welcomed the distraction and, in fact, the topic. They were both a great deal safer than Dougal Black, Duke of Thorncroft.

She smiled at Lord Forsythe. "The turnips were a success, my lord. The sheep ate the green tops as they grew, and we were still left with the root vegetable to feed the animals over the winter."

"And they grew well?"

"Very well. The soil seems replenished."

"Turnips were your second year?"

"Yes, it's barley next."

"I admit I was skeptical about the Norfolk system with all of those crop rotations," Lord Forsythe said. "But I am pleased you found success. Will you keep with it?"

"Yes, I think so. And will you try it now, my lord?"

"I believe I shall, with you to recommend it."

She could feel Dougal's surprise from across the table. He was meant to be focusing on the guests beside him, not paying attention to the spinster on the other side of the flower arrangements. The duke had chosen dahlias and roses for the ball. Or rather, his housekeeper, Mrs. Hastings, had. She had a keen eye for decorations and the duke was fussy about how he displayed his Ancient Egyptian and Roman artifacts, but not much else. He grinned at Dougal, catching his glance. "No one knows more about farming than my Meg," he said proudly.

Which was patently untrue, Meg thought, smiling at him. But she would hazard that she did know more about it than any daughter of any other viscount. Needs must and all. At harvest time she snuck into her uncle's fields to pick turnips for her larder. Turnip mash, turnip soup, turnip roast.

She hated turnips.

"I had no idea debutantes were so well versed," Dougal replied.

Tamsin and Lady Forsythe shared an eye roll. "We aren't generally," Tamsin admitted cheerfully as they rose to make their way back to the ballroom. "But being a goddaughter of a duke does afford one *some* opportunities, I suppose."

As a daughter of a duke as well as goddaughter to another, Tamsin could afford to take them for granted. And as a countess, Lady Forsythe could choose to be bored by four-crop rotation and how to best lay drainage for a field. Meg couldn't. Not when her uncle cared so little for anything but his own comforts. He collected the rents, raised them when he needed more gambling funds, and did very little to help in between.

Meg remembered both her parents tramping through the mud, arguing about soil and how the Enclosure Acts would drive farmers into cities when they weren't left with enough land to use the new crop rotation style instead of the old method of alternating between pasturing and growing grain. It might seem odd to the others, but it was one of her favorite memories. She'd read all of her mother's books on agriculture, stealing them from the library when she was fourteen years old. Her uncle had never noticed. Not exactly a surprise, that.

Still, Tamsin was right, being a favorite of the duke afforded Meg a certain amount of space to breathe. And just three months ago, Meg had been chasing a traitor to the Crown through Pendleton's statuary garden, after a ball much like this one.

What did it say about Meg that she found she preferred that evening's entertainment to this one?

It was ungrateful of her, and she felt a pang of guilt. She knew all too well how precious it was to have hours to devote to entertainment. Her uncle wouldn't have dreamed of inviting her to his soirees, not unless he needed her to act as a lady's maid. She had taking to sleeping with a kitchen knife under her bed when a certain type of guest congregated. One of the footmen had even started sleeping in her hall as her uncle's taste in friends deteriorated.

She looked forward to her visits to Pendleton Hall, even for the horrid Cinderella balls. It was a balm to see the friends whom she considered her true family. At home she saw the cottagers during the day when they were able, her uncle when he set her on chores just to prove he could, and then no one at all. She spent hours alone, painting and embroidering.

And now here she was, drinking champagne by the light of honey candles, surrounded by opulence and laughter and sugar sculptures shaped like birds. It shouldn't make her feel so…itchy. Should it? She usually loved these vacations, stolen days outside of her regular life when she could dance just for the sake of dancing. Like Tamsin who was at this very moment, gliding and turning and laughing and enjoying herself as only she could. She came alive at parties, floating from conversation to conversation and dancing until her slippers gave out. She knew everyone and everyone knew her.

Surely it was only that Meg was a little tired. It had been a grueling harvest season. She was glad for the silk gloves that covered the calluses on her palms, and the questions they would generate which she could not answer. She searched the room for Dougal. She shouldn't be doing any such thing, but she found she couldn't help herself. He was unlike anyone she had ever met. And not just for the obvious reasons.

When Mr. Hanson asked her to join him in the quadrille, she accepted and determined to enjoy herself. If she was going to be paraded about like a lonely spinster to be sold off to the highest bidder, she may as well dance. And devour custard tarts.

She danced three more sets, each with a perfectly amiable gentleman she had no intention of marrying and who had no intention of marrying her. The beeswax candles in the crystal chandeliers above them began to drip and the chalk used on the bottom of their dancing slippers made the shining parquet floor look as though it had been snowing. She declined her last partner's offer of joining him in the card room and joined Priya instead.

"I'm exhausted just looking at her," Priya said, nodding at Tamsin, who was still dancing. "Never mind the musical galloping but all that smiling." She shuddered lightly.

Meg grinned at her, feeling some of the odd mood that gripped her float away. Lady Priya Langdon was beautiful with her black hair and dark eyes, and she was also practical and sharp as a knife. There were many who feared her and many more who *ought* to fear her. But Meg knew exactly how hard Priya could be with her friends: to whit, as hard as the Blancmange pudding Meg might one day still try to steal.

There was nothing Priya would not do for her loved ones. As to that, Meg made sure her smile did not invite concern. She could hardly explain why she was out of sorts. Taking in the harvest was difficult enough when you weren't supposed to be doing it in the first place. Add to that her uncle's new friends who prowled around the estate drinking and shooting at birds, foxes, and once, someone's pig, and she hadn't slept properly in weeks. Or eaten, for that matter. It had been at least an hour since supper, surely she could sneak a pastry.

"What is it?" Priya asked, concerned.

Meg adjusted her smile. Everyone else believed her placid, polite façade without question. "I'm just a little tired," she said, and it was mostly the truth. She'd be herself again by morning. More tea, a good night's sleep; there was no better tonic. "I only just arrived today."

"Hhmph."

"Have you heard from Persephone?" Meg asked to distract her.

"I received a letter from Conall," she replied. "He says Persephone is writing a journal she plans to share with us. She's on volume three." She made a face. "I want to know that she's enjoying herself, but honestly I'd rather not read about how pyramid stones were cut and then be quizzed about it later."

Meg smiled fondly. Persephone was excessively devoted to her antiquarian pursuits and could never understand why the rest of them weren't excited to dig in the mud looking for human bones and broken pottery.

"Miss Swift, are those red birds embroidered on your gloves?" Lady Blackwell said stopping to join them by the refreshment table. "How cunning you are."

"Thank you, Lady Blackwell." She had stitched them along the top, adding a matching red ribbon. She and the others teased Persephone's grandmother about her love of ribbons, but those same ribbons she foisted on every single lady had helped them restrain a traitor not too long ago. Meg was now a fervent believer in the wisdom of always having a ribbon and a sharp pin on one's person. And truth be told, she had a closet of white dresses that had seen better days and ribbons and embroidery had become a necessity.

"You look a little peeked, my dear."

Meg stifled a sigh. Nothing like dressing up for a ball and having everyone tell you you looked tired. "I expect I've danced too much," she fibbed.

"That's what I like to hear," Persephone's grandmother approved. "Find me a footman, would you, dear? There is tea in my teacup and I would much prefer it be whiskey."

Meg had been sneaking Lady Blackwell whisky and brandy since she was old enough to realize that old ladies nearly always filled their teacups with liquids far stronger than tea. She motioned to a footman and requested spirits for the lady in the wig the color of limes who had already wandered away in search of entertainment.

"Did someone give Lady Blackwell plain tea?" he asked, darting away. "The duke will have my head."

Priya narrowed her eyes in the vicinity of the doorway. Meg raised her eyebrows. "Well?"

"That's two earls and a marquess who've just snuck out," Priya confirmed. "And very badly, I might add."

"And Tamsin has vacated the dance floor entirely. I don't see her."

"Right," Priya said with a brisk nod. "It's time."

Chapter Four

THEY FOUND TAMSIN exactly where they expected to: in the bushes.

"Took you long enough," she said, shifting to make room for them. There were already leaves tangled in the pearl pins shining in her hair. The sky was dark and low enough to touch. The mud underfoot had a decidedly frozen quality. "It's bloody cold out here."

"And pokey," Meg added, inching forward so that the thorns would stop scratching her. She didn't want to catch the embroidery on her dress either. It would take forever to mend. "Why do they always pick the parlor near the roses?"

"We might have to convince the duke to plant some larkspur," Tamsin agreed. "Something soft at least." She strained to peer through the window in front of them. It was cracked open just a few inches, enough to hear what was happening on the other side of the glass. Tamsin had run through all of the ground floor rooms before the ball started, cracking open windows and moving curtains. She'd done a fine job, as usual. "Although, I'm still not sure why we don't just tell him about this. He'd put an end to it in a heartbeat. And I wouldn't be shivering so hard my teeth just knocked together."

"We wouldn't have the advantage then," Priya pointed out. She passed Tamsin the end of her shawl, laying it across the three of them. The soft wool took the chill out of the cold garden, dressed mostly in frost instead of flowers. "And we'd never hear what they have to say."

"Or know who holds the wager purse," Meg added. She might have rubbed her palms together like a storybook villain if she weren't precariously perched on a stone. "And I mean to have it this year."

"This is our year," Tamsin agreed, supportively. "I can feel it."

The parlor glowed with lamplight, crowded with the moving shadows of a congregation of eligible unmarried men of good fortune. Or ancient ancestral titles. Occasionally both. Wine glasses clinked together, and loud laughter punctuated every statement. It was easy enough to hear every word, they were hardly subtle. And they weren't particularly kind as they discussed the duke's goddaughters. They never were. But it was helpful to know what they really thought. More than one offer of marriage had been rejected on the basis of this night's work.

Meg was most offended that the portraits she'd had painted for the duke were being used like advertisements in a horse magazine. Or cows, they may as well have been purchasing cows. *This one is pretty; this one has good teeth. This one might not produce milk.*

Those paintings had been *gifts*. And last year, some drunken sot had spilled brandy all over Lady Portia. If it happened again, Meg made no promises that she wouldn't launch herself through the window. She'd rather like to see the expressions on their faces.

She'd definitely paint that.

She might even send it to the Royal Exhibition.

"Lady Clara," shouted a man as he placed his bet down in front of a portrait. "Ten pounds she remains a spinster by the next ball."

"Only an idiot would take that bet," came the laughing reply. "That one's all vinegar."

"Good dowry though."

"She'd have to have a king's ransom. She'd talk about etiquette in her own marriage bed. Who fancies that?"

"I don't know, I like a naughty governess."

"Oh, honestly," Priya snapped. She paused. "They're not wrong," she added reluctantly when Tamsin snorted. It had to be said that Lady Clara was not an easy companion. She was notorious for preferring etiquette to all things. She noticed every social infraction. And as Tamsin flouted the rules at every opportunity, it made for an uneasy friendship at best. "Still, I hope they choke on every word."

"Lady Priya is mildly terrifying," someone said. "I shouldn't like my chances."

Beside her, Priya smiled smugly. "Bloody right."

Every year, it was the same. Sometime during the ball, a group of gentlemen snuck off to place their wagers. They imagined futures bought and sold, told ribald jokes, and placed enormous bets on the matrimonial chances of each Cinderella.

It was deeply irritating.

But educational.

Also, not terribly soothing to the ego.

"Meg Swift."

She winced at her name.

"Same odds as last year. Still no dowry."

"We will crown her Queen of the Ape-leaders!"

"That tosspot," Tamsin muttered.

Meg shrugged. "He's not wrong."

"Not only is he wrong," Tamsin disagreed. "But he'll eat those words."

"It doesn't matter. They say it every year."

Tamsin narrowed her eyes. "And last year *you* said you'd make a pie from his kidneys."

Meg wrinkled her nose. "It sounds like a lot of bother."

"Not a bit. I'll make the pastry."

"Like you know how to cook," Priya said.

"I'm sure I can!" Tamsin said hotly. "I can make...." She trailed off before laughing. "All right, perhaps not." She grinned. "I might not be able to bake pies, but I wager I'm perfectly capable of poking him in the kidneys with a sharp stick. My father's chef is forever going on about the tenderness of meat and how important it is. And he's *French*. He ought to know."

"My, we do descend into cannibalism quicker and quicker every year," Meg laughed. "Don't fret, Tam. I don't want to marry any of those men, nor do I particularly want to eat kidneys."

"Oh, very well."

"You do sound disappointed."

"I like acquiring new skills."

They shared a chuckle as the men continued to shout and wager at their expense. It didn't matter, not when she could laugh about it while crouched in the rosebushes with two of her favorite people. She would paint them like this, white roses all around, golden light at the window.

And cold rain.

The first drop landed on her nose.

"Blast," Tamsin said just as the autumn skies opened over them. "Not again."

DOUGAL HAD ALWAYS assumed the aristocracy were a flock of lunatics, but he'd never expected to have it confirmed quite so spectacularly. They danced, they gambled, they drank too much wine that tasted like cake.

And apparently, they stole almonds.

Though to be fair, theft notwithstanding, The Splendid Miss Swift seemed the least insane of the lot. She wasn't beautiful the way her friend Tamsin was, with bright curls and a creamy complexion, but Meg was pretty in a quiet way that snuck up on you and threatened to clobber you over the head if you weren't careful. Much like the lady might, he imagined. He'd been a duke for a few months now and she was the first lady to hold his interest. Scratch that. The first person entirely. She had secrets, that one. He didn't know how no one else could see it. They were taken in by that quiet loveliness, the soft manners.

And she would be in his house for the next few weeks.

He had half a mind to send Pendleton a thank you gift. What did these folks send each other when they already had everything? Fruit baskets? Pet ferrets?

His gaze followed Meg around the room without conscious volition, as if he couldn't help himself. She laughed with her friends, stopped to eat a teacake smothered with frosting an alarming shade of blue, and then danced with an elderly gentleman. Her dress was exquisitely embroidered but he noticed the thin spots where the fabric was wearing through. He'd seen them enough on his own clothing, while growing up. And his sister had done the same—attempting creative mending to camouflage the defects. But never with such style. He couldn't understand why everyone treated Meg like a sparrow when she was clearly a flame-red cardinal.

Too much wine, not enough sense, the lot of them.

Proven dismally true at this very moment where he somehow found himself in a parlor papered with yellow silk, shoulder to shoulder with a dozen gentlemen. He had no idea how he'd gotten here but that was becoming a common problem lately. When his father used to brag that they had fancy relations, he'd always laughed it off. Fancy relations didn't mean anything at the mill, and it didn't get food into their mouths.

Until it did.

On painted china plates and gold forks.

Inwardly squirming, he turned his attention back to the over-decorated room stinking of wine, perfume, and stolen cheroots. He'd kill for a pint and a walk around Manchester when it was so late there was no one but himself and the stars and the occasional cat. But this was his life now.

Meg suddenly made it seem a little less uncomfortable.

A little more interesting.

She stared at him from a portrait set up on a table under the window. Her brown hair was looped up in braids like a coronet. Her smile was crooked, charming. Exactly right. Next to her was a painting of Lady Tamsin Bell with her fire-hair and her big laugh, Lady Priya Langdon with her piercing black eyes. There were other ladies he did not recognize, all painted perfectly, wearing pearls and diamonds and the kinds of soft complexions only afforded to those who carried parasols and slept through the day in order to dance through the night.

Someone slapped a guinea in front of one of the paintings. There was an answering laugh, several shouts. "Place your bets!"

"What the devil?" Dougal muttered.

"The Cinderella Ball," someone replied as though that explained everything. "It's no secret Pendleton wants his goddaughters settled and taken care of."

"Like this?"

"Hardly," the man replied. "But what he doesn't know won't hurt him. Or us."

"It's just a spot of fun, anyway," added another gentleman, this one possibly inbred given the perfect straightness of his aristocratic nose. Dougal was having a hard time keeping them straight, they all wore the same cravats and gold buttons and tousled hair tamed with pomade. He'd never smelled so much sandalwood and bay in his life. He never thought he'd miss the stink of market day or the dust of the mill in his nostrils. At least it was an honest, straightforward smell. It hid nothing.

"Miss Swift," another man added, throwing down a handful of coins. He was blond, but Dougal could not see his face through the crowd. "Pretty enough for a tumble, but not pretty enough to marry without a dowry," he laughed. "Eh, lads?"

Dougal had the abrupt and visceral urge to plow his fist into his face.

"But Tamsin Bell will be married, place your wagers."

"You sound sure of yourself, Eaton."

Dougal turned his head sharply. The blond curls belonged to Eaton?

"Well, my grandfather was a duke and she's a twenty-eight-year-old spinster," he laughed. "Not to mention that her stepmother adores me."

"Almost as much as you adore yourself," someone retorted.

"Write your wagers in the book, lads," Eaton said. "I've got the pouch." He slipped the red velvet pouch filled with coins into his waistcoat and walked away, a bottle of wine in his hand. Dougal couldn't see his face, but he hated the set of his indolent shoulders immediately. There were too many people between them and too much cheroot smoke. Damn it. Dougal shoved his way to the door, stalking into the corridor.

The empty corridor.

Damn the man, he was already gone.

Something prowled in Dougal's chest. Something feral. Something that made him feel more like himself than he had in months.

Something he placed entirely at Meg's feet.

MEG, PRIYA AND Tamsin returned to the ballroom crowned in leaves and unruly laughter, ballgowns speckled with rain. It was most shocking.

Or would have been, if they were anyone else.

As it was, the others barely blinked. Except for Clara. She definitely blinked. And then sucked air through her nose in that way that always promised a lecture. Tamsin took a sharp left to avoid her. "It's been at least an hour since Meg had tea," she teased. "Let's remedy that before she faints again."

It was rare that Meg could be distracted from a good strong cup of tea.

The sight of Dougal stalking into the ballroom was enough to do it. She had eyes in her head, didn't she? With his bright eyes and muscular shoulders, it was difficult to look anywhere else. The way he walked made her feel warm and squirmy.

Which was ridiculous.

A walk was a walk.

Except, apparently not. He took up space without being flamboyant or intimidating. And he also seemed to be taking up what was left of the air in the stuffy ballroom because she was oddly out of breath for a moment. Just a moment. He was the early winter storm battering at the windows to everyone's placid summer rain. And Meg would choose a storm every time. Sometimes literally, she thought, picking another leaf out of her decolletage.

"Lord Eaton?" she heard the Majordomo say, when Dougal stopped to ask him a question. "Certainty, Your Grace. Right over there."

Dougal turned his head and she saw the clench of his shoulder, the calm, quiet narrowing of his eyes. Some kind of new awareness prickled through her. She felt suddenly like those paintings of the Oracle at Delphi, plucking knowledge out of nowhere. She hardly knew him, certainly not well enough to know with bone-deep certainty that he was about to do something dramatic.

Something stupid.

Her feet propelled her between the guests before she could decide what to do with her sudden and vague premonition. It put her at the perfect vantage point to see Dougal's fist collide squarely with Eaton's perfect jaw. She might have cheered if everything hadn't happened so quickly. She would definitely paint it later. On the largest canvas she could make. With the best quality oils. Never mind the canvas. She would paint it right across the front of the Parliament building.

But for now, he had no idea what he'd just done.

And she had mere seconds to undo it.

She glanced over her shoulder, meeting Priya's eyes, then Tamsin's. They rushed forward to join her without a word, as the surprised silence swallowed the cheerful chatter around them. It didn't last, of course. The musicians played on, but the dancers nearby stopped in their tracks. A lady dropped her glass and it shattered, spattering red wine. Men punching each other was generally reserved for bouts in the ring at Gentleman Jackson's or late night rambles between pubs. There were gasps, exclamations.

Eaton sprawled on the floor, red with shock and fury. Dougal stood over him, perfectly at his ease. As if he barely noticed the reactions of the aristocrats all around him.

Tamsin was the first to reach them. She fluttered like a butterfly, touching Eaton's shoulder, his red cheek. Meg knew better than anyone that she was deftly getting in his way, preventing him from leaping to his feet.

Priya was next, then Meg. Then the other debutantes, pressing lace handkerchiefs dipped in ice water at him. He preened, tossing his perfect curls off his forehead. There was blood on his cravat. Meg was fiercely glad for it. Even if it *was* unladylike of her. She could feel Dougal's eyes on the back of her neck as her hands joined the others, soothing, patting, flattering.

Eaton ate every morsel of the attention like it was an apple cake.

"WHAT THE BLOODY hell?" Dougal muttered, watching Meg kneel on the ground in her beautiful, embroidered gown.

For Eaton.

He hardly expected her to bring him roses for an act of violence on the dance floor, but nor did he expect her to comfort the very man she'd bared her teeth at not two hours before. And just when he'd thought she wasn't as cracked as the others.

The disappointment was far sharper than their short acquaintance warranted.

And yet there it was.

He ignored the stares of the other guests. And the footman, who hovered, confused. One did not throw a duke out of a ballroom.

But on the other hand, dukes did not often punch earls in that same ballroom.

"Now you've done it."

Dougal had not heard Captain Henry Talbot approach. He raised an eyebrow, leaning against the wall, the perfect picture of a languid aristocrat comfortable touching gold silk wallpaper. Except for the eyes, which seemed to never stop cataloging his surroundings: window, door, fireplace. It was a common enough pattern in the dodgier pubs, but Dougal had not expected to find it here, on a grand summer estate.

Then again, he had hardly expected to find himself with a similar garden summer estate to his name.

"That was a brilliant bit of entertainment," Henry said. "But I should warn you, it's not quite the thing."

As if he didn't know that.

As if he cared.

"He insulted Miss Swift."

Henry sighed. "Yes, I imagine he did. Git." He shot Dougal a sidelong glance. "Found the wagering room, did you?"

He wasn't nearly angry enough. "I thought Me—, that is, Miss Swift, was your friend."

"She is. But if you punch him again, which I can see you're itching too, she might thank you by punching *you*."

"And?" He failed to see the problem. She'd been insulted. Several women had.

"And then she'll punch *me* for not stopping you." Henry half smiled. "You seem a decent enough chap but I'm not keen on taking one of her punches for you."

"Does she punch you often?"

"She doesn't have to. She's surprisingly strong."

"She's like a willow branch," he scoffed. And still fussing about Eaton as he rose to his feet.

"Maybe, but she's also meaner than she looks. She used to put spiders in my shoes when we were little. And once when we were quite a bit older, come to that."

"Did you deserve it?"

He grinned. "Definitely."

"She doesn't look like she's contemplating spiders at the moment." And something about the way she was touching the other man's chest as she straightened his waistcoat made Dougal clench his back teeth together. Eaton didn't deserve a moment of her time.

Perhaps another facer though.

"Just watch," Henry suggested, as if he knew what Dougal was thinking. "Believe me when I tell you, I have plans of my own for Eaton. But the man does love a duel and he's unfortunately, very skilled. He'd shoot you between the eyes and then trot off for breakfast."

"I wasn't suggesting a duel."

"No, but he absolutely will."

"Noted." Duel or not, the man needed punching. Repeatedly.

"In fact, I expect he's coming this way for just that purpose." Henry smiled, slowly. "Or would be if he wasn't suddenly tripping over ladies."

They did seem fixated on carrying him away in a determined, relentless flurry of silk and lace and diamonds.

"Oh, well done, Tam," he murmured when Lady Tamsin deftly turned Eaton around, away from where Dougal stood. She batted her eyelashes at him. Dougal thought that was a trick from the penny papers, but apparently it worked. Eaton's chest puffed out. "But it won't save him. Not from me," Henry added softly.

Tamsin glared at Henry over her shoulder, as if she'd heard him, and motioned to the exit with her chin. Sharply. Imperially, even.

"We've got our marching orders," Henry said, mildly. He didn't seem inclined to move.

A woman wearing an entire pheasant's worth of feathers in her hair, sniffed at Dougal. "These things aren't done," she snapped. "Though I suppose one can't expect any better from you."

"Lady Watling." Henry didn't say anything else, but he didn't appear to have to. She sniffed again and waved her fan furiously, more feathers attached to the spines. She put Dougal in mind of a disgruntled Christmas goose.

"There 'll be a duel, mark my words." This time it was a man who spoke, as eager as a hedgehog digging for earthworms. His pointed nose only helped the comparison. Now that the shock had worn off, the whispers were sharpening. "The Thorncroft duchy will be down another duke by dawn."

"Good riddance," his friend replied. "He's positively savage."

"Ease off, Beaufort." Henry didn't raise his voice, but it still cut through the crowd like a bayonet, reminding Dougal that the other man had been on the Continent for the duration of the war.

"A duke should be elegant," Beaufort insisted. "This is what comes of elevating someone from the gutters. Disgraceful."

Henry pushed away from the wall, very slowly. "I beg your pardon?"

"Don't bother," Dougal said. "It's hardly the first time I've heard that."

"I suppose not." Henry spoke a little louder, and very clearly. "Though I'm sure the Prince Regent has no intention of forgiving a duel since he's taken such an interest in the Thorncroft duchy."

A fair point.

If Dougal had to marry within months, getting himself impaled or shot full of holes was likely to be frowned upon. He imagined that would infuriate Eaton even more. "Are you trying to defend me?" Dougal asked Henry curiously.

"Force of habit," Henry said. "You don't leave a man on the field."

"This is hardly a battlefield."

"You'd be surprised, Thorncroft. You'd be surprised."

"Well, much as I appreciate it, to be fair, I *did* punch him," he added. "Even I know that's hardly ballroom behavior. I should go."

Except he couldn't, because Meg had broken away from the other ladies and was walking towards him. Her expression was perfectly polite and mild. He wondered that no one else noticed the gleam in her eye. It was downright bloodthirsty. "He insulted you," he blurted out before she could say anything.

"He insults all women," she pointed out.

"Then he should be punched every time he does so." It was hardly complicated.

She looked like she might be trying not to smile. "Very true." She tilted her head slightly, like one of the birds embroidered around her neckline. "You didn't really strike him on my account, did you?"

"Of course, I did."

She bit her bottom lip, but the smile finally won out. He was entirely too pleased about that. It was like winning a prize at the fair. "Thank you," she said. She leaned closer, as if she had a secret. She smelled like sweets. It made him smile back. "I've wanted to punch him for a long time."

He was honestly baffled. "Then why did you pet him like he was a cat with a stepped-on tail?"

She opened her hand. In it was the red velvet pouch with the gold tassel. The one Eaton had taken with him after the wagers. The one he'd tucked inside his waistcoat, full of coins.

"How else was I supposed to confiscate this?" She asked, all innocence. "Since it's our future being wagered on and mocked, we should get the spoils, don't you think?" She added under her breath, fiercely. "Finally."

Dougal stared at her.

She hadn't been smoothing Eaton's waistcoat.

She'd been *stealing* from him.

"Miss Swift," he said in all earnestness. "You truly are splendid."

Chapter Five

N O ONE HAD ever called her splendid before.

Oh, she was accustomed to a certain amount of flattery when someone discovered she was a viscount's daughter, and, better, a goddaughter to the Duke of Pendleton. She had been lovely, well-mannered, pretty. But no one had ever *meant* it. And certainly not after catching her doing something peculiar.

Twice.

It would have been enough for any other gentleman to reasonably decline any association with her. Ladies who picked pockets were not generally welcomed among the family silver. But Dougal was only amused, and then impressed.

And now she was set to visit his estate. For several weeks. In the middle of nowhere. With nothing to distract her from whatever it was that shimmered between them.

Pendleton had always been sneaky. The only thing his age had done was make him sneakier still, because there was no earthly chance that she was being sent to catalogue broken pottery pieces and flints and marble busts in the home of a single duke looking for a wife merely for the historical worth of it. It strained credulity.

She couldn't afford to let it turn her head. She had to stay realistic. But if she enjoyed the warm glow still blooming in her chest, who was there to know? It felt like a rose made of fire, just burning behind her ribcage. Alone in her chambers, she pressed her hands to her warm cheeks, still smiling. What a goose she was being.

And what a lovely thing to have a secret moment to allow herself to be a goose.

However short-lived it might be.

The knock at the door was loud but cursory, even though it was three o'clock in the morning. Tamsin sailed inside, trailing Priya, and surprisingly, Clara. "I told you she'd be awake." Tamsin dropped onto the forest-green settee, her dressing gown wafting with lace. She pointed to the tea trays. "And I told you she'd have ordered treats for us."

Meg had ordered both trays for herself, truth be told. Hot tea strong enough to stain the pretty china cups and baskets of pastries and cheeses. She'd already packed away the candied violets scattered as decorations. Tamsin plucked a raspberry tart off the nearest tray. It dripped with sweet sticky icing. "This is why you're my favorite," she declared, licking the sugar off her thumb.

"This morning, *I* was your favorite," Priya pointed out drily. "When you needed to borrow my blue gloves."

Clara sat primly. "I've never been your favorite." There was a gleam of amusement in her eyes. Meg rarely saw it and each time made her wonder what Clara might really be like if she wasn't so stiff and formal. There was sense of humor lurking under the neat-as-a-pin exterior. Not that Meg was one to judge. She used manners to shield herself every day. She settled back into her chair, resigned to the decimation of her sweets. "Clara, would you like some tea?"

"No, thank you."

Tamsin rolled her eyes. "You don't want anything to eat either, do you?"

"Actually, I'll take a chocolate twist."

Tamsin narrowed her eyes. "You know those are my favorite."

"I do."

Tamsin paused, then burst out laughing. "Well done. There's hope for you yet."

"I'm sure I'm relieved to hear it."

Meg poured tea for the others. She added cream, a touch of honey, and took her time stirring it. A sip, a slow perusal of the pastries, another sip. "Meg!" Tamsin burst out.

"Seven minutes," Meg laughed.

"That's the longest she's been patient for in ages," Priya said over her cup. Her dark hair was braided over one shoulder and she wore a paisley shawl.

Tamsin sat back. "You are both terrible friends," she informed them loftily. "*Meg Swift*," she added desperately when Meg didn't say anything else.

"All right," she grinned. "Yes. Yes, I got it." Meg held up the red velvet pouch more than a little triumphantly. The coins inside clinked with all the joy of a Christmas carol.

"Well done, you!" Tamsin crowed. "Oh, it serves him right, the ass."

Meg dumped the coins out. Clara frowned. "What's this?"

"Meg finally reclaimed the wager purse," Tamsin said.

"Stole, you mean."

Tamsin sniffed. "It's ours. We're the ones they are betting on."

Clara tilted her head, her pale hair glowing in the lamplight. "I suppose that's true."

"It's entirely true," Meg said, dividing the coins into four small piles. "And so, to the victors go the spoils."

Tamsin rubbed her hands together. "I hope he knows it was us."

"Who?" Clara asked.

"Eaton."

"How was he even invited?" Priya said indignantly.

"Pendleton must not know what he's like."

"That, at the very least, I can rectify." Her left eye narrowed, the way it always did when she was thinking. Or plotting. "There must be something I can use against him. There's no conceivable way he's smart enough to hide *all* of his misdeeds."

"Not from you, anyway," Tamsin agreed. "I think the real problem is he barely bothers to hide them at all. Last time he tried to grope me, we were waltzing and surrounded by nearly a hundred other dancers. So, either no one believes it of him, or they are too used to it to be bothered."

"You might be right."

"Uh oh."

"What?"

Meg nudged her. "I know that look." Priya smiled innocently. Meg shook her head. "That innocent expression makes you look dyspeptic."

"Well, never mind, innocence never got me anywhere anyway."

"You'll shock the Mamas."

"Good."

"This only proves that we need to be careful with our reputations," Clara put in. "And our chaperones."

"Rubbish," Priya disagreed. "What it proves it that men need to be held to a higher standard of behavior than they have been." She smiled again, this time grimly. "And that our vengeance be swift and bloody."

"I don't see what we can do about it," Clara said. "Though clearly, Eaton is not marriageable. I shall strike him off the list."

"You have a list?" Tamsin asked, curiously. "It is alphabetized?"

"Naturally."

Priya looked interested. "I should like to compare notes one day."

Tamsin snorted. "Between the two of you we shall have our own secret Debrett's."

Priya tilted her head. "Tamsin, that is brilliant," she said. "Instead of a list of peers, it will be a list of fortune hunters."

"And jackasses."

Clara's entire spine tightened. "Language, Lady Tamsin."

"Oh, bother it, it's an apt word under the circumstances."

"We each have twelve guineas," Meg interrupted, trying to steer the conversation to safer ground.

"I might splurge on new ribbons, now that we know how useful they are," Priya said. "And some orchids."

"*More* orchids?" Tamsin teased. "Are there any left that you don't already have? I should think the South Americas are plucked bare."

"I could buy paints," Meg said. She could, but she wouldn't. It was nearly winter, and she needed to save the money for something practical, like potatoes for the tenants. But it was nice to think of proper pigments and drawing paper and new pencils. Or, best of all, a watercolor set from Ackerman's in London. "What about you, Clara?"

"I should like to finally have a beautifully bound copy of Childe Harold," she admitted. Although Byron was fantastically popular, he did seem rather risqué for Clara—both his reputation and his poetry. Neither of which were the reason Meg, Tamsin and Priya all paused with identical expressions: narrowed eyes and pursed lips. Clara's eyes widened. "What did I say? I know it's frivolous but—"

They replied as one, firmly, acidly. "We do not read Byron."

Clara was momentarily taken aback. "Why not?"

"He's a self-indulgent git," Tamsin muttered.

"That's hardly news."

"And he was rude to me." Also, not exactly news about a man known for his temper and his dramatic outbursts.

"Ah."

"*Very* rude." Tamsin did not elaborate. Clara did not press. Meg changed the subject entirely. "What will you do with your ill-gotten gains, Tam?"

"I have my eye on a haunted artifact."

Clara shuddered. "How gruesome."

"I agree." Priya wrinkled her nose. "I prefer orchids to ghosts."

Tamsin shrugged cheerfully. "I like the idea that we're not alone."

AFTER A BREAKFAST of toasted muffins with honey among a dozen bleary-eyed guests, Meg, Priya and Tamsin cornered their godfather in his study. He was drinking coffee and reading through a stack of letters. A fire burned cheerily in the grate and fog pressed against the glass.

"This is cozy," Tamsin said, greeting him with a kiss on the cheek. "And you look fresh as a daisy. The others are positively haggard this morning."

"Bah, the younger set can't hold their drink."

This from a man who had been acting like an elderly grandfather just last night. Meg regarded him steadily. "You tricked me."

He sucked in an offended breath. "I would never."

She raised an eyebrow. "You never told me the collection I'm to draw for you belongs to the Duke of Thorncroft."

Tamsin sat up. "You're staying with Thorncroft?"

"Apparently so."

Tamsin grinned at Pendleton. "Well done, Your Grace."

He looked both proud and perilously close to sulking. "It wasn't a trick. Is it so wrong to want you to have the same happiness I had with the late duchess?"

"No." Meg softened. He still missed his late wife terribly and she had died seven years ago. "But you have to be realistic, Your Grace."

"I want my girls married," he insisted, stubbornly.

Meg laughed before she could stop herself. "I'm not marrying Dougal."

"Dougal, is it?"

"He's a *duke*."

"And thus nearly good enough for you, my dear."

Meg shook her head. "You are incorrigible. And you know very well that dukes don't marry penniless girls."

"I can dowry you."

She shook her head again. "That's kind of you, Your Grace." It was a tempting daydream, even if Dougal wasn't involved. To have options. Add Dougal with his confidence and his kindness and those wicked eyes and it was too good to be true. She must remember that.

"So stubborn."

"Almost as stubborn as you," Priya said drily.

"Meg is still a viscount's daughter," Pendleton continued. "And he has to marry. Soon."

"You did seem to get along well," Tamsin pointed out.

"Traitor," Meg muttered. They could never know that he'd punched Lord Eaton partially on her account. She refused to blush just thinking about it.

"He is a little violent," Tamsin allowed.

"There, you see," Meg said.

"Which makes him even more perfect for you."

Meg frowned. "I beg your pardon."

"You're the blood-thirstiest of us all. And *I* collect body parts."

Pendleton's smugness was palpable. He glanced at Priya. "Before you get any ideas, I'm not marrying again," she told him flatly.

"Don't you want companionship?"

"I don't need marriage for that."

The duke choked on his coffee. "Priya! You'd say such things to an old man?"

"Find me an old man and let's see," she returned.

"You can't mean it."

"I am a widow with a considerable fortune. Why on earth should I give that up?"

"For love?"

"Would you give up your fortune for love? Your ability to make decisions for yourself? Sign contracts. Be an actual person in the eyes of the law?" He sputtered. "Exactly so," she said smugly. "Now about these Cinderella balls."

He looked mutinous. "Tamsin and Clara and Meg and the others might want to marry, even if you do not."

"True, which is why you cannot invite Lord Eaton to these affairs any longer."

"I hazarded as much when Thorncroft laid him flat," he said. "Though no one will tell me why."

"He's lecherous."

Pendleton's scowl was thunderous. "Has he touched you? Any of you?"

They didn't reply. He swore viciously, which he never did in their presence. "That's why Henry…"

"Henry did what?" Tamsin asked.

"He drove Eaton clear out of the house. He left at dawn for London. Henry too."

"Whatever for?"

"I believe Henry means to make life very complicated for Lord Eaton," he replied. "I approve, of course, but how am I supposed to know these things if no one will tell me?"

"Clara has a list," Priya said.

The duke looked at Meg. "Thorncroft is not like that."

"I know."

"I had him vetted."

"Did you?" Priya said. "You *are* serious."

Meg groaned. "Don't encourage him."

Pendleton patted her hand. "Be a good girl, now. I need to sort out his artifacts. That's as true as anything else."

Meg sighed. She knew that. And she knew when she'd been beaten. "Of course."

"You'll leave today."

"I still need a chaperone."

"Lady Blackwell has agreed to join you. She's gone home to pack her wigs and secure that spaniel of hers."

Meg was surprised. "But she hates to travel." Lady Blackwell's phobia of carriages was notorious. She rarely left Little Barrow and when she did, it was generally in an open pony cart, regardless of the weather. She had been trapped in a London riot years ago and the experience had never truly left her. Meg couldn't imagine her willingly entering a closed carriage for several hours and it was too cold for a pony cart, no matter what she might say about it.

"She wouldn't go to London for love or money," the duke said. "But as it happens, Conall has sent funds to help with some rebuilding and redecoration of her house."

"If Lady Blackwell wishes to be away from the dust and clamor, surely she would prefer staying with Lady Culpepper." Persephone's grandmother and Henry's grandmother couldn't be more different, but they had been lifelong friends. And Lady Culpepper lived just on the neighborhood estate.

"She might, but she has decided she would prefer an adventure. And she feels that a carriage ride north in broad daylight is something she can contend with."

"And she wants us married off almost as much as you do," Priya pointed out.

"Persephone's grandmother!" Tamsin grinned. "Oh, that *is* going to be a visit to remember."

"And the rest of it?" Meg asked pointedly.

Pendleton fiddled with the handle of his cup. "Ah, that."

"Yes, that."

"What exactly?" Priya demanded.

"That's what I'm waiting to find out," Meg said, not turning away from their godfather. He was entirely too slippery.

He winced. "As to that… there may have been an incident last night."

Each of the women leaned forward, abruptly and preternaturally alert. "What's happened?" Meg asked. "Did someone insult you?"

He smiled. "My Furies. I don't know why they call you the Cinderellas." He sat back in his chair, sighing. "Nothing's happened to me, but I was informed someone broke into my study during the ball."

Byron himself could have strolled into the room and demanded a kiss and they could not have been more offended.

"Someone stole from you?" Tamsin asked.

"What did they take?" Meg said.

"Who?" Priya added, darkly. "Who was it?"

He held up a hand. "Nothing was taken, but as you know, there were several antiquarians and collectors among the guests. And there was a letter on my desk here from the late Duke of Thorncroft."

Meg narrowed her eyes. She did not like where this was going. "And?"

"It was about a hoard of Tudor artifacts he believed was hidden inside the abbey somewhere."

Meg tilted her head, confused, and suspicious. "Why should that be a problem?"

"The footman later identified Lord Eaton as the man who was chased out of this room."

"He was certainly busy last night," Tamsin scowled.

"Worse, he went straight to Lord Allensby."

Priya groaned. "I've never met such a gossip in my life."

"He's also a collector specializing in the Tudor period."

"Of course, he is," Meg said. "Why is this such a dilemma?"

Pendleton rubbed his face wearily. "Who knew who he has already told. Thorncroft is about to have treasure hunters swarm his estate. I need you to help him."

"Me?" Meg asked. "What can I do? Tamsin is sneakier than me and Priya knows everyone's secrets. I'm not even an antiquarian!"

"But you'll already be there sketching the Roman collection so it won't be obvious. And if we can find the treasure before the others, Thorncroft needn't be inconvenienced."

Meg knew exactly how inconvenienced Dougal was about to be. Antiquarians were bad enough; treasure hunters were even more relentless. They would invade his house under any pretext. And Eaton now had a personal vendetta against him. It would not end well if he was left to his devices. "I still don't see why you don't send someone more suited."

"You are perfectly suited. Leonard preserved the art of Thorncroft Abbey religiously, if you'll pardon the pun. And he added paintings to every available wall and ceiling, even though his father did not leave him much space. I trust you to see where a painting might be off more than I trust even an expert in Tudor houses. It's as likely to be behind a wall as under a floorboard."

"I'm not investigating old privies." She heard stories.

"Of course not," The duke was flushed, getting agitated as he often did over these matters. "But we cannot let historical artifacts like these fall into the hands of collectors who barely deserve the title, who would sell them off to aristocrats with more money than sense so they might redecorate their drawing rooms." Big words for a man with several drawing rooms full of artifacts. He sucked in an offended breath. "Lord Allensby recently had a soiree where they unwrapped a mummy he brought in from Egypt."

"You bring in mummies all of the time," Priya pointed out drily. "And you have soirees."

"And I'm always jealous," Tamsin muttered. "*I don't have a mummy.*"

"Allensby used it as tinder when they were done."

"He *burnt it?*" Tamsin wailed, equally agitated.

"Who knows what he or his cronies would do the Thorncroft treasure!"

Meg and Priya exchanged a glance as the others worked themselves into a fit.

"It needs to be properly preserved!"

Since Pendleton was turning an alarming shade of puce that Lady Blackwell would have coveted for her next wig, Meg already knew she was going to agree. Lord Eaton needed to be stopped, and Dougal didn't deserve to be saddled with such a problem. She felt a tiny bit guilty that Dougal had laid him out partly on her behalf. If she hadn't told him what he was like, he would have had no reason to punch him.

As delicious as it had been, it probably wasn't worth the hassle of having Eaton at his heels like a rabid badger.

"What is this treasure supposed to be, anyway?" She had vague recollections of her governess talking about the Dissolution of the Monasteries. "Gold coins? Silver plates?"

"And art. Precious Medieval and Renaissance art. The abbey was a scriptorium in its heyday."

He knew perfectly well how important art was to her.

She slumped, nettled and defeated. "You fight dirty, old man."

Chapter Six

IT TOOK SEVERAL drops of laudanum, a bottle of brandy at the ready, and her dog Chartreuse, but Lady Blackwell was eventually ready to travel. She fell asleep almost immediately and Meg and Dougal climbed into a separate carriage to give her privacy, following behind. A chaperone was meant to be at the ready at all times, but as Meg was no longer a debutante fresh out of the schoolroom, it hardly signified. And there was no one to fuss over it at any rate, especially since Clara had gone for a walk. It would do well enough.

And it wasn't as though she imagined Dougal was waiting to leap on her.

Although, she *could* certainly imagine it.

Quite clearly, as it happened.

His mouth would be hot against her throat, his hands firm at her waist. His weight would press her into the carriage cushions, deliciously heavy. His breath would turn ragged, filling her ear with the sound of his desire. Heat flared inside her at the thought. She wondered that her stays didn't melt.

"Are you comfortable?" Dougal asked politely, his rough voice scraping against her pulse, even from across the carriage.

She cleared her throat. "Yes, thank you."

Comfortably mortified.

She turned her attention to the carriage, over-decorated and ridiculous in its ornamentation. She adored it. The ceiling had been painted with a great many doves flying across a turbulent sky. The seats were done in a matching gray-blue, with gold paint on every other available surface. If the abbey was anything like this, no wonder Pendleton had chosen her. Dougal followed her gaze, looking embarrassed. "It came like this," he said. "The previous family's tastes were....excessive."

"I love it."

He was surprised. "You do?"

"It's entirely too much," she agreed cheerfully. "But also entirely unapologetic. Sometimes we need a little beauty for no other reason than it brings joy."

How many times had a painting, or a particularly creative piece of embroidery saved her from feeling dejected or lonely? Or vengeful, to be truthful.

"You can't eat beauty."

Except, sometimes you could. Art had put food in her belly more than once. Her embroidered handkerchiefs sold quite well at the village dress shop. No one had to know that a bloodthirsty fury sometimes lurked beneath the white threads of snowdrop flowers and prancing rabbits. And her uncle could find little fault in her "ladylike" habits, as long as her other work was completed.

She didn't say any of that, of course.

"You might not be able to eat beauty, but if your belly is already reasonably full, beauty can feed other parts of you."

"I suppose so." He leaned forward as if he was sharing a great secret. He motioned to the doves over his head. "I still don't like it."

She grinned. "Fair enough."

"But if you love this, "he said. "You will love the abbey." He seemed to stumble over the word. "I've never seen so many murals. Even in the kitchens."

"Oh, I do love that." She tilted her head. "Do you know you flinch when you say the word abbey?"

"Caught that, did you?" When she nodded, he sighed. "I get the feeling you see more than the average person."

She tried not to beam at that, but it felt like a compliment, like sunshine sneaking under her stays.

"I never imagined I would own an abbey of all things," he admitted. The road bumped by outside the window, abandoning Little Barrow for the fields and wooded glens. "Though, it's not exactly that anymore. Nor a hall, or a manor. It's more of a hodgepodge. Like someone made a stew from the week's leftovers."

"It must be quite…different from where you lived before."

"Yes."

He didn't say anything else. Fair enough. She wasn't rushing to tell him that she had to pick wild mint for her tea and that she spent most mornings cleaning the grates of her childhood home under her uncle's sneering glares. Or that she had to bribe the Cook, who was loyal to her uncle, for butter.

"Has the duke spoken to you about your treasure?" She asked quietly instead.

Dougal leaned his head back. "He was very sorry about letting that information go public," he said. "But I don't see the fuss. How bad can a historian be?"

Meg closed her eyes briefly. He had no idea.

"That bad?" He asked with a smile.

"Worse," she said. "Worse even than toddlers after too much cake. Peevish, obsessed. Tyrannical. And those are the ones I love."

His eyebrows rose. "I stand corrected."

"I hope we can avert the crisis before it begins." Honestly, she wasn't convinced.

There was a hamper at their feet, packed with sandwiches, pears, and hard cheese. And those little buns stuffed with apples and raisins that she liked so much. She wondered if it was too soon to start eating. She'd barely glanced at the basket and Dougal was already lifting the lid. "Let's see what we've got here."

He pulled the paper off one of the sandwiches. "Apple slices, cheese, and butter? That's different."

"It's my favorite," she confessed. And unlike her uncle's cook, Pendleton's cook adored every one of his goddaughters.

Dougal passed her the paper-wrapped parcel and dug deeper.

"A bottle of lemonade, another of wine. And jumbles." He grinned. "I admit, these are *my* favorite."

He bit into a sugar-dusted biscuit shaped like a Celtic knot. She eyed one consideringly. He raised an eyebrow. "It's not gentlemanly, I'm sure, but I would fight the queen herself for these biscuits."

"Would you now?"

Sometimes, a dare was as delicious as any sugar biscuit.

And she was fast.

He was faster.

She'd barely nicked one out of the hamper before his hand closed around her wrist. "Tsk," he clicked his tongue admonishingly. "Best stick to almonds, I think," he suggested mildly. The gleam of humor in his eye was wicked and every bit as appealing as the sculpted line of his jaw.

They grappled playfully. His fingers were warm, utterly unbreakable but also careful not to bruise her. She tumbled forward, caught off balance. His free hand settled on her hip, his leg sliding between her. The motion was intimate, private. Heat raced along the back of her thighs.

The moment lengthened, quiet and close. His breath stirred the hair at her temples. The blue of his eyes was arresting. She felt ensnared, but deliciously so. His gaze dipped to her mouth. She licked her lower lip. The air was suddenly charged, a soft moment gone electric. It tingled through her.

And then the carriage bumped over a hole in the road, jostling them in a most unromantic way. Dougal steadied her so she didn't pitch forward and accidentally break his nose with the crown of her head. He eased her back onto the seat. She liked to think there was some regret in him as he released her. When the moment dissolved, she sat back, smiling smugly.

He was immediately suspicious. "What's that smile for?"

"A good pickpocket always knows how to use a distraction to her advantage." She waggled her other hand, the one he hadn't bothered securing. In it, she held a perfectly baked jumble. She took a big, triumphant bite, ladylike manners be damned.

Dougal blinked for a startled moment. Then he burst into

laughter. The sound of it awakened a response in her chest. It was such a happy sound. "I see I will have to keep on my toes with you."

It was strange pleasure to be able to show off a little, to demonstrate an odd, not to mention illegal, talent that she generally kept secret. He wasn't shocked, or disgusted. And he wasn't judging her when he asked, "Never mind a treasure hunter, how does a viscount's daughter become such a knuckles?"

"A knuckles?" She asked, charmed. "Is that what I am?"

"So they'd call you in Manchester, and in London, I imagine. And with your proficiency you'd be a Dead Nail as well."

Her smile widened. "I much prefer those titles to thief and family embarrassment."

"Punishment is the same, I imagine."

Her smile slipped. "I suppose so."

"So why risk it?" he asked quietly.

She tried for a light-hearted tone, the kind a lady who danced all night and stole golden almonds for entertainment might affect. "Balls are terribly boring, aren't they?"

"Hmm."

It was obvious he didn't believe her.

Even though she was polite, impoverished spinster Meg Swift with the gentle manners, no one ever bothered to question her. How contrary she was that she liked him all the better for it. "It began as a lark," she added. "When we were children. Just to pass the time." That was technically true. "I just happened to be a fair hand at it."

"Ah."

He seemed to know that wasn't the full story, but he didn't press. She had the ridiculous urge to tell him everything. She took another giant bite of the jumble instead. His mouth quirked, as though he was fighting a smile.

And then his face hardened, his head snapping to the right.

Something was wrong.

SOMETHING WAS DEFINITELY wrong.

It had been a thoroughly enjoyable afternoon with the inscrutable Splendid Miss Swift, sharing sweets and secrets. Well, not secrets exactly. She was clearly carrying more than her fair share. But it didn't change the fact that he wasn't good enough for Meg, despite the pull between them. It wasn't just heat, but also curiosity, enjoyment. She made him smile. She even made him forget how uncomfortable he was.

But she was miles above him, no matter his new rank. He was still a street boy from Manchester, born of an unknown sailor and a drunk mother. Only Old George had kept him and his siblings alive and relatively out of trouble.

George was the reason Dougal had only flirted with crime instead of falling headlong into it. He'd shared his one room and his meager food with three strangers' children. They'd eaten porridge or a single potato for most meals for months on end until Dougal had managed to find work. Grueling, dangerous work but he'd have washed the Devil's own arse if it meant making sure his little sister was never desperate enough to join a bawdy house. And if it meant he could repay George his kindness as his little brother grew, his stomach becoming a bottomless pit never to be filled.

And now George slept on a feather mattress, Charlie was learning how to embroider (badly) and Colin had an opinion on his cravat.

The world had changed.

But not so much that he could imagine someone like Meg accepting the suit of someone like him. Even with the Prince of Wales's seal of approval. He was starting to see that the aristocracy might bow to him but they didn't have nice things to say about the prince, outside his pursuit of fine architecture. They mocked his manners and his drinking, which was the height of hypocrisy, in Dougal's opinion.

But who was he to say anything? He was wearing boots that cost more than a year's wages and flirting with a viscount's daughter.

It was surprisingly pleasant.

Until, that faint sound, barely noticeable. If he hadn't been listening to machinery for the last few years, ears constantly trained for a warning of malfunction, he doubt he would have heard it. And even now, it was probably just overzealousness on his part. Vestiges of a time, not so long ago, where one faulty piece of a loom could have injured several, severing fingers and limbs or even taking lives.

But this was a duke's lavish and over-decorated carriage filled with painted doves and gilded woodwork.

Still.

He rapped sharply on the roof. "Stop. *Now*."

It took a moment for the coachman to halt the horses. The carriage rolled to a bumpy stop, teetering slightly. Meg didn't look alarmed. Dougal, having not much experience with carriages or horses, took it to mean a little teetering was to be expected.

Even so, something wasn't sitting right.

"What is it?" Meg asked. "Are you ill?"

"No."

One of the outriders had already leapt down to open the door for them. Dougal got out, turning to offer his hand to help Meg down. She followed, glancing about curiously, when she felt the urgency of his touch. He wanted her safely out of there until he figured out what was happening.

It was a fine autumn day, full of sunshine and wind pulling at the long grasses on either side of the road. The road was muddy but passable. No highwayman lurked in the bushes. The horses were calm to the point of being bored. "All right, Your Grace?" The outrider asked. His cheeks were red from being buffeted by the wind as he clung to the back of the carriage.

Dougal nodded absently and turned for a closer inspection of the carriage. It sat, looking as much like a cupcake as it always did. Everything was painted and gilded and carved with birds and oak leaves.

Something creaked.

Dougal bent to look at the wheel. One of the spokes had a hairline fracture, like a break in the ice of an otherwise placid pond.

And just as dangerous.

The next creak of wood had a different tone.

And then it cracked like a pistol.

It was instinct more than rational thought that had Dougal grabbing Meg and pulling her behind his body, just as the spoke shattered and the wheel gave way. The carriage jerked to the side, tilting drunkenly. The coachman cursed as he struggled to contain the spooked horses. The carriage dragged through the road a few feet, then lodged itself firmly. Meg squeaked in surprise.

"'Gor," the outrider breathed. "You have the devil's own luck, Your Grace. If you don't mind me saying."

"We could have been seriously injured," Meg said, stunned. If the wheel spoke had shattered like that while they were going too fast, or heaven forbid, going down a steep hill, who knows how many bones they might have broken. Truthfully, they might have died. She stood, eyes wide, hand pressed to her chest. "You saved us."

"Just lucky," he said.

"I don't think so." She disagreed as the coachmen unhooked the horses, who snorted, annoyed. "I'm glad no one was injured." She rubbed her arms as though she was chilled.

Fury sparked up his spine. Meg was frightened.

And she might have been killed.

He schooled his expression when the outrider took a nervous step backwards. Meg didn't seem concerned. "Never mind," she said briskly, but he could see the faint tremble in her fingers. "All's well that ends well."

"We'll see to the horses," the coachman assured her. He shook his head. "It's that sorry, I am. In all my years I've never seen a spoke snap like that. The collapse took the axel out too, looks like."

Anyone at the ball could have been behind it. A guest, a stableboy, a servant. There had been hundreds of people flooding through the grounds.

"I'm sorry for your carriage," Meg said softly.

She ought to be sorry for the culprit.

Because he knew exactly what had happened to the spoke, if not who did it. He'd seen his share of "accidents" at the mill.

And he knew one thing for certain.

That wheel had been sabotaged.

THERE WAS STEEL beneath that calm, measured exterior. She'd seen a flash of it when he inspected the wheel. No, not steel, stone. Grounded, true. Easy to miss and just as easy to rely on.

And she knew just what he'd seen to make him still like that. She sent him a wry smile, trying to calm the pounding of her heart which was still convinced they had both been ejected from the carriage and were even now lying in broken pieces in the road.

Dougal's calm steadiness was eclipsed by a new leashed intensity. It radiated off him, with nearly the same warmth of his arm against hers. The collapse of the carriage had been a surprise, but what continued to send shivers through her wasn't the near-miss of an accident. It was the way Dougal had shoved her behind his body to protect her. She knew that it was in his nature, he would have done the same for anyone. But for herself, apart from the Cinderellas, she couldn't think of the last time someone had shown that kind of concern for her. She tucked it inside her ribcage, nestled close to that burning rose. Something to remember when she was an old woman, still a spinster, but one with stories.

"I did warn you about treasure hunters," she said, her tone mild, masking all sorts of emotions.

"You said historians."

"Treasure hunters are even worse."

He looked stunned. "You're serious."

"I'm afraid so. Someone at the party wanted to get to your house before you did."

"You could have been killed." He didn't raise his voice but it changed, just enough to send an answering frisson across the back of her neck. Not like the kind of fear leftover from the carriage accident, but a kind of primal awareness, close to fear and yet very different.

Perhaps she'd hit her head and hadn't realized it yet. She surreptitiously touched her hair. No blood, no pain, only her dependable braid coronet.

"Are you sure you weren't hurt?" Dougal asked.

She shook her head. "I'm perfectly well."

They were standing alone in the middle of the road. The coachman and the footman had taken the horses to fetch another carriage. It would take them some time, even if there was an inn nearby. Lady Blackwell was far ahead of them, along with the third carriage packed with belongings and her lady's maid and Chartreuse's maid. The dog had his own maid, who saw to his meals and his exercise and baths and carpet cleanings. None of which was particularly helpful at the moment. Still, all of their limbs were intact, and the sun was shining on their heads, taking the crisp out of the early autumn air. Not to mention that the company was both handsome and enjoyable. It wasn't so bad.

"Shall we walk, Your Grace?" She suggested. He wasn't acting impatient, but she could tell that he would rather be moving, doing something.

"Only if you stop calling me that," he grumbled.

"I shouldn't."

"There are only swallows and thistle finches to hear us and I'm not sure I care what they think," he pointed out.

"I suppose I can't argue with that," she allowed. "Are we far from the abbey?"

"Less than an hour by carriage," he answered. "Considerably longer by foot."

Luckily, it had been a dry week and the road was not filled with muddy holes to navigate. The wind moved through bramble bushes and tall yarrow as they followed the hoofprints. Hills rolled gently as far as the eye could see, crossed here and there with low stone walls. It was peaceful and picturesque.

"I'm almost afraid to ask but what else should I expect from these treasure hunters?"

"Some are harmless," she said. "But even they might have the numbers, if word gets out and enough of them think it worth the trip to the country. The duke once had to shoot a man who had hidden in the pond for hours and then crept through the house dripping seaweed, all for want of a specific collection of Roman coins. He broke the housekeeper's wrist when he was first apprehended and then tried to bite a footman."

"Bloody hell." He winced at his language. "Apologies."

"I suppose the duke neglected to mention who will no doubt be spreading stories of your hidden treasure?"

"Who is it?"

Meg sighed. Her godfather would owe her new paints for this part alone. "Eaton. Though I reckon he's after the trouble not the treasure. Either way, he's likely to make things difficult."

Dougal stopped. "That bastard?"

"I'm afraid so. Now that his pride has been hurt, he will make it all the worse for you."

He nearly rolled his eyes. "I can handle a toff."

"I don't think Lord Eaton is a…gentleman. Beyond his title, I mean." Not wanting to worry him she injected a note of brisk cheerfulness into her voice. It was the same tone she used when there was flooding in the fields or beetles in the cabbages. There was no use in dwelling on misfortune. One did what needed doing. The first step and then the next step after that. "Never fear," she added. "I am here to confound all plots."

She probably should not sound so confident. Seeing as she wasn't. In the slightest.

"Aye, about that."

She waited for the inevitable protest over her gender, her skills, his honor.

"Thank you," he said instead, simply.

She melted.

Damn him, she melted instantly.

He's not for you, she reminded herself.

"You're welcome. But I should probably admit to not having as much experience as might be assumed in these matters. Despite the duke's confidence." Stubbornness.

"I have every faith in you," Dougal said. "But I have a condition."

"Which is?"

"You are not to put yourself in harm's way for this bloody ridiculous treasure."

"The duke is very worried over the proper care of historical relics."

"I don't give a damn," he said bluntly. "I'll burn them all to cinders before I risk a life over them."

He meant it too. It was a refreshing change to the usual willingness to sacrifice various limbs in pursuit of history. To be fair, she was hardly better. She might give a toe for art. A little one.

He looked down at her, as if he could read her every thought. "I'm going to need your word, Meg."

Her name on his lips was like hot tea on a cold day.

"Meg."

"Of course," she said. "I'm not keen to throw myself in front of a bullet for a handful of old pottery."

"A bullet," he shook his head. "And here I thought toffs only knew about horses and wine."

"They are each to a one relentless." She paused. "But then again you have an advantage few can claim."

"You?"

"Hardly." She grinned. "But you *will* have Lady Blackwell in the house and she is positively ruthless."

"The same sweet old lady who matches her dog's collar to her gown every morning?"

"Utterly ruthless," Meg insisted. "And the dog's a biter too."

He laughed. "Duly noted."

Chapter Seven

IT TOOK JUST over half an hour for the coachman to return with a rented cart from someone's farm. He apologized as Meg climbed into the back, sitting on bits of hay.

"Don't trouble yourself," she assured him. "It's a fine day."

"You should have a fine carriage," Dougal winced, settling next to her. "One without a broken wheel."

"I like carts," she said simply, tilting her face up the sun. He watched her fondly, as though he couldn't help himself.

It took under an hour to reach the Thorncroft estate.

As expected, it was stunning. There was no other word for it. Nestled among hills and surrounded with orchards, every perspective made her want to draw. The driveway meandered through groves of willows, keeping pace along a wide river, and then through the shadows of several tall oaks before reaching the gardens.

The gardens, though in their autumn decline, still maintained their beauty. They were lush and wild even within the constraints of such formal old-fashioned arrangements. Yew hedges hid secret wells of larkspur and foxgloves. Hollyhocks stood in rows like pink-wigged footmen. Bright spots of wilting color added cheer to a house that that had been built to be imposing and impressive, to awe anyone coming up the drive, both when it was an abbey and afterwards. It succeeded.

The original structure was several hundred years old, with

wings added on either side to create a courtyard dripping with ivy and sunshine. It was partly Tudor, partly Gothic in style, with a ruined medieval tower on one end.

"It's a bit much," Dougal muttered as the carriage pulled to a stop.

"It's beautiful," Meg said as the butler and housekeeper led the household staff out onto the gravel drive to greet them.

"It's been neglected for all of its pomp and circumstance."

"I am sure you can rectify that." Though some of the stones could use repointing and the windows needed a thorough cleaning, it was hardly falling apart. The gatehouse where Meg lived had been reclaimed from a family of foxes. And the roofs of the tenant cottages were more birds' nest than thatch. "Nothing that can't be fixed," she added.

A footman offered his hand to help her down. The cheerfulness of sunshine and hay faded to sunlight on gray stones and starched aprons and polite smiles. "Welcome back, Your Grace," the butler said. He had the build of a pugilist under his plum-colored uniform. He smiled easily.

"Thank you, Mr. Canterbury," Dougal said. "Mr. Canterbury, Mrs. Hill, this is Miss Swift."

"Very good, Your Grace." Mrs. Hill looked sour. She had immediately noticed Dougal's mistake in introducing the servants to a guest and not the other way around. And that Dougal had introduced Canterbury as *Mr.* Canterbury instead of just Canterbury. She didn't seem the forgiving sort.

Meg met her gaze directly. "Mrs. Hill."

"I assume Lady Blackwell is safely inside?" Dougal asked, even as Chartreuse bulleted through the open door, barking as though he owned the house.

Lady Blackwell followed at a more leisurely pace. "There you are, I was beginning to think highwaymen had got you." She did not look remotely concerned. She probably thought they had stopped for an assignation.

"We had an adventure with a broken wheel, I'm afraid," Meg said before she could get any more ideas, or worse, say them out loud.

"Oh, dear, are you hurt?"

"Not a bit."

Mrs. Hill bobbed a curtsy. "I'll have tea brought to the drawing room immediately."

"Oh, right," Dougal said. "Good idea. Thank you."

She nodded, the lace cap on her head quivering with indignation. Meg took note, a burst of protectiveness kindling inside her. Perhaps Mrs. Hill needed a little more time to acclimate herself to the surprising new situation. Meg wasn't without sympathy, especially as she'd often been required to act as her uncle's housekeeper. But Mrs. Hill had months already to get herself accustomed. That ought to be plenty. Particularly as Meg was certain that Dougal was not an exacting employer. He could barely meet the butler's eyes, for a start.

The rules might seem silly to him, but they would be used as a weapon against him if he didn't learn them.

"Well, that won't do," Lady Blackwell said to Meg quietly. "Never mind, we'll have the poor fellow sorted out in no time."

Dougal turned. "Lady Blackwell," he said. "Allow me to escort you inside."

Lady Blackwell smiled, the silk butterflies sewn into her bodice fluttering. "Thank you, *Your Grace.*" She lingered over the title, while glancing at Mrs. Hill. Mrs. Hill flushed and bobbed another low curtsy. Lady Blackwell had that effect on people, despite the fact that she generally dressed like a slice of cake crossed with some kind of fruit.

They proceeded up the sweep of stone steps, Chartreuse leading the way with a happy bark, the diamonds on his collar flashing.

THORNCROFT ABBEY DID not disappoint.

The bones of the house clearly belonged to an abbey, one only had to look as far as the pointed windows and the arched ribbed ceilings. Everywhere was soaring grandeur, from the marble friezes to the lush Rococo gilt wooden tables to the heavy velvet draperies tied up with gold ropes. And that was just what Meg could see from the front hall. The ceilings dripped with crystal chandeliers, set against paintings of complicated skies, angels battling, golden stars everywhere. Some of the paint was cracked. The mural of a medieval hunt with peeling unicorns and faded horses made Meg want to reach for her paints immediately. Before tea, even. Such disregard was criminal. The former duke had some answering to do.

She knew now why Pendleton had insisted she come.

"I haven't been here in decades," Lady Blackwell said. "Not since that house party where…. Well, never mind *that*."

Chartreuse shot up and down the stairs in a frenzy of tyranny and fluff. He called the various members of the family from their chambers more effectively than any housekeeper or butler could dream. Meg heard the footsteps and turned slightly towards Dougal, lowering her voice. "Make sure to introduce your family to Lady Blackwell, not the other way around, if they haven't met already. They might outrank her slightly, but she is older, a countess, and also the daughter of a duke."

He looked briefly confused. "That matters?"

She nodded. "I'm afraid so."

"Devil's *arsewit*." He sounded so wearily disgruntled that Meg burst out laughing. Dougal's ears went red. "I beg your pardon."

"Not at all."

A Black man with hair turned mostly white and a kind smile joined them from down the hall. He carried a pile of books.

"Lady Blackwell," Dougal said. "May I present George Williams."

George bowed. "An honor."

Lady Blackwell inclined her head as far as she could without toppling her traveling wig. "Mr. Williams."

"And Miss Swift," Dougal added, sounding only a little as though the formality of it made him want to burn his cravat. "May I also present George Williams."

"How do you do, Mr. Williams?" Meg asked with a curtsy.

"A right sight better now, Miss."

"Ease off, you old flirt," Dougal muttered. George grinned at Meg and she grinned back, already more comfortable here than she was in her uncle's house and most of the houses she'd visited outside her godfather's. "George lived with us in Manchester. Or, we lived with him, is more accurate." He motioned to a younger version of himself coming down the stairs, with the same thick hair and blue eyes. "My brother Colin—Uh, Lord Colin Black, Viscount Henley."

"A fine waistcoat, Lord Henley," Lady Blackwell approved, for obvious reasons. Colin's waistcoat was heavily embroidered green and gold thread leaves on crimson background. The buttons were covered in matching red silk.

Colin preened slightly. "Thank you, my lady."

A sigh interrupted them from the doorway to what looked like a blue parlor. "You look ridiculous."

"Charlie," Dougal said warningly. "My sister, Lady Charlotte."

Charlotte had thick brown curls like her brother's, the same blue eyes, but her smile was slower and considerably more defiant. She wore a plain white gown and no jewelry at all. Lady Blackwell would have something to say about it. "Hello," Charlotte said simply.

"Lady Charlotte," Meg smiled.

Charlotte narrowed her eyes. "It's *Charlie*."

Meg blinked at the vehemence in her tone. "Of course. I beg your pardon."

Dougal caught his sister's disgruntled gaze and shook his head once, pointedly.

Lady Blackwell stepped closer, all butterflies and bonhomie. "Oh, aren't you a beauty? We'll have you married in a thrice, my dear. You just need to wear a brighter gown. Something with color, to attract the eye. With a blue ribbon, perhaps."

"Told you so," Colin snorted.

Charlie paused and took a small subtle step backwards. "No, thank you?"

Lady Blackwell tilted her head. "No to the gowns or to a husband?"

"Both?"

"Not another one," she sighed. She pointed at Meg, thoroughly nettled. "This one says the same to me every time I bring it up."

Meg laughed.

"I find that hard to believe in a lady traveling with my brother the duke," Charlie said pointedly.

"Charlie, that's enough," Dougal said, warning in every syllable.

"Our Dougal here is causing a stir, it's true," George interrupted smoothly. "The ladies have been applying for house tours in hopes of catching a glimpse."

Dougal looked deeply embarrassed. Meg probably shouldn't think it was so adorable.

"Yesterday we found one trying to steal the tassels off the cushions in your room," Colin said. "For good luck."

"I…" Dougal trailed off, as if entirely unable to come up with a comment. For Meg, Charlie's rudeness suddenly made perfect sense.

Especially considering the stifled squeal emanating from behind a potted tree further down the hall.

Dougal's shoulders slumped and he suddenly looked more tired than a man three times his age. He exchanged a grim glance with his sister. "Not again."

"Eh?" Lady Blackwell frowned. "Meg, was that you?"

"Er, no." Not that she wasn't perfectly capable of hiding behind trees, but she knew better than to squeal when she did so. Even when confronted with the very handsome Duke of Thorncroft.

White ribbons fluttered from behind a handful of leaves. Someone shushed the squealer, in tones no less enthusiastic. Meg and the others looked at each other a moment, at a loss as to how to proceed with a debutante and her mother hiding in plain sight. They were all eyes and teeth. Chartreuse paused on a step and growled once. Another squeal, this time less giddy.

And then a dusky purple plum sailed through the air.

It went through the leaves and landed squarely against something like a striped cap sleeve.

"Maman!" The trees shrieked.

Meg turned towards the landing where an older lady stood,

tossing fruit at the strangers with an ease that suggested practice. Another woman stood beside her, shorter and dressed in so many layers of yellow it assaulted the eye. Clearly this was the Lady Marigold whom Lady Blackwell wanted to visit. Nothing else could account for the vibrancy of her gown.

"Off with you!" The taller woman barked. The ladies fled, back through whichever terrace door they had snuck in. Chartreuse followed them, barking, just in case they had a change of heart. Meg thought she might choke on the giggle bubbling in her throat.

Mrs. Hill darted after them, exploding from the nearby drawing room where she had been organizing tea. She paused. "I do beg your pardon, Your Grace," she said. "The tours have been explicitly told to remain in the gardens while you are at home. I shall see to it immediately." She marched after the wayward garden tour ladies, her spine like an iron poker.

Dougal just pinched the bridge of his nose. "Lady Blackwell, Miss Swift, may I present Lady Marigold, the duke's sister, and her companion Lady Beatrice."

Lady Blackwell squinted up the stairs. "Well, there you are."

The shorter and plumper lady with soft white curls peered back down. "Matilda Swithings? Is that you?"

"Lady Blackwell, these last fifty-one years. You're still wearing yellow, I see."

"It's *cheerful.*"

"You'd look better in turquoise. Yellow makes you look like a lemon," Lady Blackwell said in a supreme case of self-ignorance, considering Meg had seen her wear dresses the exact shade of orange marmalade. More than once. Also: limes and grapefruit. Possibly she considered the entire citrus family hers to defend.

"She looks like a daffodil," Lady Beatrice insisted.

"More like a pat of butter," Lady Blackwell snorted. "Bea, you're still a cantankerous old goat, but you did always have the soul of a poet."

The three women stared at each other for a moment, long enough to have everyone else shift nervously, before bursting into laughter. "I've missed you too," Lady Beatrice finally said.

Lady Blackwell grinned and then turned to holler, like any good fishmonger. "Canterbury! Whisky!"

They wandered away together, still chuckling. Not just chuckling, but outright cackling, like old witches.

"Now, I'm truly terrified," Dougal muttered.

Meg had only been inside the front hall of the house for less than a quarter of an hour and it was already her favorite place in all of England.

Europe, definitely.

The world, quite possibly.

Chapter Eight

"THAT WAS SPECTACULARLY rude," Dougal said to his sister, after tea had been had, crumpets nibbled, and any number of polite behavioral riddles upheld. He'd worried that Meg would be horrified at her welcome to Thorncroft Abbey but when the marzipan fruit began to fly, she'd beamed. Still, it hardly made his sister's rudeness acceptable. "Even for you, Charlie."

They were in the upstairs parlor, the one they all found most comfortable, as it was smaller and slightly less ostentatious. And by smaller, he meant that it could still have fit their entire flat in Manchester three times over. Gold flashed off every candlestick and there was a painting of a Roman goddess in every corner, but the couches were comfortable, and the fireplace was slightly marked with soot. It soothed him. Not to mention his sister's newfound obsession with collecting seashells on the beach translated into baskets overflowing with shells on every surface and glued to lampshades and tables.

The entire house was formal and stiff. It reminded him with every flash and fussy folderol that he did not belong here. Not really. He never would. But in this room, he could let down his defenses a little.

He knew his sister felt the same way. He tried to excuse her behavior—he certainly understood it. But he couldn't overlook it. She was only going to make things so much bloody worse for herself. He appreciated her defiance. Hell, most of him wanted to indulge in a good temper, but it would only prove the toffs right, the strangers and the servants watching his every move. It was no secret Mrs. Hill considered the new duke an affront to her dignity. He didn't much care for himself, but Charlie cared too much and refused to admit it.

She sat on the settee, scowling. Her legs were drawn up, knees to her chin, feet on the cushions. He was reasonably certain ladies weren't supposed to sit like that. But they had an agreement, he, Charlie, Colin and George, that they would abide by their own rules in the family parlor. So he didn't mention it, only went to the table where the bottles of brandy and claret waited. He poured a glass of claret for himself and wished desperately that it was beer.

He poured another for George who glanced up from his pile of books to accept it with his usual soft smile. He was intent on reading anything he could find on Thorncroft Abbey. He'd already told them the main part of the house had been built sometime in the late fourteenth century long before Henry the Eighth confiscated it from the church and created the duchy of Thorncroft for an earl who had done him a service.

And now here they were.

"Damn Henry the Eighth, anyway," he muttered.

As he'd muttered the same thing approximately a hundred times since inheriting the title, no one said anything. Colin only snorted from where he was practicing lounging with the proper languid ennui. He took being a duke's brother and the next in line very seriously.

Not that it wasn't obviously nice to have a soft bed and never run out of coal in the grate, or that he'd want to return to poverty… but sometimes, he almost wished he could. At least he knew who he'd been then. A hard worker, tired, respected.

Who was he now?

It didn't matter. There was no turning back. Best to get on with it.

And more to the point, he wanted more for his family. His sister deserved choices, better choices than she'd had this time last year: work in the factory, work in a grand house where she wouldn't be protected. The pub, the bawdy house if things got bad.

He'd sell his own damn self before he'd let that happen.

And his brother deserved to play at being indolent, after spending too much time up cramped crooked chimneys as a chimney sweep. He'd been so skinny. Good for business, bad for a long life. If he wanted to eat creamed asparagus soup now and wear gold rings, let him.

And George deserved every comfort and idle moment after protecting them since they were practically in leading strings. It could have gone badly for them, so many ways and too often. Still young enough, Dougal hardly had a handle on when to fight and went to hide. And his siblings, twins, both only seven years old. It wasn't a stretch to say that George had saved their lives. From hunger, from falling into a bad crowd, from so many lurking dangers.

And so, Dougal would wear gold buttons and bow when ladies stared at him, half-frightened, half-awed. He'd marry one of them. And he'd learn everyone's titles and the goddamn order in which to introduce them. Even if he found it both dull as tombs and bordering on painful. He'd once broken his hand on a power loom and kept working. He could do this. This was *nothing*.

And if it meant spending a little more time in Meg's company, he'd learn to waltz in bloody stacked heels while wearing a lace cravat.

Maybe.

He thought of her clever eyes, her mischievous smile. The smell of mint that hovered around her. The warmth of her body in his arms when she'd feigned a swoon.

Definitely.

He'd definitely purchase a lace cravat if she asked him to.

But he'd draw the line at false calves. He couldn't understand padding his breeches with cotton to look more muscular. He could walk the fields for that.

"I wasn't rude," Charlie insisted. "I wasn't the one hiding in the shrubbery."

"That's not what I meant, and you know it."

"Why is she here anyway?"

"*Miss Swift* is here to catalogue the parade of Roman statues crowding this house." It was like being watched in every room they entered. Except this one, where he'd had them removed. The portrait hall was a special kind of hell. Blank marble eyes and the disapproving painted eyes of a long line of ancestors he knew nothing about. Charlie had propped a moth-eaten hat with a frayed feather on the corner of the frame housing the third Duke of Thorncroft, proclaiming him to be the most judgmental of them all and perfectly capable of coming to life to avenge his aristocratic line in the middle of the night. Charlie thought the hat gave him something else to judge.

"She's here to find a treasure."

Colin laughed. "Think highly of yourself, do you?"

"Not me, you idiot." Dougal said. "Actual treasure."

They all stared at him.

"You could not possibly fit more gold in this house," Charlie said.

"Well, someone did, over two hundred years ago. Might be gold, might be silver, no one's sure. But what we do know is that more strangers are about to start poking around."

Charlie groaned. "More of them?"

"I'm afraid so. I may have…punched an earl. Or a Marquess? I'm not even sure, honestly."

"You *punched* someone?" she echoed. She had the exact same expression she'd worn when she was eight years old, and he'd stolen an orange for her for Christmas morning.

"Yes." He was trying to regret his rash violent reaction.

He wasn't succeeding.

"Now *that* would be a ball I'd actually want to attend."

Colin leaned forward. "Why did you punch him?"

"Because he deserved it," his sister answered immediately. "Obviously."

"Lord Eaton is a lecher," Dougal said. "And proud and obnoxious and will no doubt fan the rumors of this bloody treasure."

"Was it over Miss Swift?" Colin grinned at Dougal's expression. "It was, wasn't it? I can't blame you. She's a pocket Venus," he said appreciatively.

Charlie rolled her eyes. "Speak *English*."

"I was," he shot back, rolling his eyes back at her. They might be eighteen years old and nearly adults, but possibly this kind of life wasn't good for their dispositions. "Would you prefer I call her a prime article?" He exaggerated his Northern accent.

She crossed her arms. "Yes, I would. And yes also to our proper accent, you pompous git."

"Charlie," George said mildly. He was the only one able to calm her and often with just a glance or a murmur of her name. No one else could quite manage it.

She sighed, shoulders drooping. "I'm sorry. You know these people put me out of sorts."

"Meg isn't going to judge you," Dougal promised.

"You don't know that."

He thought of her stealing almonds. And then stealing the wager purse from Eaton. "I really do, as it happens."

"You do like her," George said softly, in that way of his. His dark eyes were steady, knowing.

Dougal felt the urge to blush but he was fairly sure dukes did not blush. "I like her well enough," he allowed. An understatement.

"Did you propose?" Colin asked.

"I've only known her for two days."

"And you have less than two months in which to get married," Colin pointed out. "She's pretty and she didn't scream bloody murder when Old Bea, The Fruit Cannon, got to work."

All true.

"She's a viscount's daughter."

"And you're a duke."

"Through a technicality."

Charlie's feet thumped to the floor as she sat up suddenly, spine straight as a sword. "Does she think you're not good enough for her?" she demanded, affronted on his behalf.

He had to smile. "No, she doesn't think that." But he did. He knew it to be true. The things he'd done. The things he'd seen.

He didn't regret them if they had kept his family safe, but they weren't for her. She deserved better.

"Well, good," Charlie muttered, mollified but not convinced. "How was the ball aside from all of the violence?" she added, and he knew it was as close to an apology as she would get today. "Was it dreadful?"

"Entirely," he said. Well, not entirely. Not the part where he'd met Meg. "There was a plate of sheep's eyeballs at breakfast."

She shuddered. "No wonder you punched someone. I miss toasted cheese. Meat pies. Actual food."

"I'll tell the cook to make you both."

"That's why you're my favorite brother."

"Oi," Colin protested. "I'm your *twin*."

"And you wear so much scent now I start sneezing when I get within three feet of you."

"It's from one of the best London shops!"

She didn't look convinced. "You smell like roses."

"And frankincense," Colin corrected with his charming lopsided grin. "The expensive kind."

Charlie just shook her head. "I worry about you."

"I'm not the one going feral."

"I'm not feral!" She paused. "Mostly. I'm wearing lace gloves, aren't I?" They followed her gaze to her gloves, now lying in a heap on the rug. "Well, I was."

Dougal ruffled her hair, couldn't help it even though she was too old to have her hair mussed. If they'd been born to this world, she would already be on the Marriage Market, waltzing with handsy fortune hunters and avoiding tosspots like Eaton. If she wanted to hide out in the country until she was eighty years, Dougal had absolutely no problem with that.

"Never mind," he said. "But let's all try to avoid debutantes and fruit assaults during dinner."

Charlie shrugged. "I don't see how tonight will be any different just because you have guests."

Dougal sighed. She was right.

Dinner was going to be a disaster.

Dinner was exactly as entertaining as Meg had hoped.

Eventually.

After tea, she had abandoned her cases of clothes being unpacked by a maid in favor of finding the collection the Duke of Pendleton had sent her to catalogue. She found rows of busts on pedestals, gleaming white marble with perfectly carved curls and dangerous mouths. She often wondered if classical statues had once been painted, perhaps with black eyes and blue dresses and darkened slashes for eyebrows. It seemed a shame to have such potential wasted. She'd mentioned it to the duke once and he was both intrigued and horrified, as though she meant to attack his statues with her oil paints.

These particular busts sat between portraits of the duchy's ancestors. It was a disconcerting number of eyeballs in one place, it had to be said. It would take several weeks to sketch this hall alone and she needed to be back to her uncle's house when the cottage rents were due. She put that worry aside for the moment.

As with Pendleton, the previous duke housed the majority of his collection in the library. The upper floor was for the books overlooking the balcony to statues and cases of artifacts below. His preference for classical antiquities explained Pendleton's interest. But there were also flints, iron buckles, an Anglo-Saxon crystal egg, all of which Meg was familiar with, having visited Little Barrow so often. There was a reason Pendleton had built a house there and started a festival of antiquities.

It would take considerable time to draw it all. She would focus on the pieces she knew would interest her godfather the most. Finding hidden treasure would be a feat in itself, never mind before a herd of hunters who knew what they were about.

She tried not to panic. She could figure this out. She would attack it not as a treasure hunt, but as an art mystery. She would inspect the murals and the way they fit over the walls, in the corners, along boarded up windows. The type of paints used. The perspective of the subjects would tell her where the walls slanted or changed and what century they were painted in.

If she could convince the grizzled hidebound farmers in her village to try the "cursed and newfangled" Norfolk system of crops, she could do this.

Theoretically.

First, dinner.

She sat in a dress embroidered with leaves to cover a tear at the right sleeve which resisted mending. Platters stretched before her: poultry, greens, root vegetables, and a tower of sticky buns. Lady Blackwell sat at the other end of the table, chatting with the other ladies. She had changed into a glorious silver wig for the occasion. Lady Marigold was still wearing yellow. Lady Beatrice, in a dark blue gown, resigned to sitting between two exotic birds who might render her blind.

"Tell me, Your Grace, how did you come to inherit the Ladies Marigold and Beatrice?" Lady Blackwell asked, sipping her wine.

Lady Beatrice barked a laugh that was more smug than cheerful. "We refused to go."

"We haven't left the house since my brother died," Lady Marigold admitted.

"We weren't sure how the new duke might take to us," Lady Beatrice added, narrowing one eye at the new duke in question.

"As if I'd toss two old—er, that is, ladies," he muttered at his buttered peas. "Out on the street."

"Oh, well done, you," Lady Blackwell toasted him with her goblet. "We'll have you polished up in no time."

"He doesn't need polishing," Charlie snapped. Dougal shook his head almost imperceptibly. Charlie mutinied. "Well, you don't."

"Of course, he does," Lady Blackwell returned, not at all bothered by Charlie's somewhat vehement manners. She was used to Meg and the others running wild when they were younger.

And sometimes still.

"We all get a little polishing, whether we like it or not," she continued. "Life rubs at us and we can let it grind us down and make us rough, or we can decide to shine."

The Black siblings stared at her. They would come to learn that Lady Blackwell's sugary froth hid more salt than sweet.

Dougal and his family did not speak much as they continued to eat, only shifted uncomfortably on the velvet chairs, and tried to smile when someone happened to catch their eye. She spread butter on a roll of heavy dark bread and Dougal turned to her apologetically. "There's softer bread at the other end of the table, if you'd like," he said. "We can't get used to it, I'm afraid."

"I like this bread," she assured him. She was as accustomed to eating it as she was to the lighter, whiter bread that flirted with being a pastry more than bread. She wished she knew how to put them at their ease.

She'd dismiss the footmen behind each chair, for one. And Mrs. Hill, who came in once to speak to the butler and sniffed at Charlie's hair slipping its pins in a way that rose Meg's protective hackles. Especially when Charlie lifted her chin defiantly. The small rebellion was not enough to hide the tightening of her shoulders.

The formality was underlined by the dining room itself, which was long and cavernous, owing to its former abbey-related needs no doubt. She could perfectly picture monks praying in rows or tending to well-born visitors in padded doublets and hose in this space. The mural marching across one wall was definitely newer, considering the Roman gods reclining in leafy bowers and the sheer number of bare breasts. There were more stars spilling across the ceiling, as in every room she'd been in.

Dougal must have noticed the way she kept sneaking glances at the one mural. "You do not approve?" he asked.

"I like it fine. But I want to fix it," she admitted.

"Fix it?"

"The paint is peeling in the corner and that faded gray with a hint of beige? Those leaves used to be a vibrant green with bright yellow to mimic sunlight."

"I assumed it was always this... vague."

"Certainly not." Because she suddenly sounded as offended as Mrs. Hill, she smiled to soften her immediate and prickly reaction to badly treated art. "It might have originally tended towards the garish, in fact. But art needs care, like anyone else."

"Anyone?" George inquired. "Or anything?"

"Anyone," she said firmly. "Art has a soul, I think. Though your village vicar I'm sure would disagree."

George smiled. "I sometimes think this house has a soul."

"George has appointed himself the Abbey historian," Charlie said, with more than a hint of pride. And warning. "He's read nearly every book in the library on this house and the family."

"Hardly a historian," he protested, sounding a touch embarrassed. "It's not like I had much schooling. I just like to read. And I like to know where I am."

"Mr. Williams," Meg said earnestly. "I grew up around a great many antiquarians and historians. Believe me when I tell you all you need is a passion for history."

His soft smile grew softer still. "You are kind, Miss Swift."

"The Splendid Miss Swift," Dougal murmured quietly enough to have her blushing.

"Perhaps you can help me map the house," Meg asked. "I assume His Grace has mentioned the problem with treasure hunters?"

"Treasure hunters?" Lady Beatrice barked. "I think *not*." She picked up her knife with deliberate precision and attacked her potatoes. "I will deal with any such nuisance, just you wait."

A shiver must have gone through a great many treasure hunter currently contemplating Thorncroft Abbey.

"He has, indeed," George said. "Are we thinking the monks hid the Church plates and such before the king could get his hands on them?"

"A safe assumption," Meg agreed. "But you would know better. If not the monks, there might be family stories or clues in a family bible?"

"I will start right away," he promised, eyes shining. "I'll look for any drawings of the abbey over the centuries."

"That would be very helpful, thank you."

"I do wish you had a proper antiquarian to help you."

She leaned forward. "I can tell you without hesitation that the antiquarians I know with the most schooling only tend to complicate things. And they nearly always forget to come in for supper." Which was a crime, in her estimation. Dougal's cook had done marvelous things with quail and cream and chives, with a mountain of boiled potatoes and beets. The bread was soft and still faintly warm. She only just barely resisted the urge to drop it into her napkin for later. Wouldn't Mrs. Hill be scandalized then?

She'd be scandalized right now, were she still in the dining room.

Because usually the duck was meant to be served with thyme and butter.

Not fresh from the pond and landing in a tureen of creamed turnips.

At least only the turnips had been ruined. She'd had no intention of sampling those at all.

There was a startled pause.

"Is that…a duck?" Dougal asked, in the same tone one might ask if there were more peas.

Mashed turnip splashed over the linen tablecloth. A splatter arched to land on Lady Marigold's decolletage with a wet plop. She squeaked. Very loudly. Loudly enough to startle the already startled duck.

He did not seem the equanimous sort.

As everyone scrambled to their feet, except Colin, who would let nothing ruin his lordly slouch, not even a duck, Meg started to giggle. She couldn't help it. Dougal sent her an incredulous look. "There's a duck on the table."

She laughed even harder.

The footmen were all stunned, though one darted forward, then stopped. "I don't know what to do with a duck, Your Grace," he admitted.

"You cook it!" Lady Blackwell barked.

After that, Meg fairly howled with laughter. The older ladies were standing in a huddle, making offended noises. The duck flapped his wings once. They shrieked in unison, ladies and duck.

"It's like Macbeth's witches," Dougal muttered.

Meg held onto the back of her chair. "Stop," she begged, weak with mirth.

The duck honked once, very loudly and clearly affronted.

"Well, how do you think *we* feel about it?" Dougal asked it.

Meg wheezed.

The duck took off again, and then landed abruptly in the potatoes. Now that *was* a shame. Everyone talked at once, offering suggestions, yelps, curse words. The chaotic din intensified, until the butler arrived, then Mrs. Hill, a few housemaids, and eventually the cook, red-faced and panting. "Weren't no duck on the menu," she said, bewildered.

Meg was beginning to think it was possible to die from laughing too hard.

Dougal sighed, pulling a tapestry from the wall while the butler yelled for someone to fetch a shotgun. Instead, Dougal approached the table calmly, and tossed the tapestry over the duck. He scooped the wriggling pile into his arms. "Open a window," he ordered.

Three footmen rushed forward only to realize the window was already open. Dougal shoved his arms out and unrolled the duck who flapped away, all frantic feathers and offended honks.

"That tapestry is two hundred years old," George pointed out mildly.

"And useful, at least." Dougal tossed it aside. "I think we'll dine with the window closed from now on, Mr.... that is, Canterbury."

"Very good, Your Grace," he replied with cheerful calm. "Can't be too careful."

"We always close the windows at night," one of the housemaids murmured as they filed out. "I closed that one meself."

Charlie tilted her head, gaze narrowing on Mrs. Hill. "Did the house tour come through here today, Mrs. Hill?"

"I suppose it did at that."

"Did someone open it on purpose?" Colin put it, finally sitting up. "To break in later, perhaps?"

"Surely not." She did not sound so sure.

"I'll have all of the doors and windows checked, not to fret," Canterbury said.

"Thank you," Dougal said, raising his voice as the butler bustled out. "And Canterbury?"

"Your Grace?"

Dougal grinned. "Please fetch Miss Swift a refreshing drink before laughter does her an injury, won't you?"

Meg hiccupped, tears gathering on her eyelashes.

"Very good, Your Grace."

Chapter Nine

M EG SPENT MOST of the next three days sketching muscular buttocks.

As far as pastimes went, it wasn't terrible.

Her godfather had sent along a trunk of supplies, including a new set of coveted Ackerman watercolor paints. She'd nearly purred when she'd found them. Thus far she'd used them to sketch three Neptunes, four Venuses, one Jupiter, an interesting array of satyrs hidden in a back closet, and a line of nameless gentlemen in various states of Olympic sports. Several were running, to or from what, she could not say. One had a discus, muscles twisted as he turned to throw it. The workmanship was remarkable. His skin seemed real, straining against movement. What a shame to have it locked up on a private estate.

She went back to her drawings. It was such a delight to have hours stretch before her, filled with art.

And Dougal.

There was no use pretending she was not distracted by him, anytime he happened to come by. The man was sinfully handsome, carrying himself as if he could do anything. Until you got him into a formal dining room where he was all fumbles and muttered curses. Even his vulnerability was enticing.

Truthfully, she'd never known this kind of desire. A heat mixed with an interest in what he was thinking, what he had to say, what he had seen. She couldn't help watching him while he was in the room, sketching him in her mind's eye, sometimes in her private notebook when she could not sleep. A slash for his eyebrows, so often furrowed. The shadows of the muscles she knew lurked under his fine lawn shirts and plain waistcoats. She'd sketched enough muscles to know he was built as fine as any statue.

When he'd rolled up his sleeves and crouched down to inspect a bit of peeling mural, she'd had a very serious concern that she might drool.

"That is entirely too much backside before tea," Lady Blackwell announced, interrupting her daydreams.

Meg started.

If Lady Blackwell was reading her mind, she was doing a poor job of concealing her interest. And drool.

Meg set her pencil aside as Lady Blackwell made a noise in the back of her throat. She was dressed in several unfortunate shades of green, looking as happy as a four-leaf clover. She was also observing the statues of the male athletes stationed outside the portrait gallery.

"This is what happens when statues are lined up all facing the same direction," Meg grinned. "Backsides. A great many of them."

"I suppose there are worse ways to wake up." Lady Blackwell winked. "Reminds me of a week I spent in Paris."

Meg choked as the other woman wandered away in search of her breakfast.

Never underestimate an old woman.

Or a young debutante.

Meg went still, then deliberately lifted her sketchbook, pretending to compare her drawing with the lines of the statue.

She wasn't alone.

She caught a flutter of movement out of the corner of her eye. She turned slowly, so as to not give herself away. She already knew it wasn't Mrs. Hill, who marched like a general, or the footmen who didn't usually press themselves against the wall and run like they were being chased by bees.

One of the garden tours gone awry.

Mrs. Hill, as strict as she might act over etiquette, did not quite have a firm grasp of the tours, especially when they involved daughters of the peerage. A footman had been assigned to help her, but he was helpless in the face of genteel tears. Meg thought Charlie would have done a much better job and that the tours should be cancelled until Dougal was officially engaged. There had been some discussion that if the tours were cancelled, the treasure hunters would know they were found out. They might try harder, get more underhanded. Better to be underestimated so that they did not feel pressured. "Let them think me a fool," Dougal had said in that nonchalant way of his.

There would be no debutantes or skulking treasure hunters.

And certainly no one calling him a fool.

Muttering, Meg dropped her sketches and gave chase.

She wasn't quite quick enough. She caught another glimpse of a white hem, and around the corner, the edge of a straw bonnet obscuring any features, even down to the color of the intruder's hair. And then it was just a corridor with a series of closed doors. Clever girl. Damn it.

Meg wasted precious minutes opening each door: empty parlor, empty conservatory, empty room filled floor to ceiling with a collection of preserved butterflies under bell jars.

And then the dining room door swinging lightly on its hinges.

Hah!

"Got you now," she said, darting inside.

Just in time to see another flutter of a white dress, this time exiting from the open window.

Meg didn't stop to think, she only followed, scrambling out after her. She couldn't say why she was so determined to track the lady down, or what she could even do, once found. She only knew that it didn't sit right to have Dougal treated like a piece of meat: delicious, desired, and dumb.

No longer.

Meg shoved through hardy geraniums and tall spiky foxgloves, finally bursting out of the hedge partitioning the side flagstone terrace from the back gardens.

Straight into a crowd of ladies in white dresses.

Botheration.

Debutante fashions were vexing in more ways than one. She herself would have cast off her whites in seconds if she could afford to replace her old dresses. Beyond that, they were now interfering with her investigation. She counted at least seven young ladies in white, and three grandmothers who, as much as they wanted to appear younger and au courant in their thin floating dresses, were unlikely to have launched themselves through an open window.

Meg was welcomed with gasps, shocked whispers, and one extremely theatrical shriek. Annoyed, she turned on her heel, muttering under her breath. When she climbed back in through the window, she was met with three footmen, and Charlie.

"Are you the one leaving the windows open?" Charlie accused. Her dress was patterned with blue flowers today and she looked uncomfortable, unconsciously plucking at the sleeves.

"Of course not," Meg replied. "I followed a—," she broke off. Anger was like steam boiling her brain. "She damaged the paint!" Meg nearly howled. In truth, her voice was not at all genteel.

She was not feeling particularly genteel.

That sneakabout had not only disturbed the family's privacy, she had also knocked over two chairs and an iron candelabra taller than Meg. Right into the dusty mural. Bits of broken plaster lay scattered on the sideboard. If debutantes were this barbaric, she had no hope for the manners of a treasure hunter.

"You look like a steam kettle coming to a boil," Charlie remarked. "You sound like one too."

"I feel like one," Meg replied, between her teeth. She forced a smile in the footmen's direction, but they were wise enough not to believe her. "We need plaster," she said. "Now, if you please."

They scattered.

Charlie raised her eyebrows dubiously. "*You're* going to plaster the wall?"

Meg nodded firmly. "And I'm going to do a right better job than the last person who tried."

Charlie shook her head in a manner that Meg could only describe as Dougal-like. "I'll never understand posh ladies."

Meg was lost.

She was used to fine houses. Pendleton Hall stretched out over nearly an acre of space, but it made *sense*. Thorncroft Abbey was haphazard, with odd additions that jutted out over the gardens, doors that opened to brick walls, doors that didn't open at all. It was as if several generations of drunken architects had dared each other to do their worst. She loved it. Every odd, crooked inch of it.

She was still lost though.

And it certainly did not make it easy to find lost treasure.

She'd gone up too many floors, then down a narrow staircase dating back at least to Henry the Seventh, there'd been a room full of rolled up carpets, another with broken chairs, and then approximately a hundred kilometers of hallways and a single creaking staircase that led up to the roof but nowhere else. Not even back down.

She tried another door, rattling it when she found it locked. She cursed. With enthusiasm.

"Miss Swift."

She jumped, then tried to decide if she should be embarrassed. "Mr. Williams! How glad I am to see you. I was trying to find, not only treasure, but also," she glanced down at the list in her sketchbook. "A sculpture of three Venuses wearing birds as hats", which doesn't sound terribly Roman," she admitted. "But now I'm just trying to find familiar ground again."

"I got lost daily when we first arrived," George smiled, lines creasing at the corners of his eyes. There was such kindness in his face, and calmness. She could see where Dougal had gotten his steadiness. "That's part of the reason I became so interested in the history of the house." He winked. "Self-preservation. The Cook does not appreciate it when you let her food get cold, even if you were lost in the attics."

Meg smiled back. "I'll remember that."

"I haven't seen any statues up here."

"I imagine not. I was trapped on the roof for a bit when the door got stuck and then finally managed to find my way here. Which was not as helpful as I might have hoped."

He glanced at her quick drawing of the hills and rivers from the vantage point of the roof. "You're very good, Miss."

"Thank you."

"May I?"

She handed him the sketchbook, her fingertips stained with ink and charcoal. She curled them into her palms. "These are just studies, really."

He didn't flip through the pages quickly, like most people, but slowly, taking the time to really look. There were marble busts, of course, and Roman noses and curled hair and strong shoulders. Flowers, a judgmental barn cat, more statuary.

"These are lovely," George remarked. "I wish I could draw." There was yearning in his voice. He shook his head. "Foolish thoughts of an old man, forgive me."

"Why foolish?" She asked. "There's no reason you couldn't learn to draw. I'm sure Dou-, that is, the duke, would be happy to hire you a drawing master."

"Oh, I'm not so grand as that."

"I never had a tutor either," she admitted. "Sometimes all you have is paper and a pencil and it's all you need. It's all about the practice, at the end of the day. Seeing the shadows. I started with apples."

"Apples," he said. "We have an orchard full, so that should be easy enough."

"Keep your first drawing," she said, amiably. "Especially if it's awful and you despise it."

His eyebrows lifted. "If you say so."

"I do. Come back to it every so often and you will feel quite invigorated with your progress." She leaned in as if telling a very great secret. "I framed mine. My mother thought it was a beetle. My father was certain it was a badger's face. They argued for days."

"But it was an apple."

"I was very proud of my sad, lopsided smudge."

He grinned. "Then I will be proud of mine." He handed her back her book. "Shall I escort you back?" He asked, then paused, almost shyly. "Or would this be a good time for a tour? I won't bore you with all of the historical trumpery, as Colin calls it."

"I would love a tour, *and* to hear some history," she said. "Not just because it will help us on our hunt but also because you can't know how refreshing it will be to hear something that is not from Ancient Egypt or Ancient Rome. Or even a Druid's barrow full of mad spirits." She adored her friends, but they were a tad obsessive. Tamsin insisted on telling her about every place in England where someone's head had been chopped off and might have left a ghost behind. Headless ghosts were surprisingly plentiful.

"This house is not nearly so old as that, I'm afraid."

She perked up. "Sold!" She took his arm, and he straightened proudly, patting her hand softly, like a grandfather. "I cannot condone missing tea," she added. "So be sure to point out any secret passageways."

They headed down the hall, dust clinging to their shoes. "I assume this is where they hide the family secrets and scandals?"

"When they are not naming them dukes."

She chuckled. "I am sure it was high time the duchy had some shaking up."

"You have a kind soul, Miss Swift, if you don't mind me saying so."

They stopped in front of a door which George had to kick with one foot and lift up from the handle to get it to budge. It was clearly a system he'd had some practice with. It opened onto a small square room with a staircase in the center. Meg huffed out an annoyed breath. "How is anyone supposed to find their way around if even the stairs are hidden? Never mind treasure."

"I believe this was the servants' quarters over a hundred years ago but they closed it up. I guess they thought it was easier to build new than fix it."

Meg snorted. "Showing off, is what it was."

"Oh, perhaps—"

She thought of her uncle and his wagers and spending habits and nodded smartly. "Showing off." She nodded to a large hole in the wall. "Though it would seem the mice have been here since."

George nodded. "I find the oddest holes in the wall and old

trinkets scattered about."

"Curious mice."

"It would seem so."

"Hmm. Mice looking for treasure?" She wondered out loud. "I have already noticed an increase of gentlemen and ladies who do not seem to care about the gardens wandering about."

"I noticed that too."

"I still only managed to chase a debutante and not a hunter out the window."

"Might they not be the same?"

She nodded. He had a point. They investigated the holes and the crannies but found only bits of nuts and shredded paper, treasures of mice, not men. No coins, no candlesticks, no jewels.

"I suppose it would be too much to expect it to be that easy," Meg grumbled.

They finally found themselves back in the main part of the house, with its arching windows and fluted columns. And Charlie. She scowled at Meg. "What's going on?"

"I'm getting the grand tour," Meg replied, ignoring both the scowl and the warning look George sent in its direction.

"You should join the other ladies who poke about our house and steal things from my brother's bedroom."

"Charlie," George said. "Miss Swift, I do apologize."

"No need," Meg hurried to say. "It must be frustrating," she added to Charlie. Charlie shrugged one shoulder.

"You know, of course, that Thorncroft was an abbey before it was turned into a family estate. Franciscan," George continued pointedly. "I like to imagine monks praying at night. Sometimes, I fancy I can still smell the incense."

She could see it perfectly. Painting the glowing light of the candles would be the trick of it. A little white, a little cadmium yellow. The softest hint of gold along the columns.

"Miss Swift?"

"I'm so sorry, Mr. Williams, I was painting inside my own head. Terrible habit. Do go on."

Charlie was scowling again but Meg could tell she was concerned that Meg might hurt George's feelings. Since she had no such intention, nor ever would, she decided she rather liked the scowl. Charlie was protective of her family. She couldn't fault her for that. Even if she had suddenly joined the house tour, wedging herself between them.

George continued, calm as ever. "When King Henry the Eighth decided to take over the church for love of Anne Boleyn—"

Meg snorted. He tilted his head. "Not for love?"

"Not for love." Seeing as Henry had chopped Anne's head off, Tamsin had had a lot to say about it over the years. Meg knew more about Anne Boleyn than she did most of the people on her own family tree. "Maybe at first," she allowed. "A little bit. If I am feeling charitable. But mostly, he liked getting his own way, I think."

"So, you are a historian, after all."

She grinned. "No, but my friends are dedicated enough on my behalf. One can't help but listen. I can also discuss the sand composition around the pyramids and how the new modern Roman-inspired ballgowns have got it all wrong. The Duke of Pendleton considers it a tragedy of epic proportions." She winked. "I shall spare you, Mr. Williams, as I was never spared." She trailed her fingers along the leaves carved into the windowsill. "Do we know what the first duke did to gain Henry's favor? Something suitably heroic, I hope?"

"Like the Duke of Norfolk, it was reward for services rendered at the battle that killed James IV."

"Not nearly as dramatic as I'd like," Meg teased, "But I suppose it will have to do."

Henry had created titles to build a wealthy aristocratic army in his favor, just as he had seized the properties belonging to the Church, both to claim their assets and finally have the divorce he was so desperate for.

"The abbey lay in ruins before it was claimed by the first duke. Apparently, the locals had carted away most of the western wall, as it had the best stones."

"Is that why it's such a delightful hodge-podge in here?" And why the treasure might be long gone already.

"Yes, I think so. They were a small abbey and one of the first to be dissolved, though I hear they resisted at first."

"Oh good, I do like a troublemaker."

George returned her grin. "As do I, Miss Swift. As do I."

They had reached the portrait hall where the exalted Black ancestors peeked from between Roman gods with fine buttocks. Meg paused under her favorite painting, the one wearing a truly spectacular ruff and holding a ferret with an unnatural face that was more child-like than ferret-like. He held a ruby necklace with a pearl drop the size of an apricot.

"And what of him?" The discreet bronze plaque announced him to be Rupert Black, Lord Bartholomew. "Was he also very heroic?"

"Ha!" Lady Beatrice barked from the balcony. "He was a third son, and he slept his way through half of the aristocracy and then died of syphilis."

"Oh dear."

"But that necklace he holds was said to have belonged to Queen Elizabeth," Marigold added, coming down the stairs to join them. She wore yellow again, this time with layers of flounces and ribbons best suited to a cake. "It went missing. There are ever so many stories about it. Some say it might still be in this house somewhere. Perhaps that's your treasure."

"Queen Elizabeth, so, the latter half of the sixteenth century?" Meg asked George. "Or thereabouts?"

He nodded. "I can see what improvements were made to the building around that time. I've found some family diaries and a few more books about the area."

"Never mind that, she's the one you want," Lady Beatrice pointed to a lady wearing men's breeches, red dahlias on her bodice and a sharp, mischievous smile. "Marigold's sister. She ran away with a pirate."

"She was very dashing," Lady Marigold murmured. "But he wasn't a pirate. He was a privateer."

"What's the difference?" Charlie asked curiously.

"He had a letter of marque from the British government," George explained. "He could plunder ships that were from enemy nations with a full pardon as long as England received a percentage of the booty."

"A pirate with permission then?" Charlie said. "Seems like cheating. I like it."

"Sometimes I would get packages from exotic places, coins mostly, or seashell pendants," Lady Marigold said wistfully. "Our father always lost his temper when her name was mentioned. He would have destroyed this painting, but my mother forbade him on her deathbed. Dahlia came to visit once but my father threw her out after one night. They had such a row. Half the crockery was shattered."

"Who's a pirate?" Lady Blackwell demanded, sailing into the hall with Chartreuse at her diamond-studded heels. They wore matching necklaces made from russet silk roses with faux thorns painted gold.

"My sister, Dahlia."

"Lady Dahlia!" Lady Blackwell exclaimed. "Oh, I did like her. Now there was a woman could hold her liquor."

"Did you ever want to join her as a pirate?" Meg teased. She could easily picture Persephone's grandmother on the deck of a ship, holding a musket, and demanding spoils. Naturally, Chartreuse would be there, sporting a dashing eye patch. Or possibly biting a parrot.

"I do think I would have made a grand pirate but good heaven's no," Lady Blackwell replied. "I like a feather bed. And proper meals. Frequent baths." She paused, turning to George. "Mr. Williams," she all but beamed at him after an uncomfortable moment where he looked as though he might need to excuse himself from her frank assessment. Charlie opened her mouth to speak but Lady Blackwell beat her to it. "That pink cravat is positively delicious. I do admire a man who understands a little boldness is a tonic on these gray days."

The day was perfectly bright and sunny but as George bowed with a pleased, shy smile, no one dared mention it. "You may offer me your arm," she continued. "So that everyone may admire us. We simply match too well not to give them the pleasure."

Seeing as her gown might be called orange, but only if the

beholder was feeling generous and had shielded their eyes sufficiently, Meg suspected her reasons had more to do with that shy smile and handsome face. George extended his arm, looking only slightly flummoxed but also very, very pleased. Pink cravat and orange dress clashed horribly. It was very sweet.

Lady Beatrice nudged Meg with an elbow so bony as to be registered as a decent weapon of war. She waggled her eyebrows in case Meg was in any confusion as to what the elbow to the tender area under her ribs might mean. The answering bruise needed no further elaboration.

It was restful not to be the focus of a matchmaking scheme for once.

They made a merry and odd collection as they trouped through the house, with George offering historical information and Lady Beatrice shouting inappropriate comments about the family. Lady Marigold did not seem particularly bothered to have her family harpooned. They peeked behind tapestries, inside decorative boxes for hidden keys, knocked on wall panels to make sure they were solid.

Not a single treasure to be found.

"Perhaps I'm simply not good at this," Meg muttered under her breath. Persephone could spot a forgery at a hundred paces; Pendleton could date a classical statue to the year at a glance. She couldn't find one treasure in one house, even with the help of a small, slightly eccentric army.

"Don't despair," George said quietly. "We'll find it."

They continued their odd parade through the house until Dougal stepped out of his study, only to be assaulted by shouts of "inbred dukes", orange and yellow dresses, and an over-excited spaniel.

He paused.

"Is that a pink cravat?"

Chapter Ten

T HAT NIGHT, MEG carried the picnic hamper out into the gardens under the moonlight. She'd taken it from the carriage after they'd arrived and there were only a few biscuits left that would harden if they weren't eaten. There were also pears, apples, a jar of blackberry compote and a pot of honey kept from a tea tray. She wasn't likely to go hungry in Dougal's house, but some habits were simply too ingrained. She wrapped her plaid shawl more securely around her shoulders and curled cross-legged on a marble bench supported by carved fish.

"That bench might be the ugliest thing I've ever seen," Dougal remarked, strolling out of the shadows.

Meg jumped.

"You don't care for fish?" She asked which was an absurd thing to say to a handsome man in a dark garden at midnight.

"I defy you to find a fish that looks like that anywhere in nature." His disdain was very nearly ducal. She would have applauded if she'd thought he would take it as a compliment. He wasn't wearing a coat, nor a vest or a cravat, just a white lawn shirt open at the throat and rough trousers definitely not sent down from a London shop. He looked at ease in simple clothes and shadows, in a way she had never seen him. She couldn't take her eyes off of him.

"You may have a point." She forced herself to focus on the cold bench beneath her and not on whether or not his thighs would feel as strong as they looked. She stroked a fin that looked like it belonged as a ruffle on a dress hem more than propelling fish through the sea. The stone eyes bulged, slightly cross-eyed. "I like it though. It's cheerful."

"Cheerful, is it?" He shook his head, grinning. "If you say so. And if *I* may so, you might consider spectacles. That fish is clearly bilious."

"You've got the ducal tone down, I see," she teased, risking it. She liked to think she understood him a bit better now, after so many days in the same house.

He bowed with a flourish. "I've been practicing."

She knew her smile was too bright for the jest, but she couldn't help but feel a twinge of pride that she was beginning to know him so well.

Not as well as she'd like.

Honestly, when had her inner voice turned so lascivious?

She blamed it entirely on Dougal.

At twenty-eight years old, she'd had a few kisses, a fumble in the dark, all before her uncle had squandered her dowry, of course. The men had all been pleasant enough, the experiences enjoyable. But none stirred that liquid heat in her legs that Dougal did, and she'd barely touched his arm.

"You look far away," he remarked softly.

She started. "I apologize."

"Shall I leave you to your thoughts?" He glanced at the basket. "Or your stale biscuits?"

She shook her head. "Of course not. I was merely woolgathering."

About his thighs. His hands. The line of his shoulder. What it would be like to share a life with him, laughing at ducks and ugly benches.

"You know, there are probably hundreds of fresh pastries in the kitchen right now," he said, sitting beside her. "You don't have to settle for crumbly Jumbles." He glanced at her out of the corner of his eye. "Although, I distinctly remember you telling me that we had eaten them all."

She grinned. "I lied."

"Cheeky." Something about the way he said it and the way he looked at her sent a fierce want prickling through her. With only the moon and flowers for company, she could tell herself, however briefly, that her lack of dowry didn't matter. Or, more realistically, that this kind of moment need have no future. It might be enough to feel his arms around her again, this time *without* an audience of a ballroom full of dancers.

She swayed closer, infinitesimally. She might have assumed that he didn't notice, but his eyes flared, pupils widening subtly. She could smell the soap on his skin, woodsy and plain. Moonlight touched his hair, outlining each strand in silver. It caressed his cheek, the strength of his throat. The house behind him.

The house-*breaker* behind him.

"Blast and damnation," she hissed suddenly.

Dougal paused.

"Someone is trying to break into your house," she informed him.

"What?" He stood abruptly, turning to follow the direction of her infuriated gaze. "A bloody treasure hunter?"

"I don't think so."

"Why n—." He paused. "Um, Meg?"

"Yes?"

"Why is she taking off her clothes?"

"It's easier to climb that way," she replied grimly.

"How do you—that is—she can't mean to—Oh."

The lady in question was down to her chemise and her stays and had already found her first handhold, determined to pull herself up along the uneven stone wall and the trellis and the thick ivy. She might even make it.

"She's heading for my bedroom." Dougal sounded bemused again.

Like hell.

Meg poked his arm. "She means to compromise you. You're the treasure."

"Don't be daft." He barked a laugh before he realized that she was serious.

"She'll climb into your room in her underthings," Meg explained. "And then make certain that she is discovered there. Loudly."

"I take it I am meant to be asleep in my bed?"

"Yes." She absolutely would not picture him sprawled in his bed. Naked.

Maybe a little bit.

"She might not be a *treasure* hunter, but she is definitely a *fortune* hunter."

He looked towards the house, with the lady outlined by the moonlight, her white chemise all but glowing. He shifted awkwardly. "I suppose I should go stop her before she breaks her neck."

"Or before I break it for her."

He raised an eyebrow. "You *are* bloodthirsty."

"You are not the first to say so," she replied grimly. "You stay here, and I'll go handle this."

"I couldn't…"

"Do you want to marry her?"

"No, thank you."

She smiled briefly at his tone. "Then stay here. Don't let her see you."

"Why not call a footman to cart her away to the magistrate?"

"You are the magistrate."

"I am?"

"More than likely."

"Damn it." He really was adorable. "The constable then."

"You could. But it will raise the household, and they'll wonder what we were doing alone out here. In the middle of the night."

"Would that be so bad?" Dougal asked. But he asked it so softly she could pretend she hadn't heard him, even as her heart did a funny little dance inside her birdcage. She'd paint it as a red bird, bursting out of a cage.

Later.

Right now, she had a plot to foil.

Meg marched across the lawn and over the flagstones, stopping at the lilac bush outfitted in a sprigged walking dress with matching bonnet. She looked up the side of the house where the woman had paused, struggling to catch her breath. "You're going the wrong way," Meg said.

The woman gasped and nearly slipped, catching herself on the trellis. It creaked alarmingly. She may have been surprised but she was obviously made of sterner stuff than that. She glared down at Meg. "Of course, you'd say that."

"Why's that?"

"You want to the duke for yourself."

"I don't want to marry the duke," Meg said plainly. "I have people who rely on me."

"Then you contradict yourself."

"I'm not your competition."

"I don't believe you."

Meg sighed. "I'm a servant here, a duke isn't going to marry me."

"No servant has a shawl that fine."

"It was a gift," Meg said quickly. "From the old duke. He loved the plum tarts I used to make for him," she added. "I work in the kitchens."

The woman narrowed one eye, then shimmied down closer to the ground. "Prove it."

Meg had the silly urge to make sure Dougal wasn't watching them, wasn't listening. But it hardly mattered. She was proud of the work she had done. Even if no one else was likely to be.

She held her hands out.

Meg's hands were covered in marks from embroidery needles, calluses from cleaning the grates when her uncle was feeling vengeful, scratches from digging turnips and mending roofs. They were strong and capable hands, but they weren't pampered. Most of her nails were broken and then filed too short for fashion. She usually kept them hidden under her gloves so as not to attract too many questions. "Hmph. I believe you," the woman said. "No lady has hands like that."

"I'm Meg," she offered.

"Lady Iphigenia." Lady Iphigenia was sweating. She would want to believe whatever Meg said now, if only to give her shaking arms a rest. "I have six siblings," she said defensively. "All sisters."

"I understand."

And she did understand, even sympathized. But she wasn't going to sacrifice Dougal on Iphigenia's altar. "The duke's bedroom is not in that wing," she said instead.

"I've taken the house tour three times," Iphigenia huffed, dropping down to the ground with a stumble.

Meg leaned in with a conspiratorial smile. "The housekeeper lies," she said. "For this very reason. You're not the first to try to sneak in."

"I'm not?"

She shook her head. "I'm afraid not. The duke's bedroom is in the family wing, on the other side of the house. There's even a small staircase from the terrace to the second story balconies."

"You're not helping me out of the goodness of your heart."

Damn it. Lady Iphigenia was smarter than anticipated. Meg was starting to like her.

"If you marry the duke, I want to be promoted to lady's maid," Meg said. It was a reasonable demand. She'd heard the housemaids in her uncle's house whispering about it often enough. Being a lady's maid might require equally long hours, but one did not have to scrub floors, and there was a certain cachet to the title. Not to mention gifts of the lady's old gowns, some of which could be resold for a very pretty penny.

"Done," Iphigenia said. "My current lady's maid is dumb as butter anyway."

"Hurry," Meg urged. "Sometimes the footmen patrol."

Iphigenia's hard expression softened as she grabbed her belongings. "Thank you, Meg. Truly."

Meg felt only a little badly as Iphigenia darted down the path towards the side gardens. She went back to where Dougal was waiting, looking amused and impressed. "You're a fair menace."

She shrugged.

"Are we sure she's not the same one you chased through the dining room?"

"That lady was much shorter."

"Ah. You should consider working for the constable." His smile flashed. "Why send her around back? Why not send her packing altogether?"

"Because the minute she gets anywhere near the guest bedrooms, Chartreuse will start barking like her tail is on fire. And Lady Beatrice does not sleep much. She does, however, like the view from that landing."

"You are a clever one, aren't you?"

She nearly preened before reminding herself she wasn't the type to preen.

Dougal touched her hand. "I heard what you said."

She made to jerk away but his fingers closed around her wrist, warm but strong. His thumb stroked her skin, and it was deliciously distracting. "I know why I have scars," he murmured, lifting their joined hands. "Working at the mills isn't easy. Machinery bites." He turned his hold on her, sweeping his thumb over her knuckles. "But why does a viscount's daughter have so many marks?"

She frowned, trying not to feel embarrassed. If Society gave her no options, then it had absolutely no right to judge her for her choices, for what she had to do to survive. Dougal had no right. She lifted her chin, incensed.

His eyes were warm, patient. Not at all judgmental.

She swallowed the hot retort she'd been prepared to fling his way. "I know I don't have the hands of a lady."

"Better," he insisted. "You have the hands of a woman with stories to tell. With strength, determination."

It wasn't just his words that made her feel like her blood had turned to gold, all sparkling and glittering. It was his mouth, which he pressed to the inside of her wrist. His lips were soft, gentle.

But his teeth were hungry.

The scrape of them over her pulse pulled a noise from her throat which she'd never made before. It felt like he was kissing the inside of her knee, of her thigh. Her pulse turned to fiery sparks, ricocheting throughout her body. Her heart was a single coal, and she was suddenly terrified it would catch fire. That every kiss would feed it, a conflagration she both wanted to leap into and smother immediately.

There was no smothering this fire. Not when he stepped closer, the length of his body all along hers, touching her briefly, her right hip, her thighs, her collarbone. There was a tree at her back, holding her up. He didn't press forward, only leaned ever so slightly until his mouth hovered in front of hers. So close, so tempting, and yet still not touching her.

He waited, breath ragged, but patient. He wouldn't push her. He would let her walk away.

Like hell.

Like hell she would.

She kissed him lightly, so lightly it was less of a kiss and more of a brush of lips, tingling, promising. He waited a beat and then all that promise, all that potential, all that patience, exploded. He kissed her as though he'd been waiting to kiss her for days, months, years. She kissed him back with the same need, the same passion.

His hand splayed over her lower back, urging her closer against the warmth and steel of him. He was stealing her breath, filling her with fire instead. She felt it everywhere as his mouth nipped at hers, his tongue stroking, stoking. When his lips moved to her throat and that spot just under her ear, someone made a soft breathy sound, and she was very much afraid it was her. He chuckled tenderly, not mocking, but so well pleased with his discovery. It was rough in her ear, and soft as secrets. It moved down her spine and all the way down to her toes. Everything about it was delicious, anchoring her to the moment so securely that there was no spent dowry, no tenants to worry over, no uncle, no turnips to mash for her supper. She wasn't hungry or tired or determined.

She was only here. In his arms. Being devoured. *Devouring.*

"You taste like sweets," Dougal murmured, nipping at her throat. Her hands closed over his arms, all heat and muscles. His leg pressed between hers, teasing her, and she couldn't help another moan. She wanted to stay here forever, just like this.

And then the dog barked.

A lot.

Insistently.

Dramatically.

There was a pause, a curse. And then Dougal pulled back, but only slightly, smiling. "I believe Chartreuse has found our housebreaker."

He nuzzled her nose with his and she melted with a different kind of warmth. "I should have pushed her into the bushes."

"Agreed."

"Next time." She licked the line of his jaw with the tip of her tongue, just a little, just because she wanted to. "We could pretend we didn't hear anything."

"Until they knock on my door and can't find me," he said, groaning. "Or you. Damn it." He stroked his thumbs along her cheeks, securing her at the right angle to kiss her again, hard, hungry, as if he couldn't get enough of her.

"We should go," he said regretfully, gruffly. She wasn't the only one affected by whatever it was between them.

She might have tried harder to convince him to stay, even as candles glowed at the windows of the house, but voices sounded, too near. Footmen, raising the alarm.

"The duke is missing! Search everywhere!"

Dougal sighed. He opened his mouth to say something else but then the footmen were upon them, too fast. If they were caught together, she would be compromised. He would marry her, she knew that much. And it was so tempting. But also selfish of her. She saw the struggle in his face, and the moment he read the hesitation in hers.

"My reputation," she mouthed. And he didn't know her well enough yet to know that wouldn't have stopped her, not if she'd thought a penniless viscount's daughter could marry a duke.

He looked disappointed but it was so brief she had probably imagined it. Wanted to see it. When he met her eyes, as the snapping of branches underfoot and the panting of footmen increased, his expression was rueful, apologetic, very close to laughing.

She crouched in the bushes, not knowing she could feel this

way, desperate, happy, wanted. Wanting.

She didn't even care that a twig was currently trying to poke up her nose.

Oh, he was dangerous, this man.

So very dangerous.

Chapter Eleven

WHEN MEG HAD her fill of statues, she went into the dining room to continue with her restoration of the mural. A partial cleaning had revealed a satyr behind one of the trees, two more nymphs in a lake that had once been blue and was now gray. Pan, playing his pipes, reclined on the branch of a sturdy English oak surely never seen in Rome. Every dingy shadow hid another surprise: a red bird, a hedgehog far from home, three swans. Miniature goats on a distant hill. On a stretch of blue, a ship bobbed, looking as though it had been painted by someone having a sneezing fit.

Still, it was a pleasure to bring the painting back to life, to carefully and painstakingly scrape off years of candle smoke and soot. She was mixing a new batch of colors on her wooden palette when the dining room door slammed open. It startled her, lost as she was in her work, and she yelped. Loudly.

Indecorously, even.

The intruder yelped back. Louder. Much louder.

In point of fact, Dougal shouted like a cat whose tail had just been trod on.

Meg burst out laughing and nearly fell off her ladder. Dougal stared at her blankly for a long, long moment. Then his own laugh threatened to knock her off her ladder again. He steadied her, and their eyes met, fueling more chuckles.

When she snorted, she nearly killed a duke through an apoplectic fit.

She'd already laughed more in the house in one week than in all the years since she'd lost her parents, in her own home.

By the time they managed to contain themselves, they were slumped weakly, tilting towards each other. Meg caught her breath as Dougal grinned quietly. Which was when Meg could finally concentrate on the fact that his hand was on her leg. On her thigh, to be exact. Warm, strong. Comfortable. But it still felt right, as if he should always be touching her. As if he was touching her right now—in a rather unlikely place. She squeezed her thighs together, lightly, instinctively.

Dougal noticed. His eyes flared.

She was in great danger of toppling again, but for a very different reason.

The moment changed, just as intimate, but charged now. Heated.

She swallowed when his eyes traveled slowly up to meet hers. She could only hope her blush would be attributed to laughing like a drunken donkey.

Not precisely ladylike.

Or alluring.

But he didn't seem to notice.

Or if he did, it did not matter.

He looked at her as though she was lovely,—better,— *necessary*. Even halfway up a ladder, covered in paint and her hair in her usual braided coronet because it was the easiest style to manage without a lady's maid when one was pretending one actually *had* a lady's maid. And it was tidy, practical.

And deeply, deeply unimportant right now.

All that mattered was the heat and gentle pressure of his palm. Undemanding, respectful. But still somehow hungry. The juxtaposition nearly made her moan.

He was the first to pull away.

She desperately needed him to stay where he was but also desperately needed space to regain her equilibrium. Before she embarrassed herself completely.

A soft footstep in the hall had them both turning. There was a muffled giggle. Dougal cursed once, before moving to shut the door, softly. Carefully. As if he might detonate a bomb if he were heard.

Which was not entirely wrong.

She recognized that kind of giggle. She'd heard it too many times in the last few days: single ladies, young and old, roaming the halls in search of a duke in search of a wife.

When he leaned back against the locked door, she tilted her head. "You're hiding."

"You're bloody right, I am."

"Discretion is the better part of valor?" She teased.

"It is when young ladies are sneaking into my bath." He sounded so shocked, so like an aging spinster, that she had to bite the inside of her cheek not to laugh. "I thought debutantes were meant to be mild and sheltered."

Meg scoffed, turning back to Pan. A tiny bit of gold on the flute would look like sunshine. "I take it by that response that I am mistaken," Dougal said drily.

"There are a great many debutantes who have no other recourse but to marry."

"They could work."

"They could. As governesses, at the mercy of their employers'…appetites."

He winced.

"Or as dressmakers, maybe. But they have no skills because they have not been taught any, on purpose, and are under the control of fathers who do not want governesses for daughters."

"They want duchesses for daughters."

"Precisely." She added a touch of the same gold to an oak leaf, before realizing she was working dangerously close to Pan's groin. And the original painter had apparently focused on that area. With a great deal of optimism. Back to oak leaves and ladies. "Not to mention that the war has taken too many of our young men." It had nearly taken Henry. She'd gladly run Napoleon through herself for that alone. "Fewer men mean fewer marriages."

"You are very mercenary."

"Practical," she corrected, though she had to also correct a slight slump to her shoulders. Mercenary ladies who fell off ladders were not precisely in demand.

"I like it," Dougal said softly. She struggled not to blush again.

Caught between his warm attention and Pan's erection, Meg opted to change the subject. Discretion and valor and all that. "What have you got there?" She asked, finally noticing the parchment tucked inside his waistcoat, instead of the crinkle at the corner of his dark eyes.

He followed her glance, made a face. "A letter from the Prince of Wales."

"Goodness."

"With a list of his choices for my upcoming nuptials."

"Ah."

So much for a change of subject.

It was for the best. She couldn't afford to forget her place or the reality of her situation. She might like Dougal more than she ought to, and he might like her, a little bit, but it didn't change the fact that she had no dowry and one scurrilous uncle who liked it that way.

"You can't know how it feels to be forced into marriage."

Her glance was so dry it fairly crackled.

His mouth twitched. "That was an idiotic thing to say, I apologize."

She waved it away. "Who has he suggested?" The Prince of Wales was not exactly known for being selfless. He might be a fine patron of art and architecture, but he was less careful with his cronies. And his own habits. "I might recognize their names, even if we are not friendly."

Dougal leaned a shoulder against her mural and sighed. "A Lady St. Ives."

"Granddaughter of a duke. She's clever, kind."

She'd always liked Lady St. Ives. Until today.

"Lady Susan Acton."

"Her father is a nightmare. And a good friend to the Prince."

"Of course, he is."

She met his sardonic look with her own. "Who else?" she

asked. Hopeful ladies in the garden were one thing but this was something else entirely. This was duty and royal decree and a cold splash of reality. She hadn't expected to feel quite this... cross at the thought of his marrying.

"Miss Linden."

"She's a mouse," Meg told him. "She'll be terrified of you."

He visibly recoiled. "I don't want a wife who's scared of me."

If she hadn't already liked him so well, she might have loved him a little bit for that.

But she'd only known him a week.

Admiring him and wanting to lick him did not equal love.

"What about Lady Anabelle Dutton and Miss Kemp?"

"Both unobjectionable."

"But?"

"Their fathers, again. *Not* particularly honorable." And they would chafe at having Dougal for a son-in-law, duke or not. Both because of his past and the fact that they would not be able to control him. "And very snobbish."

Dougal groaned. "I might actually have to marry one of the house tour ladies."

She smiled, trying not to feel sad. "I suppose so."

He raised an eyebrow. "Tell me again why you're unmarried?"

There was a small rush of happiness that he would ask and she squashed it mercilessly. "I am not suited for marriage."

"Hmmm."

She could easily imagine living in this house, Dougal's hand on her thigh, laughter and long naked nights. She wanted it more than she could admit to herself. She turned back to the mural so she wouldn't have to meet Dougal's all too direct and perceptive gaze.

Instead, she could have sworn that Pan winked at her.

Cheeky bastard.

MEG THOROUGHLY INSPECTED the blue parlor, checking behind every column, every crack in the wall, every shadow that might indicate a secret door and found nothing but dust and a book of naughty prints under the pink chair cushion. She hadn't expected any different, not from a room that seemed to have been redecorated within the last decade, and she was nearly positive it was an addition to begin with. It had nothing of the abbey about it.

She found Colin lounging in the doorway to the back gardens, alone, smirking. For nearly ten consecutive minutes. Surely that much smugness was bad for the digestion.

"What on earth are you doing?" she asked.

He started, then looked over his shoulder at her with aristocratic languor. She knew without asking that he had practiced in the mirror. It was charming, but likely not in the manner he was hoping for. She wanted to tell him not to contort himself into the rigid confines of society's expectations because it always came at a steep price. But she knew she wouldn't have listened when she was eighteen years old either and so she only smiled.

"I am watching my brother panic."

Meg joined him on the threshold. "Why is he—oh."

Poor Dougal.

He stood on a gravel walk, hedged in by yew bushes, rosebushes, and a singular aspen tree too narrow to offer any kind of protection from approximately eleven women aged sixteen to seventy, all wearing dainty white dresses, holding dainty parasols, and wielding dainty smiles. They had found the evasive duke and only an act of biblical proportions would convince them to retreat now. There was a footman standing nearby but he was as lost as Dougal.

"They'll eat him alive," Meg murmured. "Why did he go out there? Did you dare him to?"

"He was having a cup of tea in quiet solitude and then they descended like cats at the fish market," he said, faintly mystified. "I don't know how they did it. I admit to being terrified. They must have jogged all the way from the pond. They're not even out of breath."

Dougal shifted uncomfortably, empty teacup clutched in his hand like a weapon. He was so handsome, so patient, so intent on being polite.

So utterly out of his depths.

Meg shot his brother a side glance. "Aren't you going to rescue him?"

"Did he tell you about the time he put pepper in my beer? I was nine years old, and I sneezed for three full hours."

She laughed. "And innocent as a lamb, I am certain. Despite drinking beer at the age of nine, which I suspect was the point of the pepper?"

He winked. "You must understand that I am the grieved party."

"Seeing as it's been nearly ten years," Meg said. "Perhaps we might allow a brief interruption of hostilities?"

"He would owe me."

"And think how much fun that will be."

He tossed his hair back, smiling crookedly, just like Dougal. "I like the way your brain works, Miss Swift."

"And a duke's brother is a worthy consolation prize," she added archly. "I am sure tears will need to be dried, needs assuaged, etcetera."

"Better and better. I can't very well be a buck around town when I'm so very far behind the other bucks. I've never even been to school," he added, under his breath, losing some of his usual aplomb.

She squeezed his arm. "You leave them in the dust already, my lord."

He looked as though he was struggling not to blush. She couldn't help a grin. It was so much better than forced ennui. "That, right there," she said. "You will charm them far beyond any aristocratic manners."

"Let's see, shall we?"

They stepped out onto the terrace together and the flash of their movement had twelve heads turning sharply in their direction. They both paused, momentarily.

"Bloody hell."

"Courage," Meg murmured.

"Colin! Me—that is, Miss Swift!" Meg wondered, briefly, if Dougal might weep in relief. He sounded faintly hysterical, truth be told. "Ladies, may I present Miss Swift."

A flurry of suspicious curtsies followed.

"And my brother, Lord Henley."

Far more enthusiastic curtsies.

She could hardly blame them. At least four of the ladies transferred their interest to Colin, three of the younger ones and a grandmother with a wicked gleam in her eye. He was very handsome in his bottle-green coat and perfect cravat. And he feigned arrogance and aplomb better than his brother, who did not even try.

Dougal might not have much confidence in his new title, but he had confidence in himself. It was desperately appealing. Meg wondered if the others could sense it. If it mattered to them. Probably not. They were lurking in the hedges in order to meet a duke, it did not much matter what that duke was like in the end, as long as he was courteous, passably handsome, and did not stink of onions.

Behind them were two gentlemen, tucked neatly against a hedge, and conversing quietly. They stared up at the house.

Treasure hunters.

She'd bet her set of Ackerman watercolor paints on it.

She knew that look. All too well. She did not approach them right away, instead turned to enter the fray of ladies, with her usual mild, polite smile. Dougal narrowed his eyes, instantly suspicious. In that moment, she felt more seen than she had in years, by anyone other than the other Cinderellas, and only a few of them at that. She presented a certain façade and no one questioned it, not really.

Except perhaps Dougal.

She was reading too much into a narrowing of the eyes.

Still, it kindled a warmth inside her, a shimmer inside the blood.

"Your Grace," she said. "I'm afraid you're needed inside."

She'd never seen anyone wilt with relief so quickly in her life, not even the time Tamsin had knocked a rare Egyptian glass perfume bottle off of a shelf and Persephone had defied gravity itself to save it. She'd torn a shoulder muscle too and counted it a fair exchange. Antiquarians were mad as ten cats, honestly.

"Thank you, Miss Swift." Dougal, she felt certain, had imagined himself caught in that circle of ladies under the aspen tree until nightfall. Possibly until morning. "It seems you are always rescuing me," he added to her in undertones.

"My godfather *did* send me to help you," she replied.

"I am sending him all of the wine in the cellar."

When he offered her his arm, one of the ladies sniffed. "She's an ape-leader," she muttered. "Ridiculous. The Prince would never allow it."

Her mutter was exactly as loud as she wanted it to be. That is: loud. Clear as a bell.

Shocked giggles shivered between the other ladies. The grandmother did not look pleased. Nor did Dougal. He halted. Meg stumbled to a stop, surprised. "I beg your pardon?" He said silkily. Ducally, even.

The lady blinked, caught. She tried a smile, a small laugh. "Why nothing at all, Your Grace."

"Miss Wilmington, is it?"

Her smile turned triumphant at the corners. "Yes, Your Grace."

Dougal waved the footman over. "Please escort Miss Wilmington off the estate. She has completed her tour." When she sputtered, Dougal continued. "She will not be returning."

"You didn't have to do that," Meg said softly as Miss Wilmington was escorted away.

"Bloody right, I did."

The others whispered to each other. The grandmother looked impressed. She winked at Dougal. He flushed to his ears. Meg grinned. "I'll be right back."

His eyes widened. "Don't you dare leave me."

She laughed. "I'll be right back," she promised.

She wandered towards the gentlemen, moving slowly, nothing to alert them to her interest. She was merely another lady in a white dress on the lawn. Admiring the hazel tree, the stone bench, and, oh dear, tripping over an exposed root. She stumbled, gasping.

The red-haired gentleman rushed forward to steady her. His friend smirked. She had no doubt they were accustomed to any manner of mock tripping, or dropped handkerchiefs, all for the pleasure of their attention. Meg had something else entirely in mind. But they didn't need to know that. "Goodness," she said. "I'm so clumsy today. Thank you so much."

"Not at all," the man preened.

"Are you here for to tour the gardens?" she asked.

"Of course."

"The roses are so lovely, even at this time of year."

"Almost as lovely as you are."

The roses had shriveled up and turned brown last week under the first frost. She fluttered her eyelashes, feeling like an absolute goose. She heard Dougal clear his throat, stifling a laugh. She refused to even glance in his direction. Instead, she playfully swatted the gentleman's chest, just under his cravat. "Such a flirt!"

He bowed, winking.

"My mother would not like me to tarry," she lied, sounding disappointed. "Thank you for your assistance, sir."

"A pleasure, my lady."

She curtsied and turned away, moving with sure-footed ease over the roots and the grass. Dougal caught up to her near the house. "What are you up to?" he murmured as they crossed the stones and ducked inside.

"This!" Meg exclaimed with more than a little victory. She waved a printed map of the house, with notes scrawled in the corners. It was her turn to smirk.

"Now we'll know what they know."

Chapter Twelve

IT TURNED OUT that the treasure hunters had a map of the house dating back more than two hundred years, which was only truly helpful when compared to a map of the current house—which they did not have.

Meg, however, did.

She traced the modern house on very thin paper and then laid it over the stolen map. It was easy to see the changes then, even allowing for mistakes on the part of both mapmakers. The abbey's original structure was easier to define, making it also easier to see the later Tudor additions, the Jacobean tower, the Georgian conservatory.

It had taken some time and now the house was quiet around her, only the creaking of old wood and the wind tapping at the windows to keep her company. It was long past midnight and everyone else had gone to bed. She should wait until morning when it would be easier to see, when there would be help at hand.

She already knew she wouldn't.

There was a spot in the entrance hall, mostly comprised of the oldest part of the original abbey, which was too tempting not to explore right away. Additionally, the tiled floors were Tudor-era, as was the wood paneling. One of the windows had been built into a brick fireplace. A door led to an early Stuart addition, another to the more recent Music Room.

It was the fireplace no one had bothered with which intrigued her. It had not been used in several lifetimes; the wooden mantle and attached frieze were faded and tilting somewhat to the left. A relic from earlier days.

As she descended the stairs with her candle, she tried to imagine what it would have been like to be a monk in this place. To have spent years sleeping in austere quarters, singing hymns before the sun rose, tending to huge gardens and fishponds; and then to be informed that the king planned to take it all away and give it to a nobleman.

Meg would have rioted.

Well, she liked to think she would have rioted. But her experience with her uncle suggested she would have hidden the silver and snuck out to pick all of the turnips from the garden.

This treasure hunt was turning entirely too introspective.

Where was the ancient gold? The swashbuckling duels? A ghost or two?

Be careful what you ask for.

Be very, very careful.

She didn't hear a single thing to warn her, not the scrape of a shoe over tiles, not an intake of breath. She only knew that one moment she was contemplating the fireplace and the next the tip of a dagger poked into her spine.

"Quiet."

She froze. She had no intention of staying quiet, she just had to remind her lungs and her vocal chords how to move. Her candle bobbled in her hand and then dropped to the floor but did not go out. There would be no using the cover of darkness to get out of this.

Fear snaked through her, but also indignation. Fiery, angry outrage. Someone had broken into Dougal's house in order to steal from him, and no doubt due to Eaton's incitement. "Where is it?" The man demanded. He didn't sound nervous or remotely ashamed. He was one of the serious collectors.

Like hell was he getting the treasure.

Even if she knew where it was.

Which she didn't.

If only outrage was a suitable weapon against a knife. There was a sharp prod, and she hissed a breath. Pain nibbled. She thought she felt a drop of blood stain her nightdress.

He was making a hole in one of her few nightdresses on top of everything else.

"Where's the bloody treasure?"

And then suddenly Dougal was there.

He came out of the shadows, eyes flashing. There was no posturing, no negotiating. One moment she was trapped and then the next the dagger tip was gone from her spine.

Dougal slammed his fist into the man's elbow and his arm bent sharply. His grip on the knife loosened reflexively and Dougal caught it, ramming the hilt into the treasure hunter's face. There was a sharp crack when his nose howled, and then a sputtering howl.

"Get the hell away from her." Dougal added another punch, this one hard and vicious enough to lay the man flat on the floor, unconscious.

"Did he hurt you?" Dougal asked her, alarmed, furious.

Meg shook her head and found her voice, somewhere between the cold of fear and the warmth of Dougal. "I'm fine."

"Let me see." He turned her around gently, hands brushing her shoulders. She knew the exact moment he spotted the blood. The air around him turned arctic. "You're bleeding."

She waved it off, turning back around to meet his slightly feral gaze. "It's nothing."

"It's everything." His voice was stark.

She touched his hand gently, above his hold on the knife. "It's a tiny cut. I've done much worse to myself with an embroidery needle."

"He'll pay for it." It was a promise. Simple, dark.

"*After* he tells us what he knows," she said.

His lips twitched, nearly smiling despite the fury boiling under his skin. "Practical, as always."

"Where did you even come from? I thought you'd gone to bed."

"No, I was wrestling with account ledgers that appear to be

written in some cross of chicken scratch and hieroglyph for all they make sense."

She'd snuck into her uncle's study to peek at the estate ledgers more than once before convincing him she would hate the job of keeping the books and thereby ensuring he immediately made it her first priority. It helped mitigate some of his more outlandish demands from tenants and rents.

She prodded the unconscious man with the toe of her slipper. He didn't budge, didn't even flutter an eyelash. "He'll be out for some time," she said.

"Yes."

"Well done, you."

"I'd like to do much worse to him."

"Later. We should tie him up before he wakes up and makes a fuss."

Dougal sighed. "Can you fetch the ropes from the curtains in that awful gold room? And pull the bell for Canterbury? Because I'm not leaving you alone with this tosspot."

"He's not even conscious."

"Not even then."

She couldn't deny his concern sent a flush of warmth through her. Almost as much as the grim edge to his usually amiable face, the tightening of his jaw. It probably said something unsavory about her character that she found herself drawn to him, even now. Especially now.

She ducked into the hideous gold drawing room which had yet to be used during her visit, and with good reason – no one should use that much gilt on furniture. The wallpaper gleamed, the curtains glimmered with gold thread. The ropes holding them back were yellow, with a satin finish, but also thick and sturdy. They would do. She dragged them free and then pulled the bell for the butler.

When she returned, Dougal had dragged the man into a corner, not bothering to sit him up. His cravat was spattered with blood from his rapidly swelling nose. Dougal wound the rope around his hands, binding them behind his back and then used the rest of the rope to secure his arms and his shoulders to his chest. He was trussed up like a chicken ready for the oven. All he needed was a sprig of rosemary in his mouth. "He's not dead, is he?" she asked.

"No, he'll wake up soon enough."

"Hmph."

"In the meantime," Dougal rummaged through the pockets of his coat. "I know this is your area of expertise," he added wryly. "But let's see what I can find."

They found a gold watch, a handful of coins, a snuffbox enameled with two acrobatic ladies in postures not often found in polite society, and folded scraps of parchment.

"Another map?' Meg wondered as Dougal unfolded it, smoothing it out.

"Yes," he said, tightly.

She leaned closer, holding up her candle. "It's the same one. It seems they are being printed." She peered at his face. "He's not one of the men from the garden earlier."

The candlelight moving near his face roused him and he shifted slightly, groaning. "What the devil," he mumbled through a swollen top lip. His eyes flew open, and he groaned again. "You broke my nose!"

"You're lucky that's all I broke," Dougal said flatly.

"*You* broke into a duke's house," Meg pointed out with grim cheerfulness. "He could have killed you and no one would blame him."

The man swallowed. Before she could reply, Canterbury arrived, hastily dressed. "Your Grace, what can I—oh. Well, now."

Dougal rose to his feet. "We seem to have a housebreaker."

"One of the blasted house tours?" Canterbury asked.

"No, a treasure hunter this time. He went for Meg—Miss Swift—with a knife."

"He did what?" Canterbury's jovial eyes narrowed.

"I'm fine," she assured him. "Barely a scratch."

"He *scratched* you?' The butler's outrage was climbing into fury. Meg wasn't sure what to say. She wasn't accustomed to such reactions on her behalf outside of the Cinderella Society.

Canterbury and Dougal exchanged a look before the butler added: "I'll send a footman to town for the constable."

"Thank you. And wake a few more to take this garbage away and keep him secured until the constable arrives."

The man looked mutinous, briefly. "I am a gentleman."

"You're a thief," Dougal corrected him.

"And he's a duke," Canterbury said as he walked away to rouse the footmen.

Meg shrugged. "Told you so."

Dougal crouched beside the treasure hunter. He was all coiled strength, loose limbs, patience. The kind of patience Meg imagined a cat displayed moments before catching a mouse. "You're going to tell us what you know."

He scowled. "I'm after the Tudor Treasure, that's all. This is a bit much, don't you think? Historians take this sort of thing in stride, my good man."

"I'm not a historian."

While he squirmed under Dougal's cold, deliberate glare, Meg unfolded the other pieces of parchment that they'd taken from his pocket. She read the first quickly, dread prickling through her.

Canterbury and three footmen returned as she skimmed the other pages, cursing silently.

"Edward will go to the village, Your Grace," Canterbury said. "And the rest of us will stay with this blackguard."

"Thank you," Dougal said. "Sorry to take you from your beds."

"Not at all."

"Perhaps you could take him into the Gold drawing room," Meg suggested. "In case the other ladies heard the ruckus and come exploring."

"Certainly, Miss."

They were none too gentle as they carted him away. Meg turned back to Dougal and handed him one of the papers. "Eaton isn't just telling the treasure hunters about you, he's offering a reward. A large one."

Dougal whistled. "Bollocks."

"That reprobate isn't even a collector," Meg snapped. She wasn't sure why it should matter, but it did. "He just wants to make more trouble for you."

"Apparently one hundred pounds worth of trouble. Very few people will be able to ignore that kind of money." He ran a hand over his face. "I guess he didn't like being punched."

"Next time," she said with palpable disgust, "Punch him harder."

He smiled, despite the circumstances. "Agreed."

DOUGAL HAD NEVER known the kind of rage searing the inside of his ribcage until tonight. It was physically painful. And he was reasonably concerned that every time he opened his mouth to speak, fire might shoot from behind his tongue. He didn't believe in dragons until now.

That arse had put his hands on Meg.

Had *cut* her.

It took everything in him not to follow Canterbury and the others into the Gold room. A broken nose was not nearly penance enough. All for some treasure that might not even exist. His teeth ached, reminding him that his jaw was not naturally meant to clench that way.

He'd burn the house down if meant the safety of his family. If Lady Blackwell or her coven had wandered down for warm milk—or let's face it, whisky—they might not have recovered from the shock. Colin would have chosen violence. Dougal supported that choice at the moment, but not if it put his brother at risk.

It occurred to him that he wasn't quite sure when he had started to see Meg as family. She might not agree, and he wasn't fool enough to blurt that realization for the world to hear, but he would continue to act on it. Wherever she went, he would make sure she was safe. Happy.

He wanted her to stay right here and be happy.

Wanted it more than anything.

"Oh, I quite forgot," she said in her indomitable way. "I came down here to inspect the fireplace."

Part of him wanted to ask if she needed to sit down and rest after her recent experience and the rest of him liked all of his body parts attached to him. "Why that fireplace?" he asked, trying to sound like a civilized duke and not a dragon. He was only mildly successful.

"It hasn't been used in centuries."

The crooked fireplace was tucked into the back corner of the entrance hall, under the balcony. The firebox was red brick, the mantel and surround were a rich, faded wood old enough and thick enough with polish to shine under the candlelight. The supporting legs were carved with vines and roses. Above the mantel, holding up a pediment, were two women wearing crowns. "I've been comparing maps," Meg explained. "And this fireplace is late medieval. I think it might be oldest part of this entire estate."

"That sounds promising."

"And the wall, just here? It never quite lines up in any of the drawings."

They moved closer, touching the carvings, pushing against leaves and filigrees, exploring every nook. He knocked on the decorative panels, along the edges of the mantel, and finally over the figures.

The queen on the left did not sound like the rest of the woodwork.

He knocked again.

Definitely hollow.

He traced over the crown, the arms, her gown.

"What are you doing exactly?" Meg asked, drily from where she had crawled inside the firebox only to poke her head back out to find him fondling a medieval queen.

"Exploring," he shot back, equally drily. "Isn't this what historians do?"

Something shifted, ever so slightly, under Dougal's palm. If he hadn't been so focused, he would have missed it altogether. He pushed again, and that faint give had him looking down at her and grinning. "Found something."

Meg pounced, nearly knocking her head on the mantel in her haste. "Show me!" Her candle's flame wavered, almost going out.

"I want to shove the treasure right into that man's broken nose."

Years of dust and polish had all but glued the seam that cut along the vertical length of the linen folds of the queen's skirts. The folds were carved deep, and the shadows hid their secrets. Not for long.

Or so he thought.

It would not budge.

Dougal pulled harder, worked his fingertips into the wood for purchase, but still nothing.

"Blast," Meg muttered. "Even if there *is* a secret latch, it won't open."

"I need a knife," Dougal said. "I'll be right back."

"Wait," she stopped him, darted away with her candle. She came back within moments, a dagger in her hand. "He tried to stab me with it. Least he can do is help us on our quest."

His jaw tightened again, with a near audible crack.

"There are other places I'd like to put this," he said under his breath, accepting the knife. It wasn't particularly sharp or long, but it was more than enough to have caused some damage. "We are washing your wound," he decided. "With vinegar."

"I suppose. Now hurry up," she said with anticipation. "Disembowel her."

He couldn't help but laugh. "Remind me never to anger you."

He ran the blade along the seam a few times, working through the accumulated grime. Satisfied that it was loosened, he wedged the knife in for leverage and pushed again. A soft creak, more like ancient woodwork sighing than anything else.

But it was something.

He pushed again and the queen's bell skirt unlatched, opening a few centimeters. Meg held her breath beside him, like a child on Christmas morning searching for sweets. She might claim not to be an antiquarian or a collector, but she'd clearly absorbed that need to know, to ferret out.

Part of him wanted the compartment to be empty.

No treasure meant the hunters *might* leave.

But it also meant Meg *would* leave.

He pulled the door open because there was no other choice.

Chapter Thirteen

MEG FELT LIKE she'd drunk approximately seventeen cups of tea, with extra sugar. Anticipation vibrated through her bones, right into her blood. She understood her godfather a little better. When the hidden compartment door finally opened, she squeaked with delight. She couldn't help it. They were going to show those blasted treasure hunters just how it was done.

Or not.

She craned her neck, jostling Dougal to get a better look. They were cheek to cheek, eager to discover silver plates or rubies or gold candlesticks. Embroidered priestly vestments. A painted cross.

Anything.

"It's empty," Meg said with rising disbelief. She sat back on her heels, thoroughly disgruntled. "Well, that's not helpful."

She'd been so sure. The maps showed her the secret vestibule.

It was just that there was no treasure in it.

And there was no way of knowing if there ever had been. This could have been a place to hide secret love letters. Plans of treason. Any number of personal things which Eaton could not claim or sell.

Actually, that was comforting. He wouldn't have anything either, damn his eyes.

"Wait," Dougal said softly. "Bring your candle closer."

She did as he asked. "What do you see?"

"I'm not sure." He reached his arm into the darkness. Meg lifted her candle, imagining spiders or rats. Something crinkled when he touched it, like old paper.

"What is it?" she breathed.

Dougal stepped back, opening his palm. In it lay a single dried flower, the stem gray with age, the petals crumbling.

Meg frowned. "What can that mean? Why a flower?" It must be some private jest, a secret message.

It was thoroughly unhelpful.

Although, something about it tickled the back of her brain.

She might have figured it out if there wasn't suddenly a pained yelp from the Gold Room.

"Now what?" Dougal muttered.

They found the drawing room occupied by Canterbury, three footmen, and a treasure hunter, as expected. Less expected was Lady Beatrice in her nightgown, gray hair loose to her elbows, holding a spear to the treasure hunter's midsection. She poked him again and there was another yelp. Dougal leaned in the doorway, grinning. "Where did you get a spear?"

"There's a suit of armor in the hall outside my bedroom," she replied.

"Help me!" the treasure hunter gulped. "She's cracked!"

"She is," Dougal agreed. "Make sure you tell the others."

Lady Beatrice cackled once, just to underscore the point. She didn't seem concerned when the constable finally arrived, only shot him a look over her shoulder. "About time you got here."

The constable took note of the broken nose, the blooming bruise, the blood. And the spear. "I can take it from here, Your Grace."

"Thank you," Dougal said.

"I fear there may be others," Meg told him. "Someone is telling tall tales about hidden treasure."

"Not that again," he sighed. "Every time Lady Dahlia came home for a visit, the gossips were certain there was gold under every floorboard of the abbey. She did like to tweak her father's nose. Not even a duke was enough to control her and the old duke had a temper, to be sure." He dropped his voice as though it were a great secret. "The workmen in town made a pretty penny off repairs from his fits, especially the plasterers and painters."

Lady Dahlia. Privateer. Possible pirate.

"It was rubbish, of course," he continued. "Well, the part about the gold treasure."

"Of course." Meg squeezed Dougal's hand so that she wouldn't give herself away. That dried flower was a *dahlia*.

"I'll be sure to parade him around town come morning," the constable added. "Might deter the less determined."

"That would be much appreciated," Dougal said as the constable and two of his men marched the stranger away.

"No more garden tours!" Lady Beatrice barked in lieu of a good night. She dragged the spear up the stairs with her.

It took an age for the business to be done, for Canterbury and the others to return to their beds. Meg only realized she was still holding Dougal's hand when his thumb stroked her knuckle. She didn't let go. Instead, she used it to tow him behind her when she took off at a run towards the portrait hall.

"What are we doing here?" Dougal asked when she stopped between rows of Roman gods, under a portrait of a woman in breeches with flowers in her bodice.

"Lady Dahlia," Meg announced. "Known to be the family pirate."

"There was a family pirate?"

"Yes," Meg said. "And that flower you found…"

"It's a dahlia," he said slowly.

"Exactly. She could easily have found a treasure and taken it. Or moved it. To poke at her father." She wrinkled her nose. "Perhaps I am reading too much into it."

"Only one way to find out," Dougal said.

As he took the huge painting down off the wall, Meg used her candle to light the other tapers in the room. Soon a warm glow encased them, creating an island of light where they were perfectly alone. Dougal ran his hand over the wall where the painting had hung but there were no indications of another secret compartment.

Meg sat on the floor, taking in the thick layer of paint, the brushstrokes, the dabs of red on the dahlias. Nothing was untoward or obviously altered. She touched the stretched linen carefully but there were no bumps, nothing to suggest it might have torn or been stitched together.

She had been so certain she was onto something.

She sighed. All this fuss over nothing.

Dougal crouched next to her. She wondered how disconcerted he would be if she sniffed him. The layers of cedar and soap made her want to do things to him.

She turned her attention to the frame, hoping the shifting shadows hid her blush.

That's when she saw it.

"There's something stuck inside the corner of the frame here," she said. "It looks like a bit of paper."

"Can you get it out?"

She pulled gently. "It's been there awhile." She reached out for the dagger she already knew he was handing her. "Clearly, I'm going to have to start carrying a knife on my person, along with those hair ribbons."

"Keep that one," Dougal suggested. "Let that miscreant come at me for theft."

"Good point."

She used the tip of the blade to work the parchment loose. It was just a scrap, ripped from some book or another and folded into a flat little square. Meg flattened it out, faded ink in a bold hand. She read it slowly. "*Seven seashells for your boat, Seven roses for your coat, and seven stars for your wrath. A flash of green when day turns to night; Panic not, the treasure is in sight.*"

She exhaled. "A riddle."

"You did it," Dougal said.

"Have I mentioned that I hate riddles?"

"But it looks like you were right," he said. "She found the treasure and moved it."

"Just to taunt her father. And with a riddle as an extra insult."

"You have to admire that kind of commitment to spite." He glanced at her out of the corner of his eye. "Don't ever tell

Charlie I said that."

She chuckled. "I won't." She read the riddle over again. "We're going to have a devil of a time deciphering this. For one, does she mean seven stars in the sky? As for navigation from a ship? Or seven stars in this house?" They both looked up to the darkened ceiling, the candlelight catching the glint of at least a hundred stars. Nearly every room in the abbey was the same.

"This could take months," Meg whispered.

"It looks like the treasure hunt is not over, after all," Dougal said, just as softly. He sounded pleased.

Almost as pleased as she felt.

Chapter Fourteen

THE NEXT DAY, Lady Blackwell insisted everyone get some fresh air by heading to the village, by way of the seaside.

And then she promptly stayed home with the older ladies.

Meg wondered if she should warn Dougal to check his liquor bottles, then decided that if three ladies in their seventies wished to drink until they snored on the settees, they had more than earned the privilege. Canterbury obviously agreed as he had made himself scarce within minutes—after leaving a tea tray glittering with an assortment of whisky and brandy bottles and baskets of bread and butter and pears.

Mrs. Hill, predictably, did not approve.

Of anything, it seemed.

As Meg made her way down the main staircase, she could hear the housekeeper's voice, pinched and fretful. "You must wear these gloves instead, miss. Your arms are far too muscular for a lady."

Meg could read Charlie's spine perfectly well as it curved inward and then snapped straight. Before she could form a retort, a knock sounded at the door.

Lady Beatrice poked her head out of the drawing room. "Who's that?"

"I don't know," Meg replied as Canterbury greeted the visitor. Meg caught sight of a beaver-crowned hat, white teeth flashing in a charming smile that made her itchy.

"I'll see if His Grace is at home," Canterbury said in measured tones. There was nothing of the cheerful pugilist about him today, just the pugilist.

"My good man, I went to school with the duke. Cambridge."

Meg knew for a fact that none of the Blacks had gone away to school, never mind Cambridge. How would they have even afforded it?

"We're old friends, he'll want to see me."

The visitor pressed forward but Canterbury did not budge, as expected.

Moreover, Lady Beatrice marched down the hall, nudged him aside, and then barked in her best bark: "The duke doesn't have any friends!"

Then she slammed the heavy door in the startled man's face, patted Canterbury's arm, and marched back to the drawing room. Meg grinned at the entire spectacle, even as Mrs. Hill gaped. She soon regained her fortitude and went back to pushing elbow-length pearl-white gloves at Charlie, who was already wearing fingerless mesh gloves, perfectly acceptable for a daytime trip to the village. "Mrs. Hill," Meg said plainly. "Those are evening gloves and not suitable."

Mrs. Hill shoved them into her pockets. "Miss Swift," she curtsied.

"It's fine," Charlie mumbled under her breath.

"Thank you, Mrs. Hill," Meg said pointedly.

The housekeeper hesitated, met Meg's steely gaze, and walked away. Meg turned to Charlie. "Does she do that often?" she asked. She didn't think Charlie realized that she had clasped her hands behind her back.

"I can take care of myself," Charlie muttered, scowling. She shoved a bonnet on her head and marched outside, as if off to battle.

"I'll take that as a yes," Meg murmured. Someone was going to have to speak to the housekeeper. The Black family might have to learn society's rules but there was no reason they needed to be made to feel inadequate in the process. Anyone could see Charlie was wilting under the pressure, not because she wasn't strong enough, but because she was miserable.

And Meg never could abide a bully.

She was ruminating on a plan when George came out of one of the parlors, a stylish crowned hat sitting snugly on his white hair. He smiled kindly. "She didn't mean to snap at you."

Meg smiled back. "It hardly signifies."

"I heard what you said to Mrs. Hill. And that *does* signify."

"I'm sure she's trying to help but her methods are…" she struggled to find a polite word. She failed.

George winked. "Exactly right."

"Will you be joining us to the village?"

George shot a glance at the drawing room currently exploding with hoots of laughter and "don't keep that whisky to yourself, you old termagant!" He raised his eyebrows. "I wasn't under the impression that I had a choice, Miss Swift."

Meg grinned. "There is that."

"It's good to hear Lady Marigold laughing," George said. "It's the first time she's done that since we arrived."

"She was afraid."

"So were we." He held out his arm and Meg took it. "Shall we, my dear? I believe the others are waiting outside."

IT WAS DECIDED that they would walk to the village and take the carriage back, both to save time and because Dougal didn't want to tire George, who would walk across the very sea if he thought he was being coddled in any way. He'd once taken on three street thugs to save Dougal a bash to the skull; the least Dougal could do was provide a carriage and an excuse that it would be more comfortable for everyone. When George narrowed his eyes, Meg jumped in. "Oh, that's lovely. These are not my most comfortable walking shoes," she said.

Her leather walking shoes were soft as butter, and worn in perfectly, like a favorite pair would be. When George snorted, Meg only shot him a sunny smile.

And that's when Dougal knew he was truly lost.

He tried not to dwell on it, as the party made their way along the path that skirted to the ocean. Charlie and Colin were up ahead, bickering fondly. George took his time, but he always took his time. You may as well try to hurry a boulder.

The sea offered a hundred shades of blue and green and gray beneath a serene sky. Birds wheeled overhead, searching for fish below. The gentle roar of the waves was both insistent and soothing. It could not be ignored and yet did not call particular attention to itself.

Much like Meg.

She occupied an alarming amount of space in his head. The smell of mint and lemon soap, the perfect tiny stitches of the red birds and green leaves and purple flowers embroidered on everything she wore. The way she focused when she was drawing, a tiny frown between her eyes, the tip of her tongue peeking between her lips.

The glimpse of her tongue never failed to do things to him.

He'd been hungry through many a winter, but never as hungry as he was for her. For her touch, her giggle, the spot under her ear that he longed to bite, just once.

Maybe twice.

Every day.

Dougal watched her fingers twitch as she faced the sea. "You want to paint it."

"Desperately," she admitted. There were freckles on her nose. "See that violet there? That would be the key to it. Matching that color. Oh, and it must be glorious under a full moon."

He wanted her to have every single thing that made her happy. The force of it staggered him more than the wind buffeting at them from the cliffside.

She smiled at him, that same wind teasing a strand of hair out from under her bonnet. It was a pretty enough bonnet, tidy, with a bright red ribbon, but it was not new. The trunk of paints the duke had sent along with Meg were the only new things about her. She was a mystery, this viscount's daughter with the threadbare hems and sumptuous embroidery.

"I hadn't realized how much I missed the seaside," she continued. "My grandfather took me once when I was twelve years old. We had footraces in the sand and ate strawberry ices until our tongue went numb."

"You must have made a sandcastle."

"At least three," she admitted.

"And decorated them with seashells?"

"Naturally."

He couldn't imagine her not bringing her unique artistic flair to everything she did, even as a child. Did she have new dresses then? She must have done.

"I made a crown of seaweed," she added with another smile. That quiet, soft smile that made him want to scoop her right up into his arms. "It did *not* smell nice."

He chuckled. "I imagine not."

"I wanted to be a mermaid and sing a pretty song."

"To drown men under the waves, you mean."

She started, then laughed. "I beg your pardon? I feel certain you know perfectly well that is not the sort of thing you can say to a lady."

He shrugged because she didn't look offended, and he knew she wouldn't be. "You've fooled everyone else, haven't you?"

"I'm sure I don't know what you mean?"

He leaned close, closer than was allowed by propriety and all the damned rules. "Meg Swift, with the polite, gentle manners, all pretty flowers and patience." His mouth was so near to her ear that he had to fight not to nip her lobe between his teeth and tug. For now, he'd wait. Torture them both. Just a little. Her breath caught and he smiled. "They only see your shining hair, they think your silences are filled with acquiescence. But I know you, Meg. You don't want pearls and sonnets, you want shipwrecks. And they are fools if they don't see the power in you."

He pulled back and offered his arm. "Shall we?"

She was briefly disoriented. "Um." She had to clear her throat and he'd never been happier. She felt something, reacted to him, just as he reacted to her.

"Perhaps they have strawberry ices in the village," he said. "We will eat them all."

Eventually.

But first, George appeared to be taking off his shoes.

Again.

At least it wasn't his trousers this time.

Charlie and Colin stopped, turning to see what had held them up. He saw the moment Charlie saw Meg watching George. She started forward, hand clasped to her hated bonnet, brow stormy. As usual. She'd never been so moody in their awful cramped flat, not even when they were hungry as nine bears. But she needn't have worried. Dougal could have told her that. Meg was unfailingly kind, and she saw more than people gave her credit for. She wasn't the type to fret and fuss because an old man had taken off his socks.

In fact, she joined him.

When she kicked off her own boots, Dougal smiled. When she unrolled her stockings and left them in a heap in the sand, her ankles bare, her toes wiggling, he groaned. Then she knotted her skirts up at her knee and all he could think of was licking a line from her ankle to her knee, into the warmth of her thighs. All because of a moment at the beach.

Undone by a bare foot.

Hardly ducal.

As the sun broke through fitful clouds, Meg waded into the cold sea beside George, laughing and gasping.

"You're a brave girl," George approved. "The others won't touch the sea."

"It's…refreshing." Her teeth threatened to chatter but she didn't look bothered by it.

"Because Dougal used to tell us stories about the kraken growing up," Colin shouted lazily. "How it would pull us under and eat our bones in a seaweed stew."

"I was trying to keep them out of the rivers," Dougal shot back. "Where they were likely to drown."

"Is that why you snuck seaweed into my bed?" Charlie asked.

He grinned. "Of course. I was merely being a good big brother."

"You could have just taught us how to swim."

"Where's the fun in that?" He had taught them, not long after a boy drowned while searching for lost baubles. It might not have been the Thames, but it was just as dangerous. And just as tempting to think you might find some lady's lost brooch to sell in exchange for eating all of the potatoes you could buy.

"Seven shells to find your boat," Meg quoted the riddle. It had been running through his head all morning as well. They'd told the others who had the spent breakfast tying to remember lullabies with the number seven. She nodded to the beach, thick with seashells. "I really do hate riddles. All I'll see are seashells and it won't help at all."

George smiled. "Did you know that in the Caribbean, there is a green flash on the horizon when the sun sets? Not every night, but still, often enough."

Meg's eyes widened. "Truly? That's brilliant."

"I read it in one of the books at the abbey. There are shelves of stories about the island, and shipwrecks."

Meg stared at the edge of the sea, thick with periwinkle clouds. "*A flash of green when day turns to night.* Do you know, if Dahlia took the treasure to the Islands, I'm going to be very cross."

The waves pulled and pushed at George and Meg, frothing like lace. They clung to each other to stay upright, laughing.

"I like her," Colin said, no longer shouting.

"I do too."

Charlie snorted. Dougal raised an eyebrow. "She's not terrible," she allowed. "But all that genteel embroidery. Ugh."

Dougal shook his head. "Look closer."

"What does that mean? Besides, if I do that, she'll try to teach me how. They all do. Embroidery, dance, watercolors, French."

"Just look closer." It continued to amaze him how little people saw the actual Meg. She enjoyed embroidery, a genteel pastime that his sister derided, but she was just like the others in this instance. She saw only the roses and the violets and the red birds. She never noticed the wolves with red on their paws, the unicorn stitched on a hem, horn sharp as a dagger and dripping blood. The poison berries around a neckline.

"Why not marry *her?*" Colin asked. "Since you have to marry anyway."

She wouldn't have him. And why should she? She was of gentle birth, and he had been born in an alleyway. She insisted she wasn't marriageable. But he knew he wasn't good enough. He wasn't good enough for the ladies on the Prince's bloody list either, to be sure, but he didn't crave their happiness the way he craved Meg's. Whatever it took. Whatever it meant for his own happiness.

None of which he was likely to tell his younger siblings.

"Ducal silence," Colin rolled his eyes. "And he's pulling the wiser older brother face again."

"Which means he's almost certainly got everything backwards," Charlie added archly.

Some people feared dukes.

Or so he'd been told.

"We're going ahead," Charlie tossed over her shoulder. "I mean to get an ice before you eat them all."

The sea had darkened just enough to send George and Meg scurrying for their footwear. Meg dried her calves with her dress and Dougal told himself it was wrong to watch. His body stirred, demanded. He shifted his gaze to the horizon, thought of krakens and pirates. Meg tied to a mast, laughing teasingly. In her wet chemise.

Damn it.

He was grateful for George's distraction, if not the topic he introduced, still out of breath from the shock of the cold, turbulent water. "How is a viscount's daughter skinnier than a chimney sweep?" he asked quietly as Meg picked her way towards them.

He'd noticed too. Of course, he had.

"I don't know, George," Dougal said. "But I mean to find out."

Chapter Fifteen

T HE VILLAGE OF Perchance-By-The-Sea was as picturesque as they came. It had winding cobbled streets, a handful of quaint shops selling sweets, ribbons, and other finery, and houses with white curtains and cheerful flowers in pots by the front door. It smelled of salt and was lulled by the sounds of the ocean.

It was also overrun with unmarried ladies of good birth.

In other words, a nightmare.

When Dougal shifted uncomfortably, Meg sent him a sympathetic smile over her strawberry ice. It was cold and sweet and delicious, and she could have immediately eaten two more. If there'd been any left. Some villages specialized in traveling book libraries, or fishing nets, or baked apples.

Perchance-By-The-Sea currently specialized in ladies eating ices.

Meg might have thought herself in London at Gunter's with the most fashionable set stopping for a treat. There were bonnets, there were ribbons and lace, smiles and sidelong glances. Fluttering eyelashes.

And virtually no ices left to be had.

And with garden tours no longer allowed, the ladies clustered around, turned in Dougal's direction as though he were the sun to their sunflowers.

"It's not usually like this," Dougal muttered, looking both bemused and embarrassed. Adorable. "This is a little town with seashell art and a single bathing machine to rent."

"And a single duke under royal decree to marry," she reminded him. As if he needed reminding. As if she did. The bright day dimmed a little. Which, again, was ridiculous. Nothing had changed. Even if the strawberry ice turned to dust in her mouth and she put the cup down, unfinished. *Get ahold of yourself, Meg.*

"I'm just going to pop in here for a moment," she said brightly, motioning to the dressmaker's shop.

"Are you abandoning me on the field of battle?" Dougal asked, as the ladies began to press closer.

"Bloody right," she shot back, but she wasn't really abandoning him. She just needed a moment to put herself to rights again. She didn't want him to see her reaction, her utterly absurd distress. She needed to be quiet, practical Meg again. Not whatever this version was, who wanted to gnash her teeth and throw ices at perfectly pleasant women. Who wanted to lick strawberry ice off of Dougal's lower lip.

Clearly the cold sea water had disordered her. No wonder people thought it was dangerous.

The bloody riddle wasn't helping either. But at least it was a suitable distraction.

Miss Chan's Haberdashery was cozy and neat and soothing. There were more seashells than the usual shops Meg had been in, but it had the same smell: dust, candle smoke, linen. She took a deep breath, calmed herself. Glass cases displayed pins and brooches and carved pearl buttons. Ribbons dangled from ceiling latticework and bolts of fabric lined the walls of the back room, with an abundance of painted silk. There were tiny paintings of ships and anchors and gulls, and yet more ships cradled cleverly inside of bottles. Seashells, and more seashells.

She wished again that Dahlia's riddle had involved something a little less ubiquitous in a seaside town.

"Good afternoon, Miss," the Chinese woman behind the counter smiled. She wore a dress made with the most marvelous pink plaid. Promising, that.

"Hello," Meg smiled. It was usually best to buy a little trinket before trying to convince someone to buy something from her, but she didn't have enough money on her to risk it, being so far from home. "You have a lovely shop."

"Thank you."

Meg waited until the other customers had wandered out of earshot before taking a pile of twenty or so handkerchiefs out of her reticule. She laid them out on the counter. "I wonder if you might consider these for your clientele?"

Miss Chan had a sharp eye, a knowing smile, and a very faint accent. "These are very well done." She nodded to the embroidery on Meg's pelisse. "Your work?"

"Yes," she said. "You won't find anything like it." It still felt strange to boast about her own work, but she had learned to do so, around the same time she had learned to scrub out a stove and use madder root to dye her own threads.

"It would appear not." Miss Chan touched a fat hedgehog, red birds, holly berries. "I am certain I can sell these. I could sell more if you have anything with seashells."

"I'm sorry, I'm afraid I don't." She should have thought of it. She wasn't sure she would have time to make any before she had to leave Thorncroft Abbey. Which would be soon. Sooner than she liked, and already later than was probably wise.

Meg felt a little better when the transaction was complete. Every penny helped. Her uncle, after all, could not be relied upon to see to the tenants' needs, especially when it came to leaky roofs and empty larders. Meg might not be able to grow enough blackberries to consistently feed a person, but she could embroider them well enough. They sold decently when she could find herself in a little village who did not know her or her godfather. Trade, after all, was not to be trifled with when you were a viscount's daughter.

Even if the thought of eating one more spoonful of mashed turnips was enough to make you scream.

And since her purse was finally a little full, she was perfectly justified in giving some back to Miss Chan in exchange for one of the travel pamphlets in a basket by the door. *Tours of Thorncroft Abbey, Historic and Scandalous Ducal Residence!* The drawing of the abbey was rough but earnest. Inside were snippets of history and details on how to apply to the housekeeper for a tour. Not entirely unusual. Except for the promise of scandal. Clever, that.

She darted outside to show Dougal, but stopped up short when a tall, statuesque lady smiled brightly at her. And Dougal.

"Lady St. Ives."

Lady St. Ives was a widow in her early thirties: stunning, clever, kind. She was known for taking in kittens.

Kittens for heaven's sake.

And she was at the top of the Prince's list of future wives for Dougal. For good reason. Not only did she have an obscenely large inheritance, but she wasn't fussy or cruel. She'd make a perfect duchess. And she had seen enough of life not to be frightened of Dougal's strong thighs and scarred hands.

Meg could see Dougal marrying her. Being happy with her.

Bollocks.

"Oh, Miss Swift," Lady St. Ives said, in her husky voice. Even her voice was delicious. Double bollocks. "How good to see you. Now we may be introduced, and no one will be shocked by my forward behavior." She winked at Dougal. Because widows could wink at strange men. And be shocking. Whereas spinsters like Meg, only a couple of years her junior, still had to lower their eyes meekly and follow the rules.

Triple bollocks to that.

"Your Grace, may I present Lady St. Ives."

Lady St. Ives curtsied. "Your Grace."

Dougal bowed, somewhat flummoxed, with a sidelong glance at Meg. He would recognize the name from his royal list. "A pleasure."

"Since I gather there is every chance I am being sold by the prince, or else you are, and to each other possibly, I thought I may as well take the bull by the horns as it were."

"Erm."

Lady St. Ives smiled at Dougal as though he were charming. Meg wanted to stab her a little less. She wouldn't let him marry a ninny or a bully. It mattered not a whit that she had no say in the matter. Facts were facts.

Lady St. Ives and Dougal continued to chat until the widow

tilted her head. "You are more handsome than I expected and have not tried to look down my gown once. We shall suit quite well." She curtsied. "It was lovely to meet you, Your Grace. And to see you again, Miss Swift. As always, your dress is both unique and fanciful in a way I could never pull off and I am quite jealous."

She sailed away, a liveried footman in tow. There was a beat of silence.

"I gather she is not the one who would be scared of me?" Dougal asked drily.

"No," Meg replied in an equally dry tone. "She would not." She wanted to be back in the ocean where she could dunk her head in cold water and get herself together.

"Your Grace," a man interrupted, stalking out of the alley between two shops. "I was hoping I'd run into you."

Dougal sighed. "No."

"I beg your pardon?"

"Just no."

He forced a laugh. "You think me one of the usual treasure hunters. I promise you I am not."

"Aren't you?"

"Not like the others," he assured him in a smooth voice. "If you'll let me search the estate, we could split the profits. Seventy five-twenty five."

"Let me guess, you'd get the seventy-five percent."

"Exactly. I would do all of the work. You wouldn't have to lift a finger!"

Meg nearly rolled her eyes. That was exactly the wrong tactic.

Dougal's expression was shuttered and hard. "And your name, sir?"

"Mr. Willows."

"Mr. Willows," Dougal's voice went sharp. Mr. Willows recoiled. "Ask the constable what I think of treasure hunters."

"Erm."

"And about the last treasure hunter's broken nose," Meg put in helpfully.

Mr. Willows swallowed. "I see."

"And if *I* see you anywhere near the abbey, I'll set the dogs on you. Good day."

They walked away, Meg fighting a laugh. "You don't have dogs."

"You were the one who assured me Chartreuse was a biter."

"Never mind that, I think it's Lady Beatrice's spear they should worry about."

He grinned." That too."

"But that man won't be back," Meg said. "He's not a real treasure hunter."

"No, I suspect not."

"He gave up too easily. No proper collector would let himself be scared off like that." She sounded disdainful; she couldn't help it.

"Noted. Now what's that you got there?"

She'd forgotten about the pamphlet. She handed it to Dougal. "I thought it might interest you."

He read the title, sighed, then read the author. His jaw ticked. And then his voice positively boomed. "Colin Black!"

SINCE THE OTHERS had already walked down to the carriage, they were not there when Meg came to an abrupt halt in the middle of the street. Dougal, still intent on cuffing his brother on the back of the head, did not notice until her hand, placed around his arm, nearly upended him like a teapot. "What is—."

"Dougal."

He looked down at her puzzled. "Meg."

"Look."

He followed her focused gaze. "Oh."

They stood in front of a seaside pub: The Rose and Anchor. The creaking wooden sign was painted with roses around a black anchor, as expected.

Seven red roses.

"We have to go inside!" Meg had already darted towards the whitewashed building, heedless of the disapproving glances of a few debutantes currently trailing behind them like brightlybonneted flotsam.

"Wait for me," Dougal insisted. The pub wasn't likely to be rowdy at this time of day, but nor was she likely to have been inside one before. Even the fanciest ones had sticky floors, drunken patrons, and the stink of smoke and stale ale.

She waited for him just inside, as her eyes adjusted to the dimness. She may as well have been at St. James Palace if the brightness of her smile had anything to say about it. Several men turned to appraise her frankly until Dougal shook his head once, pointedly. He was just behind her and she did not see him. He wasn't an idiot.

The pub was a single long room with dark rafters, a fireplace in one corner, and windows opened to the constant chatter of the sea. There were simple roses painted on the pitchers, on the wall around the fireplace, and over one of the stools. Ropes of dried roses were tucked here and there. Meg's face shone.

The floor was, as expected, sticky as they crossed the room. Meg counted roses under her breath but no matter where she started, seven roses later, she was nowhere more helpful. There were no benches with secret compartments, no hidden niches in the wall. She sighed.

The owner joined them, wiping his hands on his work apron. His smile was genuine but quizzical. "Can I help ye?"

"Oh," Meg smiled back. "I was only admiring the decorations."

"Me wife painted those," he said proudly. "Can I get ye something to drink? I wouldn't recommend the wine for such as ye, but we brew a fine ale. Sometimes, we put rose petals in it, where there's a special occasion."

Curious, Meg followed him to the counter. Dougal slid coins across the polished surface in exchange for two glasses. Meg sipped the potent ale as if she drank it every day. Dougal was impressed despite already being impressed with pretty much everything she did.

"The Rose and Anchor is such a lovely name," Meg said. "Is there a story behind it?"

The bartender preened, just a little, under her attention.

Dougal sympathized. There was something intoxicating about those dark eyes, that curious interest. "Me wife's name is Rose," the bartender explained. "When I bought the place ten years ago I knew she'd crown me if I didn't name it after her."

"Ah." Meg's enthusiasm dimmed though Dougal fancied only he would have noticed. "That's very romantic."

He looked very close to blushing.

"Get a lot of toffs in here lately?" Dougal asked.

He snorted. "Aye."

"Treasure hunters?"

"Seems so."

Dougal leaned closer, grinning. There were more coins in his hand. "I'd be obliged if you'd send word to the abbey if any of them seem particularly unruly."

"Aye. The abbey, is it?"

"This is the duke," Meg offered distractedly.

"'Gor, a duke drinking me own ale," the man returned. "That's a story to tell."

"Tell them I enjoyed it very much," Dougal suggested. "And then charge them double."

"Aye, you come back to the Rose and Anchor any time," he said. "Me wife makes the best fish pie in all of England."

"I will," Dougal promised.

"Lads," they heard him bellow as they stepped back out onto the street. "If you see a treasure hunter, thump 'em!"

"I was sure I was onto something," Meg grumbled. He hated to see her frustrated—even when it made her nose crinkle in that charming way. "Where else are we likely to find seven roses?"

"We could have a look around the greenhouse," Dougal suggested. "It's a right jungle in there."

"Good idea."

She glanced at the harbor, dozens of fishing boats bobbing on the waves. A ship sliced through the water, further out. She sighed. "Too many boats and too many seashells."

"Damn the riddle," Dougal said.

She smiled at him warmly, quoting his own words back at him. "And damn Henry the Eighth."

THE GREENHOUSE WAS full of roses.

They reached to the glass ceiling, thorny arms scraping against the glass, against each other, against the other flowers foolish enough to try and fight for space. They came in all colors: red, seashell pink, yellow as Lady Marigold's dresses, a dark so deep it was nearly purple and white as the sky in winter. The perfume wafted in the humid air, kept warm with charcoal braziers and stoves beneath the floor, the smoke piped through the walls.

Meg gaped at the profusion, a veritable forest of roses. "So much for that idea."

Dougal brushed leaves off his shoulder. "I feel as though we've just walked into a perfume bottle."

Meg sighed. "Perhaps there are seven varieties of roses?" Her shoulders sagged. "But what is the likelihood they would have not only survived but in the same spots as nearly fifty years ago?"

They meandered down the walkway, patterned with stones underfoot like a mosaic. The sun had set, and the windows were shuttered, and the lamps had been lit.

"There are too many options," Meg added. "Too many boats in the harbor, too many seashells, too many roses." She pinched the bridge of her nose. "I'm going to let Pendleton down. And you."

Dougal stopped abruptly. "You could never let me down."

"You say that now. Wait until the abbey is crawling with treasure hunters."

He shrugged. "It would be worth it to have you here." He said it easily, simply. As if he wasn't devastating her. She swallowed. She wasn't sure if he was disappointed when she didn't reply. What could she say? There was nothing and everything to say. While she was damning riddles and King Henry the Eighth, she would damn dowries and greedy uncles. "If there are too many options," Dougal continued, "then we'll have to narrow them down and pick a starting point. It doesn't even have to be the right one."

She let the knotted muscles of her neck relax. He was right. She was spinning in circles because she was afraid to do the wrong thing, to take the wrong path. But you had to start somewhere. Retracing your steps, starting again, changing your mind when new information came to light; these were all good things.

She wouldn't let a riddle defeat her.

"You're right," she told him. "Of course, you're right."

"Might you remind my siblings that such a thing is possible?"

"I'll be sure to mention it." She chuckled, the last of her frustration fading away. Begin, begin again.

"I've never been inside the hothouse," Dougal admitted. "If nothing else, I'm glad for that."

"It's lovely." Meg said as they passed giant urns filled with ferns and planters of gardenias and night-blooming jasmine. The hothouse itself was larger than some of the mansions in Mayfair. "The Earl of Dunmore has a roof carved from stone in the shape of a two-story high pineapple."

"But does he have approximately ten thousand stars painted on every ceiling of his house?"

She smiled back. "No, I don't think he has." She paused, steps faltering. "Nor does he have *that*."

That referred to what she could only assume was some Ancient roman orgy. She'd never seen that many naked bodies intertwined, and she'd been sketching nude statues for weeks now. Marble buttocks were dimpled, held in strong hands, a hard nipple rested on a tongue, mouths touched the backs of knees, thighs, and considerably more intimate places.

She felt oddly flushed to see it. Not necessarily embarrassed, though she couldn't meet Dougal's eyes right way, but curious. Aware. Heat throbbed between her legs, not because of the sculpture, but more because she could imagine him doing all of those things to her. And more. She wanted it. *Craved* it.

Dougal cleared his throat. "That's…something."

Meg had to swallow before she could be sure her voice would be even. "Art."

"Yes. Art."

They skirted it, casting about for something else to look at, to talk about. Meg felt it burning behind her, all hands and teeth and smooth skin. Open mouths.

This is what came of wandering around without a chaperone.

Not that she thought for even one moment that Lady Blackwell wouldn't have found a way to make this more undignified.

"The Prince Regent had a hothouse built for his ceremony that has a stream and several miniature bridges," she blurted out. She never blurted things out. "He filled it with goldfish."

Dougal glanced at her, looked away. She realized there was a marble inner thigh behind her head. "Did he? Have you seen it?"

"No, but Priya talks about it all of the time, even five years later. She's convinced his orchids aren't being properly treated." There was a row of orchids placed on stones just ahead of them, all pinks and lavenders and cream. "Don't let Priya know you have a hothouse," she warned. "She'll take over. It won't matter that it's not hers and that you're a duke. She is a fiend when it comes to flowers."

"Duly warned."

"I want to paint her as Flora, the Roman Goddess of Nature. Flora is nowhere fierce enough, but it will have to do," she babbled. She'd decided she'd paint Dougal as a knight the first time she'd met him and that hadn't changed. But he would be a knight who knew how to take care of his own horse, no pageboy required. There'd be leaves in his hair. Roses all around him. "Persephone would be a priestess of Isis and Tamsin… maybe a spirit of some kind? Or Anne Boleyn haunting Hever Castle, her head under her arm?"

"And you?" he asked quietly. "Who will you paint yourself as?"

It seemed too obvious to say Cinderella.

And he would ask questions. Clever ones.

She still offered him a truth, but a different version of it.

"I don't know. It's hard to see yourself sometimes, isn't it?"

They had stopped walking. They were alone with the lamplight and the roses and the naked writhing bodies.

"Do you know what I see?" Dougal asked, turning so that he faced her. She recalled the feeling of his mouth claiming hers and tried not to lean forward, then wondered why she was fighting the connection. A kiss could be just a kiss.

"I see a woman who is clever and caring and so beautiful it makes my bones feel like they are on fire." She swayed closer. How could she not? She wasn't made of stone. She was flesh and blood and want. "I can still taste you on my lips," he continued ruthlessly. "Tea leaves and sugar. I want to taste all of you."

Her lips parted on a shaky breath and his mouth descended on hers or she reached up to him or both. It was enough that finally that space between them burned away. She molded her palms to the hard planes of his back. When her breasts grazed his chest, her nipples tightened, pulling an instant response from her quim. Need pulsed inside her, especially when he used his teeth to tug at the neckline of her gown. He traced the top of her stays with the tip of his tongue, dipping down to swipe against her sensitive nipples. She squirmed closer, the bulge in his breeches pressing in the hollow of her hip.

She was backed against the cold, hard marble sculpture but it may as well have been made of fire. Strangers frozen as they found their pleasure, hands grasping just above her, legs parting behind her, tongues seeking. It made her feel everything Dougal was doing to her, everything they were doing to each other, so much more keenly.

His manhood touched the soft place between her thighs and even through layers of cloth, she felt it intimately. When she moaned and tried to squirm closer, he reached down and lifted the hem of her skirts. He paused, waiting for her to refuse him. She palmed him in response and would have undone the placard of his trousers to finally feel him in her hand if she'd been able to form a coherent thought.

She wasn't.

He skated his fingertips through her triangle of hair, gently, teasingly. She trembled when he reached her bud, circling, stroking, slipping one finger inside her, then two. Sensations shot through her, as he pushed deeper, changed the angle and whispered desperate and filthy words in her ear. She'd never felt like this, tightening around him even as her thighs loosened and opened. She wanted more even as she raised on her toes, not sure if she could handle it. A beautiful kind of pressure built in her core, dragging her along.

"That's it," he murmured. "Come for me, Meg."

His thumb worked her bud, the rhythm of his fingers never changing until she gasped, little sounds of pleasure that built into a silent tremble that overtook her completely. When she caught her breath and opened her eyes, he let her gown drop. She was dressed like a viscount's daughter again, demure, elegant.

She felt anything but.

She reached for him. "I want to touch *you* now."

A noise at one of the windows startled them. A branch, a bird. Or someone from the house, out for a walk. They weren't as private and secluded as they felt. Reality was a cold bite that she thoroughly resented.

Dougal shook his head regretfully, before kissing her once more. "We should go."

Chapter Sixteen

M EG MIGHT NOT obsess over Ancient Rome like her godfather, or Ancient Egypt and ghost stories like her friends, but she had to admit that the abbey was growing on her.

Dougal, of course. But the house too. That last part was a surprise.

And probably a good thing too. Anything to distract her from the memory of his fingers and his mouth. Not that she *wanted* to be distracted exactly. But she couldn't moon about feeling tingly all the day long either.

Well, she *could*. She discovered she was perfectly capable of it. That was the problem.

The faded mural of St. George and the Dragon which she had found over a walled-in window might have been a replica of an earlier medieval stained glass. She longed to brighten the colors, to make it shine again. There were figurines carved into the posts in the main chapel area, now the front hall: ladies with long braids, men praying, a Green Man with a mouth full of oak leaves. She was charmed with every dusty, secret corner.

Except for perhaps "Neptune's Parlor." Charming wasn't quite the right word.

She poked her head in, hearing the sound of voices. The older ladies sat with Charlie, a fully stocked tea cart nearby. Behind them, stampeding from every corner, were fierce white horses, their huge painted teeth bared. White seafoam flung from their manes and the sea boiled with all the colors of a bruise under their hooves. The background was black clouds and silver glints of light. Stars were hard pinpricks of silver above. More stars, of course. But mostly, teeth.

"Gah." Meg couldn't help a small start.

Charming definitely wasn't the right word.

It was dramatic, overdone, mildly violent. Bordering on awful.

She loved it.

"We're having tea," Lady Marigold said, sweetly, as if she wasn't in very great danger of being trampled by angry mythical horses.

"Speak for yourself. Ahoy!" Lady Blackwell waved her empty teacup at the footman, who already knew the lay of the land and rushed to fill the cup with whisky.

Charlie met Meg's eyes and mouthed "Ahoy?"

Meg grinned. Charlie grinned back, caught herself, and shuttered her expression.

"Do join us," Lady Marigold said. "You must be tired. I see you all day, drawing away. My hand would cramp."

"Sometimes it does," Meg admitted. She took a seat because she had never refused tea in her life, and she wasn't about to start now. She looked around. "Was your brother an art aficionado, Lady Marigold?"

Lady Blackwell followed her gaze. "Clearly not."

"It's… unique."

"It's hideous," Lady Marigold said, cheerfully. "But my father was so proud of the art in this house, and my brother after him. Father told us stories about the horses of the sea. That's why we named this parlor for Neptune." She lowered her voice. "We used to doodle on the murals when we were younger. My brother went through a phase where he would eat nothing but strawberries and he painted them everywhere. If you look in that horse in the corner there, you'll see strawberries in his teeth. Father was furious."

Although Meg could understand that as an artist, she still found the sketches charming.

"Did your sister Dahlia also sketch on the walls?" she asked casually.

"I think so," Lady Marigold replied. "But she was a bit older than I was, and I was away at school the last time she visited. She didn't stay long."

"Bah," Lady Beatrice said. "Why would she? You were the only one who could stomach your father's temper." She scowled. "He tore a hole through my favorite embroidery hoop once."

"I'm sure he didn't mean it."

"He absolutely did mean it. But you're sweet, my dear. You always have been."

It might not be much to go on but at least it was becoming clearer as to why Lady Dahlia might have gone to the trouble of finding a treasure only to hide it away again.

"Was he as keen on the Tudor treasure as they say?" Meg prodded gently.

"I'm afraid so," Lady Marigold said. "It broke his heart that he didn't find it, even though he did find several packets of old letters and a chest of gold candlesticks."

"And Dahlia?"

"She was always poking around the house, helping to get my brother in trouble. He had his strawberries, she preferred hedgehogs and seashells."

Seashells.

"She painted seashells."

Lady Marigold nodded. "The angrier my father got, the more she painted them. She also liked to find clams on the beach and sneak them into his bed."

Interesting. Beside her, Charlie also perked up.

Dougal appeared in the doorway before she could figure out what to do with this new information. "Do I smell blackberry tarts?"

Charlie rolled her eyes. "How do you always know?"

"Because if I'm to get any after you and Colin demolish them, I have to be quick." He flared his nostrils comically. "I've had to hone my senses. Needs must."

"Donkeys have a keen sense of smell too, I've been told."

"Are you calling me a donkey?" Dougal asked, plopping down beside her. "Again?"

She laughed. "Who, me?"

He nicked a tart from her plate. She pinched him in retaliation. He ate two more tartlets. Lady Blackwell watched him for a moment, smiling and looking like someone's flighty grandmother.

Meg was instantly suspicious.

"What a lovely pianoforte," Lady Blackwell said, drawing attention to the instrument in the corner, the piano cushions dusted but faded. "Do you still play?" she asked Lady Beatrice.

Deeply, *deeply* suspicious.

"Every single day," Lady Marigold replied for her, beaming. "She is truly talented."

Lady Beatrice, who did not seem the type to blush, blushed to her hairline. They exchanged a fond, loving look. It was intimate and private and quick as a lightning beetle.

"Play for us, won't you?" Lady Blackwell asked. "Perhaps some handsome gentleman will ask me to dance."

As the only gentleman currently in the area, Dougal paused, another blackberry tartlet halfway to his mouth. "It would be my honor, Lady Blackwell, but I'm afraid I don't know how to waltz."

"What a pity," she said. "Every gentleman should know how to dance."

Meg narrowed her eyes.

"Meg will teach you."

Dotty old grandmother indeed.

"Oh, how lovely," Lady Marigold agreed. "Do play for us, my dear." She squeezed Lady Beatrice's hand. "How exciting! I've never seen a waltz. Is it as scandalous as they say?"

"Almack's in London requires permission be granted to a lady from one of the patronesses," Lady Blackwell whispered.

"Goodness!"

Meg met Dougal's gaze and it was patient, amused. Knowing. She wondered if she should be embarrassed and then decided she would rather enjoy the moment as a joke between them.

Would rather be in his arms again, truth be told.

"Subtle as Zeus's lightning bolt," Meg muttered as Dougal offered his hand and led her to the parquet floor near the windows. "You don't have to do this."

"I want to," he said softly. His expression turned wry. "And I am not equipped to take on the wrath of three old women."

"Smart."

"Is it very complicated?" Dougal flashed her a grin. "I'll try not to step on your feet."

"We start side by side," Meg said as Lady Beatrice seated herself with a dramatic flourish.

She played a few notes before barking "This pianoforte is not as good as the one in our chambers."

"Never mind, dear. I know you're more than up to the task."

"Well, of course, I am!"

Dougal bit back a chuckle. Meg tried not to look at him, fighting her own laughter. "This is serious."

"Deadly."

"Take my hand in yours."

"Gladly."

"Flirt."

"I thought that was part of the lesson," he said, innocently.

"Hmm." She moved her left hand so that it was behind her back and his arm reached behind her.

"Now what?"

"We promenade for four steps." Once they had done that, she added. "Now we turn to face each other. And the steps will be in three quarter time with the accent on the first beat. *One*, two, three. *One*, two, three." She cleared her throat. Her body remembered exactly what he could do with those hands. "Right hand at each other's waist."

Their eyes met again. They were so close that she could see the ring of lighter blue around his irises, the grain of his beard where it had been shaved close to his jaw. This was why the waltz was so dangerous. It was a private moment, a public and yet clandestine pause where anything might be whispered. And frequently was.

"I could get used to this," Dougal said, softly.

She had to swallow before continuing. He was filling up the space, she could see only him, smell the soap-and-cedar scent of him, even his voice, soft as it was, overcame the music.

"Now step back with your left foot, and then our left hands touch," she added. "Above our heads," She had been sketching and she was not wearing her gloves. His fingers were warm around hers. "And now we turn."

They turned until she was a kaleidoscope of secret feelings, wants and desires, heat and need. She'd never felt drawn to anyone the way she felt drawn to him. She wanted so much to steal the Prince's blasted letter from him and add her name to the list. To cross out all of the others. To stay here with him.

She stumbled to a halt, forced a smile.

"And that is waltzing."

She dropped into a curtsy. He bowed, silent. There was too much to say. Not enough words. Not enough of the *right* words, at any rate.

"I should go," she added, her voice feeling strange in her mouth. "I have more statues to draw. A treasure still to find."

"Of course. Any luck?"

"None at all. Well, that's not true. Lady Marigold made a comment about Dahlia's fascination with seashells."

"And George is looking through the family bibles and journals for anything to do with Lady Dahlia."

"That should help."

He watched her walk away. There was a small, irritated sigh at his shoulder. "Dear boy, what are you waiting for?" Lady Blackwell said.

"Pardon?"

She tapped him with her bejeweled and feathered fan. "You're a fool if you don't marry her."

As if he didn't already know that.

Meg and Charlie were in the front hall when Dougal found them. He was glad for his sister's presence, as he was quite mad with the need to touch Meg again. He might have tugged her into an abandoned room, even the hideous gold drawing room. She was everywhere, the thought of her, her scent, the soft sounds she'd had made when she came among the roses.

On second thought, he wasn't at all relieved to find his sister in his way. Surely, she had something else to do.

"We are working with a new clue," Charlie said. "Lady Dahlia painted seashells."

Meg glanced at him, registered the hunger in his eyes and licked her lips.

He was absolutely going to go mad if he didn't get to do the same. She raised an eyebrow, half-smiling. "Devil," he whispered. Her smile grew. God, this woman.

"I'm taking your advice," she said as if they were proper as two governesses in a vicarage. "I have to start somewhere and it got me to thinking that since Dahlia must have wanted her father to find the treasure, or at least look for it, why not start here, where she left her first clue?"

"Seven seashells for your boat," he quoted.

"Exactly." They had all of the windows open and candles burning in every candelabra even though it was the middle of the day. The medieval hunt marched across one wall, and a seascape frothed and boiled on the other. "I don't know what the boat part means yet, but one thing at a time."

Meg and Charlie each held up a candle, examining the fireplace thoroughly and the walls around it. "Four strawberries," Charlie said.

"Two hedgehogs," Meg added. She paused, turning triumphant. "And one seashell."

"Where?" Charlie pounced. He hadn't seen her this animated since they'd left Manchester. Something unclenched inside of him.

"In that hedgehog's mouth," Meg pointed.

"Oh, brilliant." They shared a small bounce of anticipation.

Dougal joined the hunt, trying to peer through decades of soot darkening the paint. "Here," he said. "Second seashell."

"And I have the third!" Charlie exclaimed. "There, on that fellow's tunic."

"That's a terrible seashell," Dougal shook his head, amused. "Looks more like a fish head."

George joined them by the fourth seashell. Colin was in Perchance-By-The-Sea, flirting with the girls, as usual. By the fifth seashell, Chartreuse had also joined the game, even though he had no idea what it was, only that he enjoyed racing up and down the hall with company this time.

The sixth seashell was in the top corner, tucked under the edge of a frieze and took over half an hour to find. Dougal had to stand on a bench. A beeswax candle dripped wax in his hair. Charlie wouldn't let him down until he'd found something.

The seventh seashell was low to the ground, hidden in a tangle of painted leaves. They might have missed it if Chartreuse hadn't stopped to lick a drop of beeswax right in front of it.

The seashells had led them to a part of the hallway that opened up to three different rooms, a drawing room, the dining room and the ballroom, each more cavernous than the last. The ceiling was a maze of carvings and moldings and stars. No fewer than three ships hung in frames on the wall. Dougal had no idea how old they might be.

None of them had roses. Not the paintings, nor their frames, nor the murals.

Charlie crossed her arms, annoyed. "Are we looking for boats or roses or stars now? Or coats?"

"We'll find it," he assured her. "Whatever it is."

"I don't think I like riddles."

Meg snorted in sympathy. "Me neither."

"It's roses, but not the kind of coat you wear," George said softly.

"What other kind is there?" Charlie demanded.

"A coat of arms," he replied, lifting his chin towards the top of the door leading into the dining room. "I should have realized sooner."

The coat-of-arms was painted above the lintel, faded but still clear enough: A rampant lion, a unicorn and a circle of seven roses.

"George, you are definitely a historian," Meg said. "And

completely brilliant."

They nearly got stuck in the doorway in their haste to stampede inside.

The dining room, predictably, was so much larger than Dougal remembered. The table where they had welcomed the wayward duck seated thirty-six. There was a shipwreck on one wall and no fewer than nine rowboats scattered among pastoral ponds.

And the stars.

"Seven stars for your wrath," Meg murmured.

The only place with more stars, and more murals, was the ballroom.

Even the floorboards were painted with stars.

Dougal ran a hand through his hair.

"This is going to take a while."

Chapter Seventeen

THEY COUNTED THE stars in the dining room and reached three thousand seven hundred and two. That was too many possible patterns of seven, none of which immediately jumped out at them. Everyone spent most of the dinner with their necks craned at the ceiling or bent over staring at the floor. Chartreuse was concerned as there was no food on the floor. The footmen were confused because the family appeared to be mad. The wine was tasted, the potatoes examined, the trifle checked and checked again.

In the morning, Meg decided she needed fresh air to clear her head. And stretch her aching neck muscles. She was surprised when Charlie accepted her invitation to go for a walk. She knew the girl did not entirely trust her. She was protective of her brother and Meg fully supported that. She also felt rather protective of Charlie when Mrs. Hill clucked her tongue disapprovingly. It was a sound far too often heard in the house.

That was likely why when Meg interrupted the latest lecture, bonnet in hand, Charlie rushed to join her. "You'll need a footman," Mrs. Hill intoned. There was no other word for it.

"I hardly think that's necessary," Meg said when Charlie sighed, already looking as though she was regretting her impulsive decision to join Meg. "We aren't traipsing about London, after all."

Mrs. Hill did not look mollified. "But…"

"Pshaw," Lady Blackwell said from the hallway. Chartreuse was nestled in her arms, the diamonds flashing off his collar. It was an unfortunate puce color, to match lady Blackwell's wig. The effect was... alarming. So was Lady Blackwell's smile, perfectly suited to the daughter of a duke, even if that duke had died decades ago. "Miss Swift is a country girl. She's perfectly able to navigate around a few cows." She nodded imperiously. "Do carry on, my dear."

Meg grinned as Mrs. Hill spluttered. "Would you care to join us?"

"Certainly not. I have no desire to track the inevitable result of a cow on my new slippers."

Meg bobbed a friendly curtsy.

"Don't forget your ribbons," Lady Blackwell added. "One can't be too careful."

"Ribbons?" Charlie inquired as they finally made it out the front door.

"Yes," Meg replied, securing her bonnet with a long hat pin. "Very useful things."

"Penknives are useful," Charlie muttered.

"They are," Meg agreed. "One need not cancel the other out. They can both be useful."

"I suppose."

Charlie was disgruntled but Meg was beginning to understand the Blacks a little better, having spent so many days under the same roof. The more bored Colin looked, the more annoyed Charlie looked, the more calm Dougal looked—the more uncertain they felt. They expected to be mocked or stared at like the elephant at the Royal Menagerie at the Tower of London.

Meg kept her own expression impassive which she realized was what she did when *she* felt insecure. She didn't want to say the wrong thing. Charlie was like a baby bird flung out of the nest into an ocean instead of the expected field. She could easily drown here.

Or she could become the most interesting bird anyone had ever seen.

"Would you rather ride?" Meg asked as they passed the stables. The smell of hay was strong, the sounds of happy horses heartening. Her uncle wasn't keen on letting her anywhere near his prized horses. She was not very steady in a saddle, but she'd make do.

Charlie wrinkled her nose. "No, thank you." She paused. "I'm still learning."

"I'm not very good," Meg admitted.

Colin cantered past them on a playful mare, urging her into a gallop. The wind picked up his hooting and tossed the happy sound around. Charlie smiled. "Colin, on the other hand," she said, "has quite taken to riding."

"I can see that. What about Dougal?"

Charlie sent her a sideling glance. "He's absolute rubbish."

Meg grinned. "Is he?"

"He practices but he's like a wooden doll. The stablemaster always has to have a fortifying nip of ale after a lesson." She stopped. "Don't tell him I said so."

Meg shook her head. "I won't."

They walked in companiable silence until the grassy hill changed to harvested fields. "Is this where the tenant farmers live?" Meg asked, nodding down a well-walked track. Smoke lingered in the distance. A baby cried. The smells of dirt and hay were familiar.

Charlie nodded. "I think so."

"You haven't visited?" Meg was surprised.

"We didn't want to be a bother," Charlie said. "I'd have wanted to wallop a toff who came into the mill to gawk at us at our work."

"You must have a very good steward then."

"Mr. Clarke certainly thinks he is. He told us everything was in hand."

"I see. Let's say hello then."

Charlie followed, looking uncomfortable.

"Has Dougal been?"

"I don't know. He spends most days reading letters and muttering about devil's arsewits."

Meg chuckled. "I've noticed that. Being a duke with as many

estates as your brother owns is daunting, even for someone trained to it since birth. It's villages and tenants and crops and field drainage and flour mills. Deer parks. Cattle."

"Is that what Dougal does all day in that study? No wonder he looks as though he wants to poke his own eye out with a pencil."

"Running an estate is hard work—if you do it properly," Meg amended, thinking of several estates who were most definitely not run properly. She was grateful that her uncle's land agent, Mr. Campbell, was usually happy to help her navigate around his more outrageous demands.

"He won't let us help," Charlie said, disgruntled.

"I imagine he wants you to enjoy yourself."

"Oh yes, embroidery and walking with parasols," she replied drily. "I am complete." She frowned. "You don't do this sort of thing *all* day, do you? Draw and change your gown and write letters?"

"Sometimes," Meg said gently, though it was mostly a lie. She rarely had idyllic days such as the ones she'd known at Thorncroft Abbey, wandering ducks and wall-scaling debutantes, and treasure hunters included. But plenty of people did. "There are some who enjoy leisure," she added. She could see how it might be more complicated for Charlie. "You used to work the weaving machines, but now you could weave by hand, if you wanted. You have the time. It would be a kind of art that produced something warm and practical at the end of it."

Charlie looked intrigued. "I'm not a Luddite but I suppose I could."

"Or you could help your brother, despite what he might say," she added with a wink. "You don't strike me as the kind of girl to take orders."

Charlie positively beamed a smile. "*Thank you.*" Her smile faltered. "I never used to be."

"Is that what you're worried about? Changing?"

She nodded. Meg nodded as well. "It's perfectly fine to change, if you want to. And it's just as fine to decide that there are parts of yourself you won't change, for anyone."

"You make it sound easy."

Meg snorted. "Nothing's easy."

Bees buzzed happily as they continued to walk, darting in and out of the last of the autumn flowers. Meg noticed a hive, set just at the edge of the trees. They must be very near to the village now. "There's an orchard at the Abbey, you could see at the cider-press if they need help. Or talk to the Head Gardener, if you like gardening," she suggested.

"I think there's already an army of gardeners."

"Very likely."

"But maybe we could expand the kitchen gardens into medicines. Mints and comfrey and the like." She pointed to the embroidery on Meg's sleeves, all bright petals and leaves. "You like flowers."

Meg smiled, waiting. Charlie frowned, looking closer. "Miss Swift."

"Yes?"

"All of those flowers are poisonous."

Meg inclined her head. "I call it my poison dress." Priya had helped her with accuracy.

Charlie smiled again, that true bright smile. "My brother did tell me to look closer."

Before Meg could ask her to elaborate on that mysterious statement, one of the farmers approached them. "Good day, ladies." He took off his cap. His hair went every which way, wild with curls. "Are ye lost?"

"Good day," Meg replied. "We've come from the abbey. This is the duke's sister, Lady Charlo—Lady Charlie," Meg introduced her.

"She's a viscount's daughter," Charlie blurted out, pointing at Meg. "Miss Swift."

Meg bit back a smile. The farmer was surprised, as were the other villagers, drawing closer. Meg was instantly more at home with mud underfoot, the smell of leaf fires, the shouts of men nearby wrestling with heavy work. A dog trotted past.

"Welcome, your ladyship." The man bowed. There was a flurry of curtsies and curious glances behind him. "I'm Angus

Blue."

"A pleasure to make your acquaintance, Mr. Blue. Are those your beehives we saw down the lane?"

"Me wife's," he said proudly. "Best in the shire."

"Does she sell her honey in the town?"

"That she does."

"I'll be sure to stop and buy some before I leave for home. My godfather has a sweet tooth." He had no such thing, but no one needed to know that.

"A kindness that is, Miss."

"Does Mr. Clarke know you're here?" A woman asked sharply. Her gray hair was wrapped in a braid like a crown, just as Meg wore hers. Her gray shawl was expertly made but mended. Her eyes, the same gray, were sharp as thistles.

"Never mind, Agrimony," Angus said, widening his eyes in warning at the old lady. She did not look particularly warned.

In fact, she waved him off like he was one of his wife's bees. "Bah. Off with you, Angus."

As he wandered away muttering, the children crept closer, all wide eyes and expectant grins. Meg had a feeling that Agrimony's temper was part of the daily entertainment. She'd know all there was to know, though. And Meg had a few questions to ask. Charlie remained quiet and uncomfortable, trying not to be noticed or to take up too much space.

Meg, always one to have sweets in her pockets, pulled out a handful of lemon candies. "Oh dear, I seem to have too many lemon drops. It would be a shame if they should go to waste." Two of the braver children barreled closer. "Might you help me?"

Meg nearly lost two fingers and a toe in the ensuing rush. As the children occupied themselves with sugary sweets, Meg looked at Agrimony. "Clever, you are," the old lady allowed.

"May I ask you something?"

"I expect so. Seeing as my grandson has a gob full of candy." She eyed Charlie. "First, I've a question."

"Yes?"

"What's with this one? She looks peaky."

Charlie did look peaky. Also not terribly thrilled to be singled out. "I'm used to working in the mill," Charlie finally said. There was a twinkle in her eye. "I'm not used to all this fresh air."

Agrimony narrowed one eye. There was a pause where even the birds seemed to hold their breath. Then she barked out a laugh. "That's all right, then. Bit of sun will sort you out."

"Yes, ma'am."

"Ma'am!" Agrimony howled. "Like that, I do."

"Why should the steward need to know we are here?" Meg asked since it seemed Agrimony was as amenable to conversation as she would get.

She spat in the weeds but there was a twinkle to her. "Caught that, did ye?" She scowled. "Thinks we complain, he does. But before the old duke got sick, when my grandson there was still just a baby, we lived in good sturdy houses. The fields drained properly."

"And now?"

She shrugged bad-temperedly. "Walls crack, windows won't shut anymore because of the damp. And roofs leak, don't they? But no one fixes them anymore." She pointed across the path to a small cottage with a garden full of fading marigolds. A very, very pregnant woman leaned against the wattle fence, thick with raspberry cane. "Her man died recently and with the harvest, no one's had the time to climb up and fix her roof. Clark don't care and Mary's too pregnant to do it herself. None of the littl'uns can reach the spot."

Meg stood up, carefully tracking the line of the roof. "I could do it."

Agrimony blinked. Charlie blinked. There was a lot of blinking.

It was not particularly encouraging.

"I might not be able to fix a window casement, but I can plug a thatched roof. I've done it before." She knew something about roofs, having a disaster of one for herself.

More blinking.

"Honestly. I just a need a ladder." She turned to Charlie as Agrimony hollered for a ladder. "And your hat pin."

"My… hat pin?"

"Yes, please." She removed hers and twisted her skirts, pinning them together between her knees. The second pin helped secure it into something resembling a loose trouser of a sort. Certainly good enough to pop up a ladder. She adjusted Charlie's pin. "These are good for stabbing too."

"That's surprising."

"You didn't know?"

"Of course, *I* knew that. I have two brothers and a George. But it's surprising to find that *you* knew that." She tilted her head. "*You* are surprising, Miss Swift."

"Realistic," Meg corrected with a small shrug. "After all, some people are vexing."

"Enough to be stabbed?"

"Most definitely."

"I admit I didn't realize ladies were allowed to be realistic."

"We are not encouraged to be which is all the more reason why we *must* be so. The world would eat us whole."

Agrimony's sister's husband's cousin arrived with a ladder and a plug of straw. Meg scampered up the rungs and onto the roof in question. She stayed along the timbers, knowing full well that thatched roofs did not always consent to hold the weight of a full-grown adult. This was not her first rooftop adventure.

The thatch was thickly laid, many families having added to it over several decades. There was some moss but not enough for concern. There didn't appear to be any serious damage, just the usual wear and tear. But it would only get worse. Meg wriggled into position, stretching out on the steep angle, the straw poking through her dress. "Where's the hole?" She called down.

"It leaks just to your left there, near the ridge."

The furthest point from any kind of safe perch, of course.

And with the nature of water, the hole could be anywhere really, but one problem at a time. She squirmed, inching forward until there was ominous creaking below her. She let out a breath. "All right up there?" Charlie asked.

"Right as rain," Meg returned, sounding far more confident than she should. She felt around the thatch, through the thick straw, around bumps and worn spots. "Found it! The birds have been at it. Shouldn't take a moment to fix."

The hole wasn't very big, fortunately, but it also wasn't particularly easy to reach. They never were. She stretched as far as she could, until her shoulder protested. It would be too easy to lose the plug of straw at this point, and watch it roll down the steep roof and have to start again. She held tight, knuckles aching as she maneuvered. A spider crawled past her nose. "If you come any closer, I will bite you."

Wisely, the spider took a sharp detour.

Meg shoved the plug into the offending gap and pushed down. The straw scraped at her hands, prickling and biting. It was hardly professional work, but she was confident that it would at least slow the progress of water. Until she had herself a little chat with Mr. Clarke. Well, Dougal would talk to him.

She had to remind herself that she was leaving, and she had no say here.

It stung. Nothing to be done for it. She inched back down to a more secure perch on the ladder and took a moment to admire the picturesque sweep of hills and fields and sun on harvest grasses. And Dougal. He rode towards them, his horse prancing energetically. The sun glinted off the red buried deep in Dougal's hair. He was so handsome, so *himself,* even at this distance.

But Charlie was right. He was a terrible rider. She wasn't sure why that should be so endearing, but it was. She supposed she had been subjected to too many lectures from various earls and viscount's second sons on the proficiency of their riding ability, stables, and horses, in that order. She always cared more about the state of the fields they rode through, and the damage done by hooves and what kind of manure was used. None of which she could say out loud.

Although she wouldn't hesitate to say it to Dougal.

Perhaps not at this precise moment, however.

Not only was she halfway up a house, but he was currently halfway off a horse.

"Dougal!"

Meg had not known before that moment that she could shriek in quite that pitch or throw herself down a ladder quite so quickly.

She ran down the path, Charlie at her heels. The horse shook his head as though he was confused, then lowered his head to nibble on the grass next to the heap that was Dougal. Fear lit a fuse along her spine. Had he cracked his head open on a rock? Broken both his legs? His back?

He groaned. Her breath hitched.

And then he cursed to make any storybook pirate proud. Or scandalized.

Really, she'd never heard such words, or in such an order.

It was poetry. Pure poetry.

Charlie stopped running, hand to her chest. "Oh, thank God. He's all right." She panted for air. "He'd never invoke the devil's balls if he was really hurt."

Meg fancied she already knew that.

And what a thing to know about a person.

Dougal sat up, disheveled and cross. "Bleedin' bloody donkey's—Meg! What are you doing here?"

"Learning new words, I wager," Charlie replied, helping her brother up. "You're a right mess."

"I reckon I could tell you exactly how many ribs I have and where they are. I think one of them may have wrapped itself around my left kidney." He stretched his neck and groaned. "Can you bruise your arse?"

Meg couldn't help herself. She hurried forward, ran her hands over his arms, picked a burr off his collar. "You might have been seriously injured!" In truth, he could have been killed. She didn't say it. But the knowledge of it ran ragged through her, like a rusty wheel.

"No wonder the stablemaster winces every time he sees me." He brushed at the grass and mud on his coat. Meg plucked grass out of his hair. She looked so worried, he smiled at her. "Nothing's broken but my pride. And possibly my arse."

"Next time land on your head," Charlie said drily, though there was a tremble to her voice that she fought to hide. "You're not using it anyway."

"You have me confused with Colin."

"Oh, right."

They grinned fondly at each other.

Dougal's horse lipped his shoulder companionably. "See you're still here," Dougal said mildly. The horse replied with a snort. "Couldn't agree more." Meg picked up the dangling reins and handed them to him. "I think I'll walk home," he said. "Safer all around."

"We'll join you," Charlie said. "Someone has to look after you."

"I once had to fetch you from inside a well."

"I was rescuing a baby badger!" She turned to Meg. "Someone had tossed it into the bucket for sport."

Meg narrowed her eyes. "Another reason to carry a hatpin on you." They exchanged bloodthirsty nods.

"Speaking of which," Dougal looked down at Meg. "Are you after starting a new fashion?"

She followed his gaze, then flushed. She pulled the hat pins free hastily.

"While you were pretending to be an acrobat, and a bad one at that I should point out, Meg was fixing that roof." Charlie said. "All by herself."

He frowned at the roof in question. "It doesn't look very sturdy."

"It's not," Meg agreed.

"Then why on earth did you climb it?"

"Because someone had to."

"With thirty-seven cottages on this estate alone, don't I have a thatcher to do that?"

"You might have once," Meg said, grimly. "You'll want to speak to your land agent."

"It appears I might at that."

"Are you sure you didn't injure yourself."

"I'm fine. We weren't even going that fast, it just felt like the saddle gave out."

Meg frowned at the saddle, running her hands over the leather. It was worn but oiled and well cared for. She lifted one of the straps. It was ragged, cut through in a way that leather would never do.

Someone had damaged it on purpose.

"Like the carriage wheel," Dougal said, stunned.

"Like the carriage wheel."

"But why bother? Killing me won't get the treasure found any quicker."

"But the ensuing chaos would admit any number of strangers into the house," Meg said.

"Bloody treasure hunters are a menace."

"Especially if Lord Eaton is poking at them."

He sighed. Meg and Charlie exchanged a glance. When he finally muttered under his breath, they chorused with him, in perfect unison.

"Damn King Henry the Eighth."

Chapter Eighteen

S HE WAS LEAVING.

First thing tomorrow morning.

The reality of it sat like a stone in her stocking, biting at her, keeping her unbalanced, bruised. She knew it was for the best. After that stolen moment in the hothouse which had replaced all of the blood in her body with fire and all of the air with Dougal, she had to be smart. The village was overrun with marriageable ladies, at least three of whom at last count were high on the Prince's list. Dougal was running out of time. And she was running out of ways to convince herself it was fine. And more than that, it was necessary.

The rents were going to be collected from the Swift tenants soon and she needed to be there. Mr. Campbell was kind and honorable, but even he could only do so much against the constable that her uncle always sent to scare the villagers. He was an arrogant, rigid man but he softened ever so slightly when a lady, the estate's unmarried daughter especially, was in the vicinity. And so, she was always in the vicinity.

She had obligations.

No matter what her heart wished she could do. Even without the rents, she had no dowry. Dougal might not realize how unsuitable that made her, but she knew it perfectly well. She wouldn't be one more thing for the world to use against him, to add to the reasons the *ton* might look down their noses at him when he was one of the best men she had ever known. Best *person.*

And so, she would go home.

Practical, realistic, calm Meg Swift.

It was enough to make one scream.

A maid was packing her personal things, but she would pack the art supplies herself. They were precious, breakable. She was on her way to do just that when she passed Dougal's study, the door open and a man lingering on the threshold. There was something about the way he held himself that made Meg narrow her eyes. They nearly set fire to her head when she heard Dougal murmur his name from inside the study: *Mr. Clarke.*

"If you could see to that then, Dougal," Mr. Clarke said, with a sneer he probably thought was subtle. "That'd be grand, my boy."

"I beg your pardon," Meg said sharply. She didn't care for formal rules and the fuss of hierarchy, but she would not hesitate to use it as a weapon to protect Dougal and his family as many times as was required.

Mr. Clarke jumped and turned to glance at her. "Yes, Miss?"

"I am quite certain that you meant to address the duke appropriately," she said steadily, refusing to drop her gaze.

"Oh, erm." His fluffy white whiskers trembled.

"*Your Grace,*" she supplied helpfully, with the kind of expression that might have made Lady Beatrice proud. If only there were more marzipan fruit to catapult.

She might not be able to stay, but like hell she was going to let this kind of bullying go on, even when she was far away embroidering her blasted white dresses.

Dougal would not want boot-lickers and she understood that, but this was a kind of condescending disrespect the agent thought Dougal would not notice or understand.

Meg understood it perfectly well.

And if he was going to be rude, he could be brave enough to be direct about it. Mrs. Hill was the same with Charlie.

Abruptly, she was done with it.

All of it.

"Um, of course. Your Grace," Mr. Clarke stammered. He flushed slightly. Good. He knew he'd been caught being a prat and was less likely, one might hope, to proceed from disrespect to something worse. It might be rare, but it had been known to happen. And Dougal, much as he would protest the fact, was ripe pickings.

"And I believe cottage repairs fall under your purview, does it not?" Meg continued relentlessly. When he squirmed she did not feel badly. Not a bit. She was probably a terrible person. Never mind. No one would do to Dougal's estate what her uncle had done to the Henshaw estate. There was little enough she could do about any of it, but she could do *this*. "The roofs need thatching and the windows repair. Now. Before the snow falls."

"Yes, Miss." Mr. Clarke bowed to Dougal and then to Meg, deeply enough that he might have confused her with the queen. He hurried away, heels clacking on the marble floors and stays creaking under his coat.

"Well, that's him told," Dougal murmured, from where he leaned against his desk, looking pleased despite himself. "You are a menace."

"I'll take that as a compliment."

"As you should." He tilted his head slightly. "Were you protecting me, Meg?" His voice was honey and spice. She would have drunk it in tea, if she could have.

"Well, of course, I was." She stepped into the library. The walls were papered with blue silk patterned with tiny flowers. Leather bound books marched in neat rows, interspersed with more Roman busts. She made a mental note to record their presence, as she hadn't the time to draw them properly for Pendleton.

"The Splendid Miss Swift," he said quietly, fondly. It did something to her knees, that tone. Made them shiver, made her legs heat. Made her want that honey tea. Made her want Dougal.

"Don't be silly," she said briskly. "He was rude. I merely pointed it out."

"*I* am frequently rude."

"Not on purpose. And you're never *rude*, you're just learning a new set of rules. And they may be absurd sometimes, but if someone is being unkind, I mean to use them as a weapon. I am afforded so few as it is."

"You think he was being unkind, not just pompous."

"He was. And negligent I think, after the previous duke's illness."

"I do know that, you know," he said gently. "What his manners say about him. And I mean to come back to the matter of neglect, never fear."

"You do?" Had she gone too far? There was a reason she kept so quiet; temper hadn't fixed anything for her before.

"Aye." He shrugged one shoulder. "I just don't particularly care what that old man thinks."

"You should!"

"Why? He's not the first and he won't be the last. And his opinion means nothing if he's going to act the arse."

"Well…yes. That's true."

"But?" He prodded.

"People are developing a habit of treating you and your family as if you don't matter and I won't have it." She probably shouldn't sound so vehement. Where were her usual placid tones? Her wry calm? She was all topsy-turvy, like a champagne bottle turned upside down.

"I see."

She was still leaving in the morning. She just had several things to do first.

One of which included a decision not made lightly. And yet easily enough with Dougal standing there with his steady eyes the color of the sky and the perfect line of his jaw.

The other decision was a piece of work much easier done and connected to the topic at hand. "Your Grace," she began.

He frowned, looking annoyed for the first time. "Don't call me that."

She half-smiled. "I can't very well do otherwise after the fuss I just made with your land agent."

"I'll show you a fuss," he muttered, eyes gleaming. His left eyebrow spoke volumes, dark delicious volumes. It should be illegal. "You'll call me Dougal."

His steely tone was doing nothing to cool the desire running roughshod throughout her body. She had to clear her throat. "I only mean to ask if I might do something for you before I leave, something which requires your permission."

"Anything. But only if you call me by my bloody name."

There was no reason to blush or feel as though she was suddenly standing in her chemise. She was nearly thirty years old, after all. And he had pulled the best orgasm she'd ever had from her body with very little effort. Which was exactly why she felt as though she might accidentally be naked.

And did not mind it a bit.

That decision was making itself.

First things first.

"Dougal," she said.

He was so satisfied she couldn't look away. Didn't want to.

"I found you a new housekeeper," she blurted out.

If she'd ever wondered if she was the seductive type, she did not wonder any longer.

Which might make her next proposition a bit tricky.

One thing at a time.

"A housekeeper?" Dougal repeated, surprised. "But we have a housekeeper. The indomitable Mrs. Hill."

"I found one better suited to your household." She sounded prim, even to her own ears.

He smiled at her as though she was lovable. She wanted to move closer, to lean into him.

"What are you trying to say, Meg?"

She wrinkled her nose. "I don't think Mrs. Hill is happy here. More to the point, I think she is making Charlie *unhappy*."

"And you won't have that?" he asked, quoting her directly.

"No."

"Good. As it happens, neither will I."

"Oh."

"You've found a replacement?"

"I have. A Mrs. Cricket from the village."

"Mrs. Cricket and Mr. Canterbury. I've found myself in some

sort of ridiculous storybook."

"She's very cheerful and capable," Meg assured him. She'd asked Mrs. Chan from the shop in town for recommendations. "And she can start straightaway."

"What do I do with Mrs. Hill?"

Meg swallowed her first suggestion, which was neither polite nor pretty. Noticing, Dougal laughed. "You can retire her to a cottage or move her to one of your houses that you don't frequent or else offer her a fine letter of recommendation," Meg said.

"I was sure you were going to say death by fire ant hill."

"She's not… *evil*," Meg allowed. "Just too conventional for this estate. And you deserve to be happy and comfortable in your own house, surely."

"There's a thought."

"Your Grace, would you be so kind as to take my virtue?"

Eek, no. Quite aside from the fact that she *technically* had no virtue to take, unless such things grew back, Dougal would never agree if she addressed him by his title.

"Alas, I seem to have stumbled into your bedroom naked."

That was no better.

Blast.

Why was this so difficult? Society mavens would have it that a lady was in great danger of ending up naked every moment she went about with a chaperone. Well, here Meg was, with the best chaperone—an elderly woman who didn't give a fig for convention—and she still had yet to find herself naked.

Agreeing to a night of sweaty pleasure would be so much easier than *proposing* one.

A regrettable choice of words, even in her own head. There would be no proposal. And if there were, she would have to say no. She wasn't fit to be a duchess, even were one to ignore the paint on the sleeve of her nightgown. Not lingerie or a fine transparent muslin chemise. But instead, her plain, ordinary *nightgown*, for heaven's sake.

This seduction business was harder than it looked.

And she was known for being direct, however polite and quiet she might dress up that directness. Right now, she was none of those things. She was only awkward and wishy-washy and hovering in the hall outside Dougal's bedchamber like one of those ladies on a house tour. Nothing untoward about that. Or dissolute. Merely desperate.

Honestly, she should just go back to bed. Preserve the last shreds of her dignity, such as they were. It was embarrassing enough that she hadn't managed to find the treasure. There was talk about pulling up floorboards but that could take weeks. Even tapping on the walls randomly hadn't provided any more clues. What seven stars? What wrath? What bloody boat?

Even so, the want and the need that glittered through her would not be silenced. Nor would the certainty that if she did not take this chance, she would never have it again. Dougal would be married, and she would ease further into spinsterhood and a genteel sort of poverty that was no less insidious than any other kind of poverty. She would have pride and purpose, but not Dougal. She'd also have the Cinderella Society and her godfather which was more than many had. She wouldn't feel sorry for herself.

But if she was going to have to eat turnips for most of her winters, she should at least have something delicious to remember, to hold out like a candle when her uncle's neglect turned to cruelty. She could foresee it already. Years of drink and expectations were not precisely improving upon his character.

Never mind that.

Tonight was for *her*.

For her and Dougal, if he'd have her. She'd have to ask him first. There was no way around it. He wasn't proving to be particularly adept at reading her mind through the thick oak door. Pity. Perhaps she should just knock and when he opened the door, she could step out of her nightclothes. Let her nakedness do the asking.

And if he refused, she would be stuck naked in the corridor.

Thank you, no.

Another tactic, then.

"If you think any harder, you might break something."

Dougal.

Speaking from *behind* her. He hadn't even been inside his bedchamber at all. All that fussing wasted, and she wasn't one for fussing in the first place.

"Meg?"

His voice was so soft and husky that she nearly shivered. She swallowed, forcing herself to turn around before she made even more of a goose of herself. Dougal leaned against the wall, his smile crooked and curious. She wanted to kiss that mouth. Wanted it on her. Nearly said so out loud, then lost her nerve.

Damn it, she'd chased down a murderer and a traitor with nothing but her hair ribbons. She hadn't lost her head when a treasure hunter poked her with a dagger. This ought to be simple.

"Is something the matter?"

Yes. No.

She really had to say something out loud before he called the doctor.

Diagnosed with an acute case of lust. Mortifying.

"Meg?"

"I—" she stumbled over her words, choked on them. The resulting cough was as alluring as her plain nightgown smudged with paint.

Was it too late to crawl into a hole?

Dougal took a step closer, looking alarmed as her eyes began to water. A small giggle forced its way through the coughing. She couldn't help it. The naughty books she had read made this whole process seems much more sophisticated. Inevitable. With smoldering glances which left words unnecessary. Not whatever this was. Wordless, all because she was choking on her own awkwardness. Honestly.

"Do you need water?" Dougal asked.

"Whisky," she croaked.

"I'll fetch some." He pushed into his bedroom as if she might expire on the spot. She was considering it, truth be told.

But not until she got her one night.

Her one memory no one could take from her.

She stepped into his chambers as he rushed towards her with a crystal glass filled with amber liquid. She took a single burning sip and it melted the nerves freezing her throat.

"Better?" Dougal asked.

She smiled as though this was all quite ordinary. "Yes, thank you."

She was just inside the door now, his bedroom decorated in shades of blue. Roman columns had been set against the wall and on either side of windows and doors. Venus was painted across one entire wall, rising from the fireplace in a cacophony of ocean waves and meadow flowers and frolicking cherubs with red cheeks.

Dougal wrinkled his nose. "You should see the other bed-chambers."

"Choices were certainly made."

He grinned. After a moment, he added, with one eyebrow raised. "Meg?"

"Yes?"

"You appear to be standing in my bedroom. At midnight."

She swallowed. "I am."

"You would tell me that is not done. Is there a problem? What can I do for you?"

Oh, what a question to ask.

She had many, many answers. There was just *so much* he could do for her. To her. With her.

"I...," she trailed off. *Be your own woman, Meg.* "I am leaving tomorrow."

He didn't look happy. "Yes."

"I, well, we only have tonight left. Together. I know we can't have a future but..."

"What are you saying, Meg?" He asked quietly. He was still, calm. Except for his eyes. They gave her courage.

And sent heat streaking up the back of her legs.

She took a careful breath so she wouldn't choke again. "I want to spend the night," she said, plainly, a little shyly. "With you."

He stared at her for such a long quiet moment, her courage

balked.

"If you want me."

He was so still, so quietly still.

He didn't want her. She'd been a fool. She tried to smile, as though she wasn't in very great need of more whisky and also, please God, a way to turn back time in order to un-humiliate herself. Of course, he didn't want her. He was kind, courteous. And a duke. She was wearing a nightgown that had been mended three times already, knew how to plant and grow turnips, knew how to pretend to belong to the glittering even as she felt herself shrinking every day.

But this was a choice she could finally make for herself. About her own life.

One little problem.

Dougal wasn't interested.

Chapter Nineteen

DOUGAL WAS VERY, *very* interested.

Dougal was also fairly certain he was hallucinating and needed a moment to make sure this was all real. He'd never wanted anyone as much as he wanted Meg. In his bed. In his house, in his life.

In his bedroom, at this very moment, trying to slink out unnoticed, her hair in a sensible braid, her toes bare under her hem. Desire hummed through him. Something primal unfurled, demanding that he lock the door, that he barricade it with every stick of furniture he owned in order to keep her from leaving. He wouldn't, of course. But Lord, did he want to. His voice was hoarse, and very nearly desperate when he spoke her name.

"Meg."

Just her name. It might take a moment for his brain to find other words that weren't *Meg* or *want* or *need*.

She hesitated in the doorway.

He was close enough to touch her, to wrap his fingers around her wrist, in her hair. He wasn't too proud to admit his breath stuttered in his chest. She wanted to spend the night. Wanted *him*, born in an alleyway, gutter rat, millhouse worker. With his scarred hands and scarred past, he knew full well that he wasn't good enough for her.

It didn't seem to matter as much tonight. He wouldn't *let* it matter. Not when she was so close.

Not close enough.

"Meg, are you sure?"

She was blushing, pink moving from her cheeks to her chest, dipping below the white fabric of her nightgown. He wanted to follow it with his tongue.

She couldn't quite look at him, but she nodded. "I'm sure."

"Your reputation…" Why was he still talking? Worse, possibly talking her out of it?

She finally looked at him, defiant, hungry, trusting. It floored him. Made him want to marry her right here at midnight between the velvet bed and the open door. "Hang my reputation. I deserve something just for *me*."

She was fierce then, in a way he hadn't yet seen, beyond her bloodthirsty protective instincts, beyond her need to fight bullies at every turn. This time it was about her, and *them*, and he could have eaten it like cake. Could eat *her* like cake.

His smile grew, slow, promising.

"Then close the door, love."

He spoke so softly, promising wicked delicious things with just the intonation of his voice and every word sent tingles to her core. *Close the door, love.*

He *did* want her, at least for one night. It was all she wanted. Well, it was all she could reasonably *expect*, and it would have to be same thing. It would have to be enough.

She pulled the door shut and turned to face him but couldn't quite bring herself to close the distance between them, however much she wanted to, however much that distance was instantly offensive to her. Nervous anticipation heightened the curl of lust in her belly.

He padded towards her, lean and gilded in the candlelight. He wore the plain rough trousers he preferred and a simple lawn shirt that hinted at the shape of his chest, the strength of his arms. The muscles in her thighs went hot and loose and he wasn't even touching her yet. His mouth quirked in that crooked smile she loved so much.

His fingertips were so gentle on her neck that she shivered.

"Dougal."

He trailed them up into her hair, tightening slightly, releasing. His mouth brushed over hers, just as gentle, just as devastating. Her every nerve turned to fireflies, glowing, sparking, fluttering. She leaned into him, nipping at him until he finally deepened the kiss, until his tongue slid along hers, teasing, tempting. She clutched at his arms, just to feel the play of muscles there.

He lowered his head and closed his lips over her nipple, the thin cotton dampening as he used the flat of his tongue over the tightening bud. The combination of the cool cloth and hot mouth made her moan. "There is too much of this dress," he muttered.

She couldn't agree more.

He loosened the faded blue ribbon of her neckline, his thumbs sliding along her collarbones. The ribbon was frayed, the material nearly transparent in spots. "Meg, why are the clothes of a viscount's daughter so worn through?"

She felt like she might come apart at the seams, just like her nightdress as he pushed it over her shoulders, and he was asking questions about *fashion*.

"They're just clothes." It was a struggle to focus on anything but his hands on her bare skin, the hardness of him just out of reach, teasing.

"That's not an answer." He sounded stern even as the fabric dropped to the floor, pooling around her ankles. She was naked, completely naked, and he still wore every stitch of clothes. There was something wonderful about that, something that hinted at wickedness.

She liked it.

A lot.

But she liked the solemn questions clouding his expression much less. He was still thinking about worn cloth, about mended seams, about what they all meant. "You can tell me the truth, Meg."

"Do you really want to talk right now?" she squeaked indignantly. "About clothing?"

Heat flashed in his blue eyes, like the heart of a candle flame. "No," he admitted. "No, I don't."

And then her clothes were forgotten, and she was dressed in only his hands, his heat, his hardness. He tugged her up against him, dragging his mouth over her neck, stopping to suck at the spot where it met her shoulder and along the curve up to her ear until she was gasping and melting. "I've been wanting to do that for a long time," he whispered hoarsely. "Too long. Since before the hothouse even."

"Almost as long as I've wanted you too," she replied, arching her neck slightly to give him better access. He smiled against her throat, rubbing the slight scruff of his beard against her until she squirmed, half-giggling, half-moaning. She pushed at his shirt impatiently until he dragged it up over his head and she could finally touch him, sketching him with her fingertips, until she might sketch him with her mouth.

He backed her towards the bed and when her calves hit the mattress, he lowered her down, one hand at the small of her back, supporting her. Soft blankets billowed around her and then he was there, taking up every centimeter of her view until it was all tousled hair, bright eyes, cheerful wicked mouth. She pulled his head down towards her when he took too long, happy to look at her until she turned desperate. "Dougal!"

He took her mouth with more than a hint of hunger and teeth and something inside her uncurled, practically purring. Desire throbbed through her, pulsing low in her belly, high in her throat, everywhere. His big, strong hands roamed over her ribs, thumbs scraping under her breasts, then along her hip, inside her thigh until they went lax and parted of their own volition. When he grazed the softness between her legs, her mouth opened on a gasp. His tongue invaded her mouth even as his fingers dragged through her wetness to plunge into the heat of her. Her toes curled at the sudden, intimate possession. Her back arched.

He was gentle, stroking her petals and then invading her again, the juxtaposition making her tremble.

She'd been wrong. One night wasn't enough. It would never be enough.

She wanted him in her hands, the silky steel of him, the saltiness. She couldn't quite manage the placard of his trousers. "I hate clothes," she said, viciously. He chuckled and pushed away just long enough to divest himself of the hated garments. It was too long. She grasped at him, feeling wanton, wonderful. Wicked.

He groaned, the muscles of his throat working. "You're killing me."

She felt a bit smug about it, actually. She'd hate to die alone. Which she might do if he didn't touch her again, so she touched him all the more, gliding her palms over the ridges of his stomach muscles, the pelt of his hair, arrowing down to his manhood, erect and twitching towards her hand. She closed her fingers around him, savoring the heavy heat, the tender power. She explored him from root to tip, caressing softly, then more firmly, until his breath turned ragged.

She smirked, just a little.

And he noticed.

"It's like that, is it?" He growled. The teasing glint in his eye was the only warning before he ran his open mouth over her belly button, tickling her with his breath and his tongue until she tried to wriggle away. It was amazing to her that she could be on fire, that they could be both sweaty, needful as animals but also laughing friends, and at the very same time. She giggled.

His lips curved in an answering grin against her skin and then was moving lower and lower, until his mouth was at the core of her. He ran his tongue over her petals and then slowly, so damned slowly, up to her bud. It made her tremble, in her thighs and her knees, down to her very breath. He was so careful, but his arm was solid over her hips, pinning her in place when she tried to get closer. The combination shivered inside her, like liquid waves building slowly. He worked her with his mouth, kissing, teasing, and then sucking at her bud until she started to make small noises in the back of her throat. Her inner walls fluttered, clutching at nothing until he slid two fingers inside of her, crooking them even as he rolled her bud in his mouth, sucking harder.

The waves of pleasure peaked, cresting, carrying her away for long, languid moments where there was only her body, no other worries, or cares, or wants. Only Dougal's mouth and his hands and the internal fireworks that sparked and shimmered.

He lifted his head and watched her come back to herself, dark hair spread on the pillow, lips parted on a quivering breath. She reached for him and he slid up her body. She hummed when his manhood grazed her curls. He hesitated, until she scowled. He had to bite back a grin even as he spoke. "I don't want to hurt you."

"You're not hurting me."

She was a gentlewoman, an aristocrat. And he was only playing the part.

He might have tortured himself for much, much longer on that point, if she hadn't reached down and grasped him firmly. "Do I have your attention?"

He swallowed. "Yes, ma'am."

"Good."

She arched up, nudging the head of his manhood between her soft lips, still slick with desire. "Now, Dougal."

He slid into her, slowly, prolonging the moment, wringing every delicious second of enjoyment out of it. She moved against him, gasping, as he filled her up. She clutched his shoulders when he retreated, made a soft sound when he returned, plunging deeper. No matter how she wriggled or panted, he would not make haste. They moved against each other, warm glistening skin meeting even as mouths met, as climaxes met, peaking, shattering, dragging them to the crest, over and over, until they fell together.

Dougal pushed off, clearly concerned about crushing her, before he'd even caught his breath. He lay next to her, his large warm hand on her hip. She felt sated, happy. Where she was meant to be.

Devastated.

"I wish you weren't going," Dougal said softly.

"Me too," she said and then kissed him because she didn't want to ruin the moment or the memory with the hopelessness threatening to boil over inside of her. She wanted to hold onto this, his mouth on hers, the mat of his chest hair under her fingers, his knee moving between hers. He seemed to realize that she did not want to speak about it and did not press. She wasn't sure if it made it better or worse. She wasn't sure of anything.

When she finally left his chamber, she wasn't two steps down the hall when Lady Beatrice came out of the dark. She wore a dressing gown, her hair in long gray braids like a Viking shield-maiden, carrying her spear. "Can't be too careful," she said, gruffly. "I won't have any more treasure hunters about the place." She eyed Dougal's door, then winked.

"Carry on"

Meg was halfway down the hall when she smelled smoke.

A lot of smoke.

"Fire!"

A FIRE IN town was dangerous business as it could hop from house to house and take out entire neighborhoods. A fire in a country house was a different sort of danger—they were far from helping hands, especially at night. When Meg shouted, it took very little time for the family to burst out of their bedrooms, and the servants to spill out of the attic bedrooms.

Smoke lingered at the bottom of the stairs, acrid and sharp. "Get outside," Dougal told them, as he joined the search for buckets to haul water from the kitchen and the pond, even the watering troughs at the barn would be emptied. Lady Beatrice took Lady Marigold to the warmth of the hothouse, joined by Lady Blackwell and Chartreuse.

The others refused to budge. And as Dougal did not have time to argue, there was not much he could do short of ordering the footmen to carry them out bodily. And he could not spare the footmen. But he considered it.

The fire, thankfully, was currently contained to the Music Room. Thick velvet and brocade curtains sent out plumes of fire and more smoke. A pianoforte made strange sounds in the corner. Flames licked at the walls, touching the ceiling, eating a display of dried flowers which only fueled it further. Dampened handkerchiefs were wrapped around mouths and noses and two lines were formed, one from the water pump in the kitchen, and one from the terrace doors where footmen raced down to the pond. It was hard, grueling, awful work.

But effective.

It took several hours before they were satisfied that no embers remained, quietly menacing the house. They pulled the fiery curtains down and shoved them into the fireplace. Dougal was covered in sweat and soot and every muscle ached, including the ones he'd never thought of before. According to the pain in his chest, it took far more than he'd assumed to keep his lungs working. He tried to keep George, Charlie and Meg down the hall with the buckets, but each was more stubborn than the last. Mrs. Hill brought jugs of lemonade for aching throats. Meg kept replacing Dougal's handkerchief with a cleaner, wetter one before he could cough himself into the realization that he needed a new one.

Anger licked inside his cramping chest. Who knew how fast and far the fire might have spread if Meg hadn't been sneaking out of his bedroom at some ungodly hour of the night? It might have engulfed the entire ground floor, might have raced up the stairs and trapped his family in their beds. Might have suffocated them before they could even cry out for help. Though he was dripping with sweat, he was cold to the marrow.

"No one was hurt," George said, as they finally removed their face coverings and bent over to catch their breaths. The fire was finally out. Most of the Music Room was gutted, and there was some smoke damage in the hall, but all things considered, they had gotten off easy.

Dougal patted George's shoulder and tousled his siblings' hair, just to reassure himself that they were safe. He wanted to gather Meg into his aching arms but there were too many people around them. Family, footmen, maids, a few people from the village who had heard the bell being rung for help. He met her eyes and hoped she could read everything he felt.

"Mrs. Hill," he rasped. "Make sure everyone gets as much to eat and drink as they want."

"Yes, Your Grace."

"Do you reckon it was another treasure hunter?" he asked Meg.

"This room was built less than twenty years so I can't imagine why they would bother. Plus, it would only have damaged the treasure if it *was* in here."

It took another couple of hours to cart the furnishings out of the Music Room and onto the stone terrace, just to be safe. There were burns to be seen to, blisters to wash. By the time dawn began to flirt with the horizon, it was only himself and Meg who remained.

The wallpaper was charred, two of the windows shattered. Smoke lingered, oddly tinged with lavender and the sharpness of burned fabric. Water sluiced underfoot. Everything was dirty, damaged. "What a way to say goodbye," Dougal murmured.

She leaned wearily against his shoulder. "It was always going to be horrible," she said. "But this is rather dramatic," she admitted. "Even for us."

Chapter Twenty

T HE MORNING DAWNED bright and clear and beautiful.

It was offensive.

Meg would have preferred gray rain to suit her mood, or storms to release this gnawing energy moving inside of her. She wanted to be back in Dougal's bed, waking slowly, his warm body against hers. Instead, she'd woken from a few hours of fitful rest to a maid bringing in a tea tray and offering to comb the snarls out of her hair which stank of smoke.

If only she could comb the snarls out of her mood.

It soured her mood further to discover that the plaster she had used in the dining room was already cracking.

She was rubbish at plastering.

And finding treasures.

Everything.

And now here she was, standing with Dougal, both stiff and awkward under the gaze of his family, her chaperone, a butler and three footmen. As if the muscles of her thighs weren't still pleasantly sore under her white dress. As if she didn't already miss him.

She smiled, composed, because what else was there to do? Weeping or gnashing her teeth, railing at the heavens—none of it would change the facts. She had no dowry, only responsibilities. Best get to it.

She curtsied to Colin who bowed, with a wink. She curtsied

to George next and handed him a small package. "What's this, then?" he asked.

"A gift," she teased. When his eyes went a little teary, she rushed to add. "It's only drawing pencils and good strong paper. For you to practice on."

A little teary turned to downright drippy. Meg bit her lip. Had she offended him in some way?

"Never mind," Dougal spoke from behind her, his voice in her ear stirring the little hairs on the back of her neck and chasing tingles down her spine. "George weeps on the daily."

George sniffled. "Rotten boy," he muttered. He bowed to Meg. "Thank you, Miss Swift."

"You're very welcome."

Charlie was next, frowning.

"It was lovely to meet you," Meg said. "I hope—"

Charlie cut her off by throwing herself at Meg and hugging her tight. She didn't say anything, just hugged tighter still, then stepped back abruptly.

Everything about saying goodbye was harder than she'd even imagined. She'd only been here for a month, but she wanted to wrap herself around the nearest sturdy object and refuse to be moved.

Dougal was last. She turned, meeting his eyes, that patient blue, like the ocean she had so wanted to paint. On a clear day when the sunlight pierced through a wave.

"Thank you for your hospitality, Your Grace."

His eyes flashed a warning at her use of his title. She raised an eyebrow. The easy, silent rapport mended a small part of the tearing inside the fabric of herself. Goodness, how melodramatic she was. She would miss him. It was that simple. It hurt but it hardly required theatrics and bad poetry. She straightened like a soldier. A small, determined soldier covered in embroidered hedgehogs baring their teeth. She'd add seashells and roses later for him. For all of them.

"I'm sorry I never found your treasure," she said. Oh, that rankled. She'd managed to sketch the statues for her godfather, but she hadn't succeeded in doing the thing he'd really wanted her to do. She needed more time. But the rents were due and real life called.

"We'll keep searching," Dougal promised.

"You'll send word if you find anything, won't you? Please."

"Of course. And you can always come back and keep searching."

"You'll be married by then," she murmured.

And there it was. Nothing left to say. Meg turned blindly to the carriage, taking Dougal's hand when he offered it. He squeezed her fingers, a secret message. A private farewell.

When she settled onto the seat, Lady Blackwell was already leaning slightly to the left. The laudanum she had taken was making its way through her system. Meg felt a rush of affection for the old woman who had braved her own fears just to escort her to a duke's house. Chartreuse woofed once, softly, and then launched himself across the space between them to land on Meg's knee. She caught him, pressing her cheek to his warm face. It was easier than looking out the window to Dougal and his family, standing there on the drive. She hoped the little dog would stop her from hurtling herself straight out of that same window.

Lady Blackwell surveyed her, only slightly blearily. "Margaret Swift, I never took you for a cabbagehead."

Meg raised her eyebrows. "I'm sorry?"

"As you should be." She harrumphed, before adjusting her impressive wig so that it served as a pillow of sorts. "I came all this way only to fail dismally at chaperoning. Here I am, returning you uncompromised." She sounded truly disgusted.

Meg couldn't help a smile even though she felt wretched. "I think you might be confused as to what constitutes a good chaperone."

"Bah. Shows what you know."

Chapter Twenty-One

S HE WAS HOME again.

She knew it was for the best. It was simply too easy to want to belong with Dougal and his odd jumble of a family. To want it all, so desperately. But she was accustomed to making meals out of morsels. This would be no different, in the end. Her gatekeeper's cottage was the same as when she'd left. It was she who was different. She'd felt like she belonged at Thorncroft Abbey but now she was back on the Henshaw estate.

And she would *not* mope about it.

Well, not *much*.

She tried not to resent everything that was not Thorncroft, that was not faded paintings, not the sea, or Lady Beatrice's temper. Treasure hunting. The fish bench.

Dougal.

She did love her little cottage, even if it only boasted a bed, a dresser, a table and a single chair with frayed rushes. But the walls were a kaleidoscope of colors, red birds, blue flowers, green leaves, rabbits painted under the eaves and tucked into corners, dragons on the ceiling. It was like living inside a storybook. And it was so much better than the room she'd had inside the house proper, where sometimes her uncle's male guests wandered the hallways, looking for sport or mischief, or simply an unlocked door.

Anyway, she didn't have the time to fuss and feel sorry for

herself.

She was needed at the main house.

Inside, Henshaw Hall was like a dollhouse stuffed with every pretty thing that had caught a child's eye. There were too many golden candlesticks, too many statues, too much furniture, too much decoration, all competing to demonstrate the importance of their owner.

Uncle Dermot.

His last house party was winding down, if the sounds of voices and cutlery coming from the dining room were any indication. Not to mention the smell of cheroot smoke and perfume and spilled wine. She bit back a sigh and made her way down the glittering, opulent hall. The study was no better, lined with oak shelves filled with ornate, gilded books that had never been opened. Gold ducks crowded between them. She'd always hated them but now they made her think of that dinner at Thorncroft. There was also yellow silk, carved mahogany, crystal decanters. It tired the eye.

"So, you've returned from your gallivanting," her uncle scowled at her. His graying hair was heavily pomaded, forced into elaborate curls he imagined made him look both dignified and somehow younger. The emerald in his cravat pin gleamed. It had belonged to her father once. She refused to look at it. "I'm not sure it's seemly."

"One does not refuse a duke," she reminded him.

"See that you don't get airs."

She swallowed back a retort. There was no use in arguing with him.

"Sleeping all hours of the day," he continued, needling her. "It's nearly eleven o'clock. No one wants a lazy wife."

As if he had any intention of letting her marry and leave his house to the mercy of housekeepers and maids who expected wages for their work. She kept her tone even, mild, never letting him see how he annoyed her. "You wanted to see me?"

He narrowed his eyes. She waited patiently. Patience, she had discovered, was an overlooked weapon. "You've work to do," he finally snapped. "I've had guests. Some will be staying on and all of the grates need to be scrubbed, the linens seen to, more silver polished. I won't have you lollygagging about and taking advantage of my kindness."

"Yes, Uncle." He always set her to clean the grates when she returned from the Pendleton estate. It rankled that he had never been invited and never would be.

"And where the devil is that constable? I need those deuced rents."

Which meant he had already gambled them away, likely in this very house in the last few days. He'd been barred entry to some of the more popular gaming hells in London for not paying his debts and had resorted to hosting lavish house parties with anyone who would play at cards.

"One more thing, niece."

She paused in the doorway, tensing. "Yes?"

"You'll join us tonight, in the parlor."

She hated his parties. Hated standing by the wall and waiting for orders for more wine, evading pinches to her backside, tolerating the sneers and whispers. Fetching things that didn't need to be fetched merely to demonstrate her uncle's power over her.

"Of course, Uncle."

You'll be married by then.

What had she meant by that? Would it bother her to know he would be married? Was it enough to make her change her mind that she wasn't for him?

He didn't know. It chased itself around his brain for hours, days, and he still didn't know. And like the idiot he was, he hadn't asked her. He hadn't stopped the carriage and demanded she clarify her statement, explain herself. Give him a chance to fix whatever the problem was. He was a bloody duke now, wasn't he?

Instead, he'd stood there like a lump, her voice reverberating inside his skull.

And now he was on the back of a horse, cursing his fate and poor choices.

And like to have his teeth rattle clean out of his head. He'd known it was too soon to leave the paddock, but he needed the distraction. Holding on for dear life as the trees and fields whizzed by seemed the thing. It was his third morning in a row, and every time he rode away, Colin stood by the gate and shouted at him. "Don't forget to hold on! I don't want to be the duke, it's entirely too much bookkeeping!"

He was improving, if nothing else. His seat was much more secure. His horse had even stopped shaking his mane and shooting him dirty looks. It was therapeutic. Painful, but therapeutic. He rode for hours, stopping at the cliff to watch the sea. There were no pirate ships, no green flash to mark the way. No Meg itching to paint the changing shifting colors of the water.

No Meg.

No, he wasn't supposed to be thinking about her.

Or the fact that he had less than a month left in which to choose a wife. For the rest of his life. Or to have her chosen for him by a drunken prince he'd never met.

He would never miss the hunger or the hollow look to his siblings' faces, but there were other aspects of his old life that he would miss. The ability to choose his own wife for one. The responsibility for three people, not several hundred. The fact that this new world had given him Meg, only to take her away again.

At night, he spent hours haunting the house, searching for more clues, for stars and secrets. Lady Beatrice continued her patrols, and he merely nodded a greeting when they passed each other in the small hours. Secretly, he placed footmen near the front doors, back doors and kitchen doors. Both in case of intruders, and to help her regain her feet if that bloody big spear tipped her over.

He had found countless spiders, dust, one startled mouse, three beetles, and a packet of racy love letters wedged behind a mounted frieze but no treasure.

As if he didn't know the treasure was Meg herself.

And now, when he couldn't rest, he locked himself in the dining room, counting stars like sheep for the sleepless, and then attacking the floorboards one by one with a crowbar by lamplight. It would take days, weeks even to rip them all up and then out them back together, but he couldn't see to care.

Sometimes Colin stumbled in before dawn, stinking of wine and perfume and smoke, and gave him a hand. They didn't speak much, only worked until they were covered in sweat and dust.

Still no treasure though.

One night, as they worked side by side, there was a sound at the window, just before it opened. They stood quietly, stepping back against the wall as a treasure hunter pulled himself into the room. He was graceful enough, right up until the moment that Colin leapt out of the shadows with a shout of "Oi!". The intruder jumped, tripped over a floorboard and sprawled ignominiously in one of the many coffin-like holes in the floor.

Colin smirked down at him. "Serves you right, tosspot."

"CINDERELLA, ANOTHER BRANDY. And something sweet, eh?"

If Meg were to draw Lord Piers she would draw him with Lady Beatrice's spear through his eye. Spiders in his mouth. And perhaps with a lobster attached to his more delicate places.

To say she loathed the man was an understatement.

He attended every one of her uncle's parties, drank more wine than a pirate drank rum, and groped the ladies under the table. And he wasn't the only one. Currently the ballroom had converted into a gaming hell with tables and chairs from every part of the house, and candles burning throughout the night. It was four o'clock in the morning and the guests did not appear to notice. Card games continued, increasingly dangerous bets were placed, couples meandered into the shadows (mostly) for sport. Perfume and cheroot smoke thickened the air.

Though footmen took care of the serving of drinks and delivering of food, lady's maids were always being summoned by the women to fetch various items such as shawls and nose powder and thread for dropped hems.

And Lord Piers always took advantage.

He lay in wait like a kraken made of hands.

She did what she could to mitigate his behavior at the best of times but tonight, when her mood was sour, and gloom threatened to spill through her like spilled ink, she was abruptly done with everything. Everyone. The whole lot of them.

Especially when his smile turned a smirk as a particularly pretty lady's maid, clearly out of her depths, arrived with her mistress's pearl earrings, lately lost on a hand of cards. Her curls were flaxen, her cheeks pink as she tried to avoid looking at anyone or anything. Not all of the wagering was done with coins or jewels. There was a large pile of clothing in the back corner. Meg did not begrudge them their entertainment, but she did begrudge them the hours they expected the staff to remain alert or what they expected them to overlook. She'd already set the housemaids and footmen on rotating shifts so they might catch a few hours of rest.

And now Piers was reaching for the maid. Her mistress rolled her eyes. "If it will buy back my favorite pearl earrings, I'll look the other way," she said.

Meg stepped closer, just as his hand closed around the poor girl's backside and then began to wander. She jumped and squeaked. The other guests at the table laughed. Meg inserted herself between them on the pretext of snuffing a candle that was gutting out and belching black smoke. She had already pulled her hat pin from the folds of her dress.

This was not the first time she had worked one of her uncle's parties.

By God, it would be the last.

She stabbed down with the pin, dragging it hard across the back of Lord Pier's wrist. He snatched his hand back with a loud curse. Meg widened her eyes as innocently as she knew how. "My Lord, I apologize. I left a pin in the sleeve of this dress accidentally and quite forgot."

"A dress pin? I had no idea you had such a delicate constitution, Piers," someone laughed.

He scowled but she knew he wouldn't want to make a fuss. Even though a needle could not have drawn quite so much blood, he'd still look the fool. She pressed a clean napkin to the wound and raised her eyebrows pointedly at the maid until the girl caught on and fled. "Let me bandage that for you, my lord."

"It's fine," he muttered. "Just a scratch."

Meg curtsied when he waved her away.

"Niece," her uncle snapped from the next table. "Have a care."

"Of course, Uncle," she said. "It's only that I've been awake for nearly twenty-four hours."

And in that time, she had done the job of a scullery maid, a lady's maid, and a housekeeper. Not to mention assorted little errands for her uncle that he could have done himself only it pleased him to see her scurrying back and forth in front of his guests. She decided she wasn't above burning the entire ballroom down if it meant she could get some rest. Her uncle must have sensed it because he narrowed his eyes, before forcing a loud guffaw. "Getting old, my girl. Off you go."

Meg left before he could change his mind. She did not have to feign the shuffle to her steps. She could have slept standing up, propped against the wall. The lady's maid was still in the hall. Her name was Beth and she blurted out her life's story in under a minute. Meg tried to pay attention, but her eyes were burning, and Beth was getting blurry.

"It's that grateful I am, Miss," Beth finally wound down. "My Da warned me to look out for fancy blokes but I can't very well punch them like I'd punch them in the village, now can I?"

"I suppose not," Meg said. "When you find yourself in London next, go and speak with Lady Langdon. Tell her I sent you and she will find you a safer position."

"Oh, thank you, Miss." Beth bobbed a curtsy.

Meg made her way down the hall and out into the cold night. Cold morning. The darkness was already fading to gray in the east. There was frost in the garden and the brisk air helped revive her. She might not have to curl up and sleep in the hydrangea bushes after all.

The gatehouse cottage was nearly as cold as the garden. The fire had gone out and she hadn't had a chance to sneak out to tend to it. She added more kindling and twists of dried hay until it eventually crackled back to life, dancing over the painted walls. She ate a pear from the basket on the table and a hunk of cheese she had stolen from the kitchen when Cook was busy fussing over lavender water jellies requested by one of the guests.

She flipped through her sketchbook for a moment, seeking the comfort of Dougal's face. Just for a moment. In the morning, she would be composed again. She would go on with her life. Not just go on, but really inhabit it. Control it.

But for now, she just missed his smile. His steady and patient gaze. His everything.

She had sketched him by the sea with the wind in his hair and his trousers rolled up above his ankles. In the town, surrounded by ladies with strawberry ices. At dinner, looking vulnerable and determined. In his bedroom, his shirt tossed aside, ridges and contours of muscles dusted with hair.

They had made each other laugh. She could see building a life with this man, having him in her bed on cold nights and winking at her from across the table over breakfast. She genuinely *liked* him.

Loved him.

She could admit to herself, here in the cold darkness, if nowhere else.

She had convinced herself for so long that it just wasn't possible for her. She tried to convince herself again that it was for the best. That he needed someone different.

A soft knock at the door interrupted her woolgathering. Wallace stood outside in his rumpled footman's livery. "I didn't see you leave the house," he scolded. "You should have said."

She smiled and stepped back to let him in. "You're meant to be sleeping already. I put Simon next on the schedule."

Wallace shrugged. "I can sleep here. But I didn't want to startle you if you saw me outside."

"I do lock my door every night." Sometimes, she even shoved her chair under the handle.

"You know the last nights of these parties are the worst."

He wasn't wrong. It was safer now that she wasn't in the house proper, but at the same time she was further from help should she need it. And she *had* just angered a very drunk and sullen Lord Piers. Choosing pride over logic seemed silly under the circumstances.

"It's too cold to sleep outside," she said. She eyed the bench in the small, crooked foyer, barely big enough for him to stretch out. "Although that can't be much more comfortable."

"Sight more comfortable than my room," he assured her. "I share with Anthony and he snores like a bull." He sat down stubbornly. "I don't like the feel of the house, Miss. We've set someone outside the maids' quarters too."

"You're very kind, Wallace." She ought to have thought of that. "Do they really go into the attics?"

"A few of those guests, gentlemen and ladies alike, will go anywhere when they're soused enough."

"Let me at least get you a blanket."

She also brought him a pillow and what was left of the mint tea from the kettle before shutting herself up in her narrow bedroom. It would have shocked the gossips of the *ton* to know she was sleeping under the same roof as a single man. Even if he was below her rank and she was an aging penniless viscount's daughter. But she trusted Wallace and the closed door of her bedroom would serve propriety well enough.

She finally lay down, her feet throbbing. Her lower back felt like the hollow cup of a spoon at the end of the hot metal of her spine.

She had been brave to stay. There were people who had needed her here.

And now she had to be brave and go.

If she could leave Dougal, whom she was in love with, she could leave her hateful, selfish uncle.

✦

Chapter Twenty-Two

How was anyone supposed to survive dinners like this, never mind look forward to them? The starched cravat Dougal had hired a valet to tie for him, the stiff formal talk about the weather, smiles that said too much and nothing at all.

It was torture. Worse than the burn of his muscles from days of hard abuse. His horseback skills were improving through sheer force of will and repetition. Some days he stumbled home, barely able to walk. His thighs spasmed at night, his knees hated him from the hard floorboards of the dining room. They'd had to convert the breakfast room into a dining room for this gathering.

And all of it was still better than missing Meg, which bit at him in every unguarded moment. Better to be exhausted. But this: formal gold painted plates, crystal goblets, the crisp white gloves of hovering footmen. It was a different type of pain.

He longed for a dinner with Meg, wayward duck included.

He longed for Meg, full stop.

Instead, he was seated at the head of the table, acres of polished wood and lace cloths, and ladies wearing pearls. There were roses from the hothouse that made him think of Meg, lilies that perfumed the air. He missed the wildflowers that Meg brought into the house. His sister stifled a sneeze and sat back, looking as though she was sitting on a hedgehog.

He knew exactly how she felt.

Colin, more pragmatic than he appeared, was basking in the

attention of women eager to praise everything they saw and heard, if it meant being noticed. After all, as he said, only one of them would get to be a duchess and the others might not mind being a duke's sister-in-law. And a viscountess.

Dougal understood the mercenary aspect to the whole business. Aristocratic marriages were about land and contracts and power. Love was for affairs, or so he'd been assured. It was a neat system, but not one he had any experience with. It wasn't that people in his former life didn't also sometimes marry for comfort or a nine-month necessity. Love grew.

It was just that none of them were Meg Swift.

He was starting to feel as though this might not be love, but the ague. It was too soon for love, wasn't it? And he felt ill, tired, irritable, with a certain jagged edge that threatened to cut anyone in his vicinity. It was with great willpower that he swallowed another sharp comment and drank fine wine and nodded amiably when someone spoke to him. He didn't even know what they were saying. He didn't care.

But he had to care. Like it or not, this was his life now. And he owed it to any future wife to not be a complete ass.

Not that he had any intention of marrying Miss Spencer, who watched him as though he were a rabid wolf inexplicably loose in the dining room, or the girl next to Colin who kept giggling and fluttering her eyelashes. Someone had clearly told her it was the best way to flirt. He wanted to call for a doctor in case she scratched her retinas. Colin didn't seem to mind. He was taking it all in stride, making the best of a situation Dougal knew full well hundreds of men envied. Thousands even.

None of them had met Meg. Had heard the sound of her laugh, even the same night she'd been threatened at knife point, or knew her determination, her secret whimsy. The sounds she made when she came, spread out on the bed beneath him. He was going to have to get rid of that bed. Or switch rooms entirely. He couldn't bring a wife to a room that held such memories. Not when he wanted to hold onto them so badly.

What was the use in being a bloody duke, if he couldn't have the one thing he wanted? If it wasn't for his family, he'd walk away from it all now just to find her.

Except he wasn't good enough for her.

That hadn't changed.

He wasn't technically good enough for the others either, but they were so intent on catching him for a husband that it seemed to balance out.

Except for Lady St. Ives. She was sophisticated, droll, beautiful. They would rub along together fairly well. He might never feel for her what he felt for Meg, but he would be a good husband. And she wasn't jittery over his background. They could be friends. Good friends.

It was more than so many others got.

For some reason it made everything worse.

He was greedy to want more.

He stifled a sigh and turned his attention to the lamb with blackberry sauce on his plate before someone else asked what he thought of gardens, or horses, or London. He'd never even been to London. The idea of taking his place in the House of Lords, of making parliamentary speeches soured his mood even further. So did the knowledge that Meg would scold him to think of all the good he might do with the power to fight laws made by people who didn't know the first thing about the Norfolk farming system or going to bed hungry.

"Is the dinner not to your liking?" Lady St. Ives inquired.

He glanced up, hastily arranging his expression into something less feral. "It's delicious, as always. Is there anything you need?"

She shook her head and then leaned a little closer, lowering her voice. "You're doing very well." When he only stared at her she smiled. "I've been on the Marriage Mart," she reminded him. "It's gruesome. The trick is not to take it too seriously." She studied his pained expression. "Oh dear, have I gone too far? I apologize. I am too outspoken."

"Not at all." He drank more wine. It gave him something to do with his hands. "I prefer it."

"That is encouraging." She watched him drink more wine for a moment. "I hear there was some excitement about a treasure recently?"

"Yes." He should say something else. He was just so tired.

"We routed that bugger!" Lady Beatrice said, smugly. Several of the ladies gasped at her language. One of the footmen choked. "I poked him right in the spleen with my spear."

"She was very brave," Lady Marigold added, though she had slept through the entire incident. As had Lady Blackwell, who was vexed that her Chartreuse had not had the opportunity to prove his mettle.

"Is there really treasure?" Miss Aisnworth asked, eyes wide. "Truly?"

"Rumors of treasure," Colin replied. "Which is half the fun, wouldn't you say?" He winked. She blushed. Her mother set her fork down with a clatter.

"We have been ambushed," Charlie added. "Strange men trying to break into the house. It isn't safe."

Someone gasped again, louder. Dougal shot her a dry glance. He knew exactly what she was doing. She just smiled at him, innocent as a baby lamb. Fear would have shot through him at the sight of that smile, but apparently he'd managed to drink just enough wine to make it interesting instead of foreboding.

The footmen cleared the plates and brought out the last course: a flummery made of rosewater custard, a fish pond platter consisting of gold flecked jelly in the shape of a goldfish, cheeses, nuts and a display of marzipan fruit which Lady Beatrice eyed with considerable glee. She had insisted on bringing her spear with her and it leaned against the wall behind her chair. She had already instructed the footman not to block her access to it. Lady Marigold wore yellow, of course, and she twinkled at everyone like a merry Christmas lantern. George was seated on Lady St. Ives' other side. Dougal had quickly realized she was the only lady currently in attendance who would not make him feel uncomfortable. She was quiet and polite as a dowager. Scratch that. Dougal had yet to meet a dowager who was not more wolf than little red riding hood.

Dougal felt a rush of warmth for his odd, eccentric family. Whoever he married, in the next few weeks, would have to respect them. Each of them, for all of their quirks. Including Charlie, who was even now pulling a sneaky, mildly rude trick. Footmen had been asked to present a gift to each lady, an exquisitely embroidered handkerchief.

At least she'd improved to only "mildly" disrespectful. In a house where marzipan was a projectile weapon, he supposed he should be grateful for small mercies. And in truth, no one else would realize that the gifts she was having brought out had been stitched by Meg. He would recognize the fat hedgehogs, the roses and secret poison berries, anywhere.

Charlie was needling him, not their guests. Well, not so they would notice, anyway. He thought Lady St. Ives might notice, but she didn't say anything.

The rest of the night was a blur of bowing and curtsying, compliments, and more wine.

Too much wine if the fact that he found himself stretched out on the settee in the family parlor had anything to say about it. If it didn't, his siblings certainly made up for it. George just shook his head and rang for strong coffee.

"Have they gone?" Dougal groaned. He'd made his goodbyes and fled the moment the guests were on the drive, waiting for their carriages. Colin had gone out to wait with them. He probably should have done the same, but he'd been afraid he'd bare his teeth and start growling. A perfect end to a perfect evening.

"How much did you drink?" Charlie asked. "You don't even like wine."

"I like wine fine." He didn't. He found it cloying. But it was something dukes were supposed to like, wasn't it? Wine and artfully tousled hair and gold rings on every finger. "Damn Prinny, anyway," he added. "Damn his eyes."

"Damning the royal family," Colin remarked. "And not just King Henry. Is this about Meg?"

"Of *course* it's about Meg," Charlie put in.

Colin leaned against the sideboard. "Tup her already, mate," he said.

Dougal sat up. His face changed. It was the expression he'd

had on the daily, before George had taken them in. One that promised retribution and pain to anyone who messed with his loved ones. "Shut your gob," Dougal said. Colin held his hands up placatingly. "You can dress the part of a careless aristocrat, but you won't act like it. Not in this bloody ostentatious house. *Mate.*"

Colin's eyes widened. "It's like that, is it?"

Dougal would have said something else, but the sudden outburst had made the wine swim in his head, full of sugar and thorns. "Where did you get those handkerchiefs? You didn't ask Meg to make them all for you, did you?"

"Don't be ridiculous," Charlie rolled her eyes. "I bought them from a little shop in town. Don't you know that duke's sisters are supposed to shop?"

"Why would a viscount's daughter need to sell her handiwork?" Dougal wondered out loud.

"Ask her, you donkey."

They paused while Mrs. Cricket bustled in, pushing the coffee tray. It was in a silver carafe shaped like a swan. "I've added some ginger biscuits," she said, cheerfully. "My Da swore by them when he'd had the wine."

Lovely, even the housekeeper knew he was a drunken miserable sot.

She closed the door gently behind her. She was as warm and comforting as a muffin straight from the oven, and roughly shaped the same. Meg had found them a miracle. She was making his life better even when she wasn't here.

He wanted to punch something.

He never wanted to punch something.

"Why haven't you asked her to marry you?"

"Mrs. Cricket?"

"Do you think I won't brain you with the fireplace poker?" Charlie asked. "*Meg.*"

He looked away, hands cradling the coffee cup Colin had handed him. "I'm not good enough for her."

"She said that?"

He braced himself for his little sister's temper.

She only frowned. "That doesn't sound like her."

Dougal squirmed. The coffee was hot and sweet on his tongue, and it was waking up his drowsy brain. Charlie raised her eyebrows. "Dougal, did Meg actually say that to you?"

"Well, no."

"And did you actually ask her to marry you?"

"I…" He paused. "I did?" Didn't he? "No."

"But you told her you loved her? Or at least esteem her greatly? Whatever bloody dukes say?"

"I…No."

Charlie rolled her eyes. "But she's meant to fall at your feet, is that it?"

"No, but—"

"Lord, men are idiots."

Dougal turned to Colin and George for support. "Don't look at me," Colin grinned. "We *are* idiots. But mostly you."

He rubbed a hand over his face. They had a point. She made comments about not marrying, about dowries, and he hadn't wanted to pry. But maybe she thought he didn't care.

"Anyone can see how you feel about her," George said in his quiet manner. "About each other."

"And since you have to marry within the fortnight anyway…" Charlie added. "You go and ask her proper. Or I really will clobber you with a poker."

⚜

Chapter Twenty-Three

IT WAS ALL good and well to decide to run away, but she still had responsibilities to see to first. The land agent Mr. Campbell would be down in the village shortly to collect the rents. She needed to be there to help Wes get it done as quickly as possible. Her uncle sent the constable Mr. Hughes to oversee and to intimidate, before escorting Mr. Campbell back up to the Hall with his money purse. Meg was occasionally able to distract him and keep his mood sweet. She wore her best dress, white with bluebells embroidered over every inch of fabric strong enough to hold thread. Every time she wore it, he told her blue was his favorite color and he wasn't as rough with the tenants.

Meg paired it with a straw bonnet and fingerless lace gloves, so as to appear as ladylike as possible, even though the gloves itched. She walked through the fields, admiring with some pride the stubble of hay and vegetables from the recent harvest. The cheerful wind and the bright sun improved her mood, and she could almost pretend not to remember the sound of Dougal's husky laugh. Almost.

Not to wonder what he was doing right now.

If he'd found the treasure.

Or a wife.

"Meggie!" Peter crowed her name and tore through hillocks of dirt to reach her side. His blond curls were too long, as usual, and home to twigs and stray flower petals, also, as per usual. His grin was contagious and chased away the last of her doldrums.

"Peter Farthing," she crowed back. "Here's a fine lad."

"What did you bring me?" he demanded instantly.

"A kiss."

He made a loud, offended gagging sound. "*Meg!*"

She laughed. "How about a pirate's treasure, then?" she asked.

"Treasure?" He looked both excited and suspicious, as only a ten-year-old boy could. "What kind of treasure?"

"Gold." She handed him the pouch full of almonds.

His eyes widened at the glint of gilt. "'Gor!'"

"Better yet, it's gold you can eat."

His eyes widened further and were in very great danger of falling right out of his head. "I can eat these? Truly?"

"Truly."

He hugged her waist, quick as a bird, darting away before she could hug him back. "Thank you, Meg!"

"You're welcome," she said. "Mind you share those."

He was already running and shouting over his shoulder. "I will!"

He wouldn't. She'd brought sugared violets saved from the last month of tea trays, as well as biscuits, for the other children. And dried flowers she'd twisted into circlets to wear as crowns. Winters could be long and gray, and a little art could make a difference. Her cottage had been dull as tombs before she'd taken a paintbrush to every available surface. She might not be able to eat cerulean blue, but it certainly helped the monotony of three straight weeks of boiled turnips in January.

The rest of the village children descended, shouting stories about the frogs in the pond that she had missed and the crows on the hill and the fine folk who had ridden by on horseback from her uncle's party, tossing pennies. Peter lost a tooth, Mary had found a beetle and put it in her grandmother's bed. Someone had let the pig loose and it was a great mystery never to be solved.

It was Little Agatha. It was always Little Agatha.

"Give the poor woman space to breathe," Little Agatha's father, Tom, grumbled. He added a fearsome growl that sent the children running and shrieking happily with mock fear. He bowed his head to Meg. He'd washed his hair and it was still wet, curling behind his ears.

"Miss Swift."

"Tom," she returned. She'd been asking him to call her Meg for longer than his children had been alive. "Has Mr. Hughes arrived?"

"No, but my boy just came down from the hills to say he was on his way. Wes is already here."

"Oh good, that's a relief."

She found him in the small main square, perched on a stool, his ledger in hand. It was barely more than a patch of dirt with a few cobblestones and a pub of sorts operating illegally from Old Nancy's side window. The thatched houses were sturdy, the roofs mended time and time again until they were thick as angry hedgehogs. Meg was greeted warmly and offered a stool. Someone put a cup of beer in her hand. She took a hasty sip before Mr. Hughes could arrive to disapprove.

"Well, look here, it's Herself," Wes greeted her with a grin. His black hair was wind ruffled, his cravat obligatory. Cravats were the very devil when working out of doors. Or so he told her. Often. He was a handsome man with a ready smile and strong shoulders. The village was lucky to have him; there were few people who could both put up with her uncle and endure his rubbish. "You look well."

"Thank you, as do you." The villagers were already lining up to pay him the rents. No one wanted to be left straggling when the constable arrived. And he was nearly over the hill. "Hughes is on his way."

By the time he rode his pony into view, she had set the scene, like she would have composed a painting. She sat daintily, holding Tom's youngest in her arms, who was gnawing on a stale bit of biscuit to ease his swollen gums. The sun hit the embroidery on her dress just so. She was slightly out of the way so as not to seem interfering, but perfectly situated to see Wes with his ledger. Mr. Hughes liked to stand behind him, with the villagers lined up, orderly and polite. He did not like dogs or cats or Little

Agatha's pet frog. Nor her pig. Nor her spiders. Really, he was a puzzle to the little girl.

"Ready?" Wes murmured under his breath.

Meg nodded.

"Don't let my little piglet there ruin your dress," Tom added, when soggy biscuit landed on her sleeve.

"It doesn't signify," she assured him. She tried to project an air of calm, and of the kind of mildly pretentious snobbishness she hated but which Mr. Hughes enjoyed greatly. Tom doffed his cap at her with exaggerated humility. She wrinkled her nose at him.

"Miss Swift," Mr. Hughes greeted her with a bow.

"Good morning, Mr. Hughes."

"Campbell," he said to Wes. "Everything in order?"

"Of course."

"Hmph. And what finds you in the village, Miss Swift?"

"Just visiting," Meg answered, rocking the baby. "I've been away."

"It's lucky they are to have your charity."

He would never understand that they had saved *her* often enough, leaving loaves of bread on her windowsill, bunches of foraged greens, mint for her tea. A kind word. Especially that.

"Speaking of which," she said, intending to speak of no such thing. "I was nearly caught in one the traps at the edge of the path through the woods today." She hadn't been. "I'm afraid one of the children might come to harm."

"My dear, you should not walk alone through the woods! Those traps are there to protect your uncle's lands from poachers and yourself from danger."

"Of course." If her uncle didn't want poachers stealing his pheasants and hares, he ought not charge them quite so much for quite so little of everything else. She knew those appeals would fall on deaf ears. The law was the law. Theft was theft.

She, obviously, had a slightly different view of theft.

"Perhaps you might point the traps out to me?" She asked in a whisper. "So I need not be frightened."

He patted her shoulder arrogantly. "Certainly, my dear."

Wes stifled a snort. He knew she hated to be pet like an indulged lady's pug. And he also knew she would mark each trap in her memory and tell Tom the locations so they might be avoided. "I knew I could count on you, Mr. Hughes."

The collection of the rents went as smoothly as expected: villagers lining up, Wes accepting payment and ticking off names in his ledger. Old men, fit men, widows, one after the other. Gavin was three pennies short, and Wes allowed an extension, but not without Mr. Hughes giving a condescending lecture first. He had the power to reverse Wes's extensions and so no one spoke out. They stared at their boots and waited.

"The haying left its mark this year," Tom's wife, Emmaline said, nodding to the scar on Meg's forearm. They had washed their faces in May morning dew together every year until they turned eighteen and decided they were too old for fairy stories. When she'd married Tom, he'd claimed it was the dew on her rosy cheeks that did it.

"It's not too bad," Meg shrugged. Dougal hadn't seemed to mind it.

No, don't think about that.

"My Tom there would tell you the toffs can keep their gold watches and shiny shoes, he prefers the fields and a good loaf of bread. He even likes the haying."

"And you?"

"I have three little 'uns and a powerful need for quiet. Not to mention those shiny shoes come bleedin' winter. Don't see why I shouldn't have them."

"You're turning into a revolutionary," Meg teased. "Not that I disagree, mind you."

"*Turning?* Where have you been?" She leaned against the fence behind. "Tom got all of the poetry, and I got all of the riot."

"That's true enough."

"Don't see why you're still here," Emmaline added. "You went to that ball, didn't you? Surely, someone there was good enough to marry. Better than being stuck here."

In fact, there had been someone good enough, more than good enough.

She was the one who wasn't good enough for a duke.

They watched as Mr. Hughes delivered another blistering lecture, followed by a refusal to fix the rafters of a cottage he claimed was not clean enough, even though Wes had approved it and cleanliness had nothing to do with the state of the rafters. Emmaline scowled in his direction.

He wasn't a bad sort, really, but he did her uncle's bidding, which made him not particularly a *good* sort either. Lord Henshaw was a viscount, after all, and this was his land. It had been her father's land before that, and she was a viscount's daughter besides, but there was little enough she could do. "You've got that look on your face," Tom murmured, as he joined them in the shade of the oak tree.

"I'm sure I don't know what you mean," Meg returned.

"It's the same look my Emma has now, which means trouble brewing." He sighed. "There's no sense in fighting a parish constable, but will she ever listen?"

"The Duke of Pendleton's constable is a perfectly reasonable man," Meg pointed out. "Hughes ought to be kinder."

Emmaline smiled at her, fondly, and a touch drily. "It's sweet you think so."

"You think I'm naïve." Mr. Hughes despised Emmaline because she refused "to know her place" or "mind her tongue". It went without saying that she was ten times more competent and knowledgeable than he could hope to be and that rankled most of all.

Emmaline snorted. "You've had to eat too many turnips for me to think that of you."

Meg snorted back and they were like two companionable pigs.

And then Mr. Hughes said something about tripling the rents, causing a grown man to cry and two women to boil with anger. Meg wasn't clear on the details, but it had something to do with an eviction if proper deference wasn't shown, raised rents as punishment. Tom and Meg groaned in unison as Emmaline rushed to interfere.

"He had her clapped in the stocks last time she put her nose in," Tom frowned. "I'd run in there and stop her, but then they'd both wallop me."

"When was this?" Meg demanded.

"Just last week."

"I didn't even know we had stocks."

"I think he may have had them built special, just for Emma."

"Oh dear."

Emma said something foul enough to have Mr. Hughes recoil, blanching.

"Oh dear," Meg said again.

Tom shook his head. "Better let me have my boy, there, before he spits up on you. I know that hiccup all too well. Naught to be done about my wife though."

Meg stood, still cradling the baby. "I have a better idea."

Tom sighed as though he were suddenly three hundred years old.

Little Tom opened his mouth on a wail, cheeks boiling red. "His mother's temper," his father muttered as Meg sailed into the fracas, wielding a crying, nauseous baby as her weapon.

"I'll have you in irons, madam!" Mr. Hughes roared, wiping at the dirt Emmaline's temper had kicked all over his pristine white stockings and the old-fashioned buckled shoes he was so proud of. She did have a flair for drama.

One Meg was only too happy to emulate.

Especially as Wes was trying to fit himself between them but to little avail.

Meg turned Little Tom just so and when he finally vomited, he spit up on her sleeve and dangerously, dangerously close to Mr. Hughes. He scrambled back as though it was fire, thoroughly distracted from the argument. Emmaline's mouth twitched as she fought against a smile and lost. "There, poppet. Who's a good lad?"

"Control your offspring!"

"I thought I was being hauled away to your bloody stocks?" Emmaline asked tartly, never one to give in gracefully.

"Emma," Tom said, wearily. "Please."

"Control your wife!" Mr. Hughes roared.

Before an actual war broke out, Meg turned again, keeping

the constable in the line of fire, while rubbing soothing circles on the baby's back. He was already looking better, his cries more offended than uncomfortable. She finally handed him to Emmaline once Mr. Hughes had stepped back. "Mr. Hughes, I'm sure you agree that a baby needs his mother. We should not punish this little one because a mother's love makes her a little…outspoken."

"Well, I suppose…"

"It's her nerves, you see."

"My nerves," Emmaline hissed. "Meg Swift, you—"

"And I simply cannot leave this stain to ruin my dress!" Meg continued with growing alarm.

His eyes widened in horror that ought to have been comical were he not so serious. "Miss Swift! Do let me take you back up to the Hall."

"Thank you, sir." Tom ushered Emmaline towards their cottage, soothing the disgruntled baby. Wes just shook his head and went back to sorting through the rents. Meg would hop up into the pony cart and listen to Mr. Hughes intone on various concepts. Her cheeks already ached from smiling and her neck wasn't pleased with all of the nodding. She was clearly out of practice. She hadn't had to dig for her polite smile all of the many days she'd been at the Abbey.

But as no one had been fined or put in the stocks, Meg considered the morning a success of sorts.

And then that voice she would never forget, the one that she thought she would never hear again, husky and full of the North, the one that slid over her skin and never failed to make her tingle.

"Meg."

Chapter Twenty-Four

I F IT WASN'T for Emmaline poking her head back out of her garden, eyes round, Meg would have assumed she'd imagined the voice.

But she hadn't.

Mr. Hughes was already bowing low. She turned on her heel. Dougal.

He had on the fine breeches and coat of a duke, but his cravat was simply tied. He wore no gloves, no jewelry. But the carriage behind spoke volumes. It was nearly as resplendent as the one with the broken wheel, all lacquered wood and detailed carvings. It was pulled by four horses her uncle would have sold his liver to parade through London.

"Doug—Your Grace."

Oh, how she wanted to leap on him. Simply run and throw herself right at him so he was obliged to catch her up against his chest. She swallowed hard. She knew the entire village was watching them. "What are you doing here?"

"I'm here for you," he said simply.

Unexpected joy chased all through her, like a cat after a ribbon. She was afraid she might actually start purring if he stepped any closer.

Of course, he stepped closer.

She had to tilt her head up to meet his eyes, blue as a summer sky. "You forgot something," he said.

"I did?" Him. She'd forgotten *him*.

"Me."

She blinked. Was he a mind reader, now?

"You forgot to take me with you," he continued. "Because I want to be where you are." He took her hand and though she didn't say anything, she held on tightly. His nails were neatly trimmed, his scars faded like satin. "I know I *have* to get married, and soon, but I still have a choice left. And I choose you, Meg. I will always choose you." He lifted her hands to his lips. "Please say you'll choose me back."

She hesitated. She wanted to say *yes* more than anything. She knew marriages that had succeeded with far softer of a foundation than they already had together. She wanted to chase ducks through the dining room and debutantes out of the garden.

And hadn't she just decided to leave this place?

Surely this was fate.

Dougal misread her pause.

"Is it me you object to? I know I'm not good enough for you. I was—"

"Who says you're not good enough for me?" She interrupted, outraged. She wanted very much to kiss his face and to punch whoever had put that thought into his head.

He was bewildered. "No one had to say it. It's the truth."

"It's rot," she insisted. "Utter rot. I'm the one who's not good enough for you."

Dougal barked a surprised laugh. "Get off."

"If you don't marry him, Meg, you daft cow, I will." Emmaline called out from behind the relative safety of her garden fence. Several of the other women laughed and threw Dougal appreciative glances. So did Richard, the blacksmith's apprentice. Who could blame them?

Never mind a glance, she'd been contemplating throwing her entire body at him not two minutes previous.

Not wanting the audience who was drawing closer and closer under pretext of pulling a weed, moving a stone from the road, and picking late-season cabbages that had already been picked, Meg pulled Dougal towards his carriage. Even Mr. Hughes would fall right over if he craned his neck any harder in their direction.

After asking the coachman to take them to the gatekeeper's cottage, they climbed inside, enveloped in soft quiet. Also, a thousand vines of green, red raspberries and blackberries poking between tiny leaves. Meg touched one of the tendrils painted on the ceiling. "This is nearly as opulent as the other carriage." There was a basket on the ground, filled with Jumbles, gilded almonds, vegetables. "Are those turnips?" She asked, confounded.

"You seem to hold turnip crops in high esteem," he admitted sheepishly.

She had to smile. He didn't bring roses or diamond pendants, instead he brought proof that he listened. That he cared.

"Meg, what's all this rubbish about not being good enough?" Dougal pressed. "You're a viscount's daughter. And duke or not, I was born in an alley."

She sighed a little, nervous and confused. She wanted to hold onto this dream just a little longer. "Dougal, I have no dowry."

He stared at her. Just stared. She assumed he understood her until he leaned forward abruptly. "Is that what this is about? A *dowry?*"

"Dukes don't marry women without dowries," she explained patiently, even though it ripped at her. "They just don't. And the world is already trying to tear you down."

"Hang the world."

"If only it was that simple."

"Why can't it be? You're the one who keeps pointing out that I am a duke. Why can't I use this bloody title and this bloody power to do something good?"

"My uncle lost my dowry on a series of bad wagers," she explained. "And he's been taking more and more drastic measures to try to recoup his losses. He's desperate. And frankly, really bad at cards. We are not good *ton* anymore."

"I don't care about that. I've never been good *ton.*"

"But that dowry is meant to cover the cost of what you would spend supporting me as a wife. So that nothing is taken from the estate and its people."

"We'll come back to your uncle in a minute, but devil take

your dowry."

She made a face. "He already did."

"I have more estates than I care to count. I am more than sure that they can support us all." He raised an eyebrow. "If you don't want me, love, you only have to say so."

"Of course, I want you," she blurted out. "Idiot."

"There's my Meg," he grinned for the first time. Truly grinned.

"But I have duties here," she said. "My uncle would run the village into the ground and damn the tenants. Someone has to be here to stop him, even if only a little bit."

"Something can be done."

She shook her head. "I'm afraid he's getting worse, not better." She bit her lip. "Although I admit I was planning to leave."

"Then leave with me."

"It's not that I don't want to." She *really* wanted to. "It's only that there are details to consider. I still haven't figured out how to protect everyone before I go. The maids aren't safe in that house when he has his parties, and the tenants will starve if he doesn't let up. Wallace slept in my front hall last night because he was concerned for my safety."

"I beg your pardon?" That hard tone that never failed to send inappropriate heat tingling between her legs. "We'll consider them all," he promised. "Together. Let me try. Even if you refuse me, Meg, I won't leave you at your uncle's mercies. You made sure we were taken care of before you left. You found a new housekeeper who would be kind to Charlie, saved the village from Clarke. You even left drawing supplies for George. You did all that only to come here and lay yourself down like a sacrifice for your family's tenants. Who takes care of *you*, Meg?"

The sudden sting of tears behind her eyelids took her by surprise. How could she say no when she didn't *want* to say no?

He tilted her chin up gently. "You're thinking so hard there's about to be smoke coming out of your ears." He drew her closer, slid one knee between her legs, pressing gently against her most intimate place. There was an answering throb of desire. "If I've learned one thing about the peerage, it's that they like to complicate the simplest of things."

His fingers stroked her cheek, cradling her face. He glanced down at her mouth, quirking a smile when she swayed towards him. His kiss was soft, tender. It wrapped around her like the green tendrils painted over their heads. She kissed him back hungrily until he groaned, until the carriage drew to a halt and his groan turned into a curse.

When they stepped outside, the coachman was dubious. "Here, Miss?" he asked, blinking at the little crooked cottage, sturdy enough but not quite as fearsome as it might have been two hundred years ago.

Dougal smiled at the front door, painted red as a strawberry and decorated with leaves and little white flowers and a secret spider or two. "I'd know this was your house anywhere."

She tried not to be embarrassed about her stark, oddly whimsical cottage. She knew it wasn't what he would expect. And she knew the questions it kindled. It was one of the reasons she had never invited the other Cinderellas to visit. Where would she put them? On the roof? And how would she answer their questions?

Dougal stood inside the doorway, scanning the shelves of provisions, jars of mint and lemon balm leaves for tea, apples and pears she'd nicked from the orchard, a basket of pencils and paints, the bucket set out to catch the drip from the roof. There was only one chair, a small table. And dragons painted above.

"This is where you live?"

She tried not to squirm. There was nothing to be embarrassed about. It was sparse, but also tidy. "Yes."

"It's very cozy. Charming and unexpected, just like you."

She blushed. "Thank you."

"Why don't you live in the Hall? Isn't that where you grew up?"

"It is, yes."

"But your uncle."

She wrinkled her nose. "Exactly."

Something hard flashed behind his eyes, quickly followed by determination. And something very close to vengeance.

"Meg, is there a barrister in the village?" He asked. "Or better yet, a bank?"

"Yes, though the bank is in the next town. Why?"

"I have an idea."

IT WAS SEVERAL hours later that Meg paused on the front step of her childhood house, the warm yellow stone towering above her. Dougal looked calm, as if he did battle every day. He smiled down at her when she shifted her weight from one foot to the other, hesitating. "This will work," he said softly.

"My uncle is not a… good man."

"He's a bully."

"Yes."

"Can't say I'm fond of bullies."

She had to smile. "Neither am I."

"Let's have at it then, love," he said, extending his arm as though they were about to step through into a ballroom. She placed her fingertips over his sleeve, finding comfort in his strength and the sudden grim, devil-may-care quality to his smile.

The entrance to the house was an assault on the senses, as always. Gilt glinted on every accessible surface, crown molding to frieze to the grooves of the wood wall panels. Silver gleamed, crystal flashed from a chandelier, statues crowded together. One of them wore a sort of crown, made of rough-cut rubies and pearls. Dougal was faintly baffled. "Devil's tits, it's a bit much."

"Meg, that you?" Her uncle shouted from the main drawing room. "Damn gel."

Meg tensed. Dougal glanced at her. "This is the very last time you ever have to see him, if that's what you want."

An option she had never even thought possible.

"He'll be awful to you," she warned him.

He grunted. "I can handle a toff."

In his study, Uncle Dermot reclined in his favorite chair, looking bored. Also, looking too much like her father, as ever. The color of the eyes, the shape of his nose. It hurt. It always hurt. "Fire's gone out," he snapped at Meg. A collection of diamond-studded snuffboxes lined the mantel behind him. "And the grate needs cleaning. See to it."

He was in a mood. He always set her to difficult or disagreeable tasks when he had a rotten head from a long night. She didn't mind the grates so much and had taken pains that he should never realize it. "We have a guest, Uncle," she said, mildly.

"Who's this, then?"

"The Duke of Thorncroft," she replied.

He made an effort to correct his tired slump. "A duke, eh? Welcome, welcome. Come for the party, have you? Excellent, excellent."

Dougal did not incline his head in recognition of the greeting. "I've come for your niece," he said bluntly. "We are getting married tomorrow."

Dermot laughed, until he realized no one was laughing with him. "She's got no dowry."

"I am aware."

Dermot glared at Meg. "Have you embarrassed the family?"

"That's your job, I believe," Dougal said, before she could answer. "And you appear to require no help in the matter."

Dermot stared for a long moment, trying to decide how he had been insulted in his own study and how to reply when it was a duke who was doing the insulting. "You can't marry her without my consent. And I have need of her here. She has work."

"I'm twenty-eight years old," Meg pointed out mildly. "I reached my age of majority some time ago."

And Dougal came prepared. He wore his ducal crest ring, which she had never seen him wear before. It flashed gold and garnet in the light as he held up folded parchment. "A letter from the prince. I can marry whom I like, Henshaw."

That wasn't precisely true, but Meg applauded the deception. It was effective. Her uncle snorted. "You should get yourself a duke's daughter then, not this ragamuffin."

"I like Meg."

Such a simple statement but it made her cheeks warm. She wouldn't have trusted a flamboyant declaration of love, but this she trusted: kindness, respect, affection.

"And you'll be very, very careful how you speak of her."

"You're a fool, boy, but what do I care?" Dermot snickered.

"Here's the thing, Henshaw," Dougal continued. "You might care that I now hold all of your debts."

Another simple statement that held just as much weight, though of a different sort, of course.

Her uncle turned purple, sputtered, and finally narrowed his eyes. "You're joking."

"I assure you, I am not."

"No one would go to so much trouble for a spinster," he scoffed. "Especially that bony old girl."

"You really need to stop talking." Dougal's tone snapped, sharp as hidden thorns in the blackberry bush. "As I said, I hold your debts. You will repay me every penny. A reasonable schedule will be worked out. You will also make every effort to take better care of the people in your charge, both in your house and in the village."

"Mr. Campbell is a very good land agent and knows the estate well," Meg murmured.

"Excellent," Dougal said, his attention still on Dermot. "Mr. Campbell will stay on, and you will report to him. If he does not like the speed and quality of your improvements, your debts will be collected on the very next day, in full."

"That would ruin me!"

"It will, if you don't choose wisely. Your property might be entailed but I own every candlestick and snuffbox in this house. Which seems like rather a lot. You'll start selling them to make those improvements. Today."

"And Mr. Campbell will appoint a new housekeeper and butler," Meg added hastily. "If the staff in this house do not feel safe, we will know it."

Dougal nodded. "Agreed, love."

Dermot's stunned and furious gaze slammed into Meg. "This is your fault, you bloody baggage." He stood and raised his hand to shove her, as he sometimes did in a temper.

This time, Dougal was there, and without a word he caught the other man's fist. Dermot was so surprised that his eyes bulged. No one ever moved against him in this house. He was the king of his little domain.

Dougal stepped forward, pushing him inexorably back, until he stumbled over his own feet and finally dropped heavily back into the chair. He was bright red with anger and the effects of a night of hard drinking. Dougal looked down at him, disgusted, furious. "Let me make this perfectly clear, Henshaw. You will forget Miss Swift. You will not think of her or speak of her ever again. And should I have cause to hear *your* name brought to my attention you will regret it."

"Think you're so high and mighty now, as a duke. A peasant duke, how pathetic for England."

Dougal smiled and it was terrifying. His easygoing friendly manner was all ice and the inexorable weight of stone. Meg wasn't scared of the slash of his jaw, muscles clenching in anger— she wanted to kiss it.

Her uncle, of course, had a different opinion.

He was still enraged, but also frightened. Sweat beaded his hairline, wilting his artfully tousled curls. Dougal leaned closer. "As a duke, I could murder you in your bed and not be found guilty," he pointed out calmly. "But this warning, this *promise*, is one I make to you as a man born in the back of an alley."

Dermot visibly gulped.

"Do you understand me, Henshaw?"

Dermot nodded jerkily.

"Good. Pray I don't hear your name."

Chapter Twenty-Five

MEG SENT DOUGAL a sidelong glance as they descended the steps to the drive. The carriage was already waiting, her belongings packed in three chests lashed to the roof. "You're not a murderer."

"He doesn't know that." He shrugged. "As you've said, if they are going to use my birth against me, I may as well use their own misconceptions against them."

"You were brilliant," she said. She could still hear the sound of crystal glasses smashing as her uncle had vented his spleen on the furnishings before they'd even reached the front door.

"Careful, Henshaw," Dougal had shouted over his shoulder. "Those belong to me."

The last stragglers of the party had poked their heads out of the dining room. "Is that the duke?" someone whispered.

And now here they were. Here *she* was. Free. Free to make choices about her own life. Nervous anticipation sparked under her skin.

Dougal stopped at the carriage door. He looked serious, hesitant. "Meg."

"Yes?"

"Just to be clear, I am not buying the village or your uncle's debts in order to buy you. There is no obligation between us or ever will be. I can take you anywhere you want to go. I did this to clear the way for you. But if you choose to take it in my direction,

I promise to walk beside you the rest of the way and to make you laugh every day while we do so."

"Well, really," she said, sounding miffed. "How am I supposed to resist a declaration such as that one?"

"You're not." His crooked smile was vulnerable, charming. "Please say yes."

"Yes." She touched his wrist, just below the cuff of his coat. "Take me home, Dougal."

He exhaled sharply, leaning his forehead against hers. "Thank God."

THEY STOPPED IN the village so that Meg could say her goodbyes, and also to apprise Wes of his new situation. There was a smugness to his usual friendly smile, one which Meg returned with interest. Dougal shook his hand, instead of accepting a customary bow. The etiquette was entirely wrong and Meg adored him even more for it. She was beaming like a sunflower. It was probably indecent to be this happy in public, but she didn't care.

"I have one more surprise," Dougal said later when they were settled back into the carriage.

"Another?" Meg asked. "I'm not sure I can take another."

His smile was crooked. "I thought we might be married at Pendleton Hall. Priya and Tamsin are still there visiting."

She swallowed, joy making a lump in her throat that felt suspiciously like tears. She nodded, mutely. He looked satisfied. "I had to stop there to get directions to find you. I should warn you, he already has a special marriage license with our names on it."

"He does?"

"Apparently, Lady Blackwell wrote to him from the Abbey," he said drily.

She smiled. "Did she, now." Her smile wavered. "Oh, Lord, she'll have decorated for the ceremony before we even get there. Everything will be shades of clementine and puce."

He winced. "Do you mind very much?"

She shook her head, laughing, "As long as I don't have to wear one of her wigs."

"She must have the strongest neck in all of England."

They ate biscuits and drank lemonade from the basket at their feet. Turnip leaves wilted over the side, prettier than any bouquet of perfect hothouse roses. Meg broke the companiable silence. "Have you found the treasure?"

Dougal made a face. "I'm afraid not. I've scoured the dining room but to no avail."

"We'll find it," Meg said. "I am more determined than ever."

"Will you mind sharing your house with my family and old women with spears?"

She kissed his nose. "In fact, I insist."

He claimed her before she could lean back again, one hand clasped around her waist. "The Splendid Miss Swift." He dragged his lips across her throat until her head tilted back of its own accord. The soft tickling feeling traveled down between her legs, turning into a hot aching that made her squirm. His mouth moved to the neckline of her dress, the thin muslin no challenge to his teeth and his tongue, flicking down under the line of her stays. He lifted her breast out, sucking gently, pulling, his tongue working her nipple so delicately she thought she might lose all decorum. She needed *more*.

She moved against him, pulling his shirt from his breeches so she could feel the hard planes of his stomach. There was a feverishness to her, a primal desperation. His hand was on her knee, her skirts bunched up. He traced soft patterns, like she was made of soap bubbles. She felt swollen and wet. His erection strained against her hand and she curled her palm around him. It wasn't enough.

She leaned forward, shifted until she had one knee on either side of him on the seat cushion. He sat back with a smile that challenged her to take what she wanted. "Go on then, love," he said hoarsely.

She edged forward, feeling wanton and deliciously daring. He leaned back, suddenly every inch the indolent duke. She fumbled with the placard of his breeches until she could grasp the rigid heat of him. He was silk and steel and fire. He lifted his hips slightly, releasing more fully into her palm. He was still sprawled, boots planted firmly to steady her weight. He raised an eyebrow, another challenge.

She shifted closer and then lifted up slightly, fitting him to her entrance. His eyes flared, his breath going ragged. But still he didn't move, didn't thrust up, only waited patiently. "Damn your patience," she whispered, and he smiled, up until she lowered herself onto him, inch by glorious inch. The carriage wheels went over a patch of uneven road, jostling them closer. She gasped and he hissed out a breath. She lifted again, her thighs straining and then sank down, down, deeper still. And again, and again. Sweat gathered on his throat, under her stays.

The pleasure swelled and built, just out of reach, tantalizingly close.

And even as she sat astride him, riding him for her own needs, he was so careful, holding back as if she might shatter. And she had every intention of shattering. Only she meant to take him with her. She leaned back slightly, bracing herself. The new angle lit sparks of new sensation. Dougal finally moved, his hands dipping under her dress, skimming up her thighs to the place where they were joined. He brushed her clitoris and she gasped, her breaths short and sweet. She clenched around him, and he hummed with satisfaction. "Reach for it, Meg."

The ministrations of his fingers, the rocking of the carriage and then finally he thrust up to meet her, driving her into waves of sensation. She wilted over him, trying to catch her breath. A strand of hair had come loose and stuck to her cheek. He brushed it aside.

He was still hard inside of her, and she tightened around him. He lifted his hips to drive himself deeper and then stopped. She moved against him. "Dougal."

He kissed her. "We're nearly there."

She scowled out of the window and saw that he was right. They were turning onto the long driveway. As they drove up to Pendleton Hall, Meg knew a kind of happiness she had never felt before. Even with turnips and the dirt attached filling the space with that particular green smell she knew so well. "Dougal?" she said as they put their clothing to rights.

"Yes, love?"

"May I tell you something?"

"Anything."

"I hate turnips."

TAMSIN WAS THE first to greet them when they walked up to the house. She burst out of the side gardens before Basil had even opened the door. "Meg!" She rushed in for a hug. Her red curls were caught back with a wide yellow ribbon.

Meg gestured to it. "Lady Blackwell is already here."

Tamsin grinned. "You should see the ballroom. I hope you like orange."

Meg groaned. Tamsin turned to Dougal assessingly, before flashing him the wide, toothy smile she reserved for family. "Aren't you the clever one?"

"Lady Tamsin."

"So formal," she teased, which was likely a surprise to him since he had never been accused of being formal in his entire life. She slid her arm through his. "We're family now," she said. She lowered her voice. "And your shirt is not quite tucked in at the side."

He flushed and hastily fixed it. She laughed. "Oh, we're going to have fun. But for now, say your goodbyes, because we are claiming your fiancée."

"You are?" Meg asked.

"Of course, we are," Priya agreed from the front step. Meg hugged her. Basil stood behind them, stiff as a poker by the door. They were offending his sense of decorum, as usual, by chatting on the stoop. Even if that stoop was actually a sweep of impressive steps bracketed with white pillars in the shape of Vestal Virgins. The wind was cool enough to hurry them inside, even if his judgmental sniff wasn't. Still, he softened when Tamsin grinned at him. Not enough for anyone who had not known him since childhood to notice, but enough for Tamsin. "Thank you, Basil," she said, sailing past him.

"His Grace is in the library," he said. He bowed smartly at Dougal. "Lord Thorncroft."

Dougal nodded back politely. He was already losing the ease he had around Meg, and around George and his siblings. Even around Lady Beatrice and her marzipan cannon. Meg slipped her hand into his discretely and squeezed.

"Well, here you are," Lord Pendleton boomed, when they found him digging through a new chest of antiquities. "Finally." He beamed at Dougal. "Good to see you, my boy. You made good time. I knew you could do it."

Meg and her friends shared an eyeroll.

"And you, my girl," Pendleton continued. "I told you how it should be."

"You sent me to draw Roman buttocks and find a treasure. Which I did not actually manage to find," she added, disgruntled.

"A treasure you most certainly did find," he smirked.

She kissed his cheek fondly. "You're not going to smirk at me like that the entire time, are you?

"Allow me some vindication, my dear."

They managed a few minutes of polite conversation before he drifted over to the crate again. "Oh, what a beauty," he crooned. "Straight from Egypt. Persephone sent me a crate of presents." He held up a figurine of a woman with wings and feathers in her hair.

"That's the goddess Ma'at, isn't it?" Tamsin asked, crowding by his elbow. "She weighs the hearts of the dead against a feather," she explained to the others. "And if your heart is light, you move on to Paradise."

"And if it's not?" Dougal asked, not having yet learned that to ask questions was to invite hours of lecturing and an obligatory tour of several collections.

"If it's heavy with dark deeds," Tamsin continued, brightly. "It gets devoured by a crocodile." She sounded utterly thrilled by the prospect.

"I don't remember that from church."

"Isn't it delightfully gruesome?"

"We cannot ascribe our own modern values to an ancient culture," Pendleton chided gently.

Tamsin laughed. "Eating a man's heart is gruesome no matter

where you are."

"On the Appian Way they—"

"No," Priya interrupted firmly. "Absolutely not."

Pendleton and Tamsin looked at her blankly.

"We are not spending the evening talking about bones and broken bobs and the eating of hearts. *We* are taking Meg away and *you* two can do what you like."

"But what about dinner?"

"We will have a tray sent up to my room," Priya insisted.

"Two dukes in the house and neither of us are in charge," Pendleton grumbled.

Meg, Tamsin and Priya sank into identical, perfectly synchronized, very deep curtsies, usually reserved for royalty.

"And now they mock us," Pendleton said with feigned sadness. "Off with you, termagants."

Dougal caught Meg's hand and pressed a kiss to her knuckles. It was chaste, polite. It definitely should not have reminded her of what they were doing in the carriage less than an hour ago.

But it absolutely did.

THEY FOUND LADY Blackwell in the family chapel, cheerfully bossing around a battalion of maids and footmen. Built from fieldstone in the fifteenth century, it was small and drafty but charming in its own way. It was also full to bursting with the last of the autumn flowers and every rose and lily Lady Blackwell could steal from the hothouse. Which was a considerable amount. There was even a lemon tree in one corner, already incongruous, even without the spools of pink ribbons dangling from the branches. More ribbons festooned every pew and window, as expected. The local vicar was currently being scandalized by Lady Blackwell's determination to add orange ribbons to the altar. For a touch of "cheer".

"Since we can't be in London at St. George's cathedral, I'm sure you'll agree, dear vicar, that we must do all we can to prepare the chapel."

"Lady Blackwell, this is a place of God. I assure you, it is already prepared."

Chartreuse was asleep on his back on one of the church pews, snoring softly.

"Who wants to wager she'll make him cry before the end of the day?" Tamsin whispered.

"What fool would take that bet?" Priya whispered back. "She's wearing her 'dotty old grandmother' smile. He hasn't a chance. Satan himself could not stand against her."

"Lady Blackwell," Meg hurried forward, smiling fondly. The vicar hid a sigh of relief, looking baffled. After decades in the village, he ought to have a stouter disposition. This was hardly the first time Lady Blackwell had suggested some scheme. Or the Duke of Pendleton. Or Persephone for that matter, who had once snuck a jar of beetles into the village church one Sunday morning to have them blessed. She'd read that dung beetles were sacred in ancient Egypt and thought plain old English garden beetles might suffice. No one had pressed her on to what they might "suffice" for. Meg wished her friend could join them, though she was grateful to have Priya and Tamsin at the wedding. For such short notice, it was lucky indeed.

"Meg," Lady Blackwell fluttered. "There you are."

"You've been busy. And sneaky, I hear."

"It's not sneaky to be prepared," she replied primly. "You both got on so well, I wasn't going to waste such an opportunity, nor did I think you were a featherhead to waste it either. And so, good for you, my dear."

"Thank you," Meg replied drily. "I think." Tamsin leaned too close to a flower arrangement and sneezed violently. Fair enough, there were perfume shops with less scented air. "It looks very nice in here," Meg added. "Thank you."

"You're very welcome. I'm only sorry my Percy could not be here."

"Me too."

"Ah, well, never mind. She'll be back from her travels soon enough."

"In the meantime," Priya announced. "We are stealing the bride."

"Excellent notion," Lady Blackwell approved.

The vicar looked at them pleadingly. Priya curtsied. "A good afternoon to you, Vicar," she said ruthlessly.

"And good luck!" Tamsin tossed over her shoulder, laughing. "I think the altar will look very pretty with ribbons."

His heartfelt groan woke Chartreuse, who replied with a scolding bark.

PRIYA LED THEM to Meg's usual guest chamber. Her trunks had been set in the corner and a tea tray was delivered shortly after. "The Duke of Thorncroft thought you might like something to eat," the maid explained, wheeling in a full tea tray, the kind usually reserved for drawing rooms.

It must have taken several footmen to carry it up the stairs, even before it was packed with a silver tea pot, baskets of Jumbles, pears, blackberry tarts, strong cheese, salty biscuits. She was not unaware that he had been plying her with food since he met her uncle. Well, since before then even. She knew the smile on her face was silly, even before Tamsin grinned at her. "She's besotted."

Priya waited until the maid had left before pinning her with a searching glance. "We're finally alone. You do want to marry him, don't you, Meg? Because no one is forcing you."

Meg hugged her concerned friend. "I do want to marry him," she said softly. "He's a good kind man." With a wicked tongue, she nearly added. Her cheeks warmed.

Tamsin waggled her eyebrows. "Oh, I like that blush, my friend. I like it very much. I want to hear every scandalous detail."

"There's nothing to hear."

"You are such a liar."

Meg laughed. "I thought people were supposed to be nice to a bride."

"We're very nice to brides who have no other options," Tamsin said. "Since you look like the cat who got into the cream, you owe me details. Naughty one." She tilted her head. "Is he a good kisser?"

"Yes."

"See how fast she answered, Priya?" Tamsin chortled. There was no other word for it.

Priya's stern expression finally relaxed into an answering

smile. "I'm glad for you, Meg. You should have told us your uncle was such a blackguard."

Meg shifted uncomfortably. "I thought I had it handled," she said. "And I did for the most part. But he is getting worse, there's no denying it."

Tamsin frowned. "You could have come and lived with me."

"I know," Meg said, not wanting her friends to be offended. "I had responsibilities. And I didn't want to worry you."

"Well, that's just stupid," Tamsin declared. "That's what friends are for. Cinderellas, especially."

"I know. I'm sorry."

She huffed, relenting. "But you *are* happy? Truly?"

Meg nodded. "Truly. We make each other laugh. And I like his family."

"Better and better. I don't even like *my* family most of the time." Tamsin's father had washed his hands of his only daughter the day he married his second wife. And when she'd given birth to a son, Tamsin may as well have moved to Australia.

"In that case," Priya said. "It's time to choose your wedding dress." Meg started towards her trunks, but Priya stopped her. "Tamsin and I already brought you some of our dresses and my lady's maid has agreed to alter your choice before morning."

"But I have dresses."

Priya and Tamsin exchanged a speaking glance. "You can't get married in a dress with a hole in the sleeve, no matter how exquisite your embroidery might be. You deserve something *special*."

"Oh, I really couldn't," Meg said, when Tamsin opened the wardrobe, hanging with beautiful dresses. "I can't ask your lady's maid to stay up all night sewing."

Priya rolled her eyes. "It will take her an hour or two at most. She's very skilled in needlework and hostage negotiations. She's getting a week's vacation when we get back to London and a trip to Gunter's for ices." She raised her brows, going in for the kill. "It's that or one of the gowns Lady Blackwell sent over. With matching wigs."

"I would *love* to wear one of your dresses."

Chapter Twenty-Six

THE BRIDE WORE blue. Meg chose one of Tamsin's dresses and spent most of the evening embroidering a Tudor knot like a Jumble biscuit in the center of the bodice. She borrowed white lace gloves with matching blue ribbons and wove a crown of flowers stolen from the hothouse at one o'clock in the morning, along with her two half-drunk bridesmaids. She woke with a mildly bleary head and a tonic sent up with her tea by Lady Blackwell. Chartreuse wore his best gold collar and was very handsome.

Meg had to suppress the inappropriate urge to giggle all the way down the aisle. She had never thought she would have this day, and certainly not with a man such as Dougal Black, Duke of Thorncroft. He stood at the end of the chapel, waiting for her. He was patient and so handsome in his simple cravat and paisley embroidered waistcoat, but she could see the glimmer in his blue eyes. He had held out his arm when she approached, escorted by the Duke of Pendleton, who was openly weeping happy tears.

The vicar had put his foot down and there were no ribbons on the altar. He no doubt wished he had reacted differently when he spotted the ribbons tied around the neck of the original Medieval carvings of the baby Jesus and Mary.

To Meg, it was all perfect, down to Chartreuse being whisked outside by a footman when he lifted his hind leg to bless the vicar's left shoe.

They spoke their vows, exchanged simple rings, and shared a wedding supper with the others. Seeing as they had a special license along with a special dispensation, they did not have to marry before eight o'clock in the morning and chose a more civilized afternoon ceremony. There was plenty of champagne to go with the roast lamb, cucumber salad, thin slices of ham, trout, potatoes and apples fried together, followed by poached pears drizzled with cream and honey.

As night fell, the Duke of Pendleton gave one last toast and send them off to the privacy of the Dowager cottage, which had been cleaned and filled with flowers and beeswax candles. A cold rain tapped at the windows and Meg was encased in a warm cocoon gilded by firelight. Priya's lady's maid came to help her out of her dress and her stays, leaving her in her chemise. After she'd left, Meg found a package wrapped in paper on the edge of the bed with her name on it. It was from Lady Blackwell and took her love of ribbons to an entirely different level. Meg unwrapped a nightgown of white muslin so thin as to be transparent, edged with soft lace and held together mostly with wide satin ribbons, all in a bright strawberry red. She ducked behind the decorated screen (painted with ducks, one of whom had three legs) and slipped it on.

She could hear Dougal moving around, removing his coat, pouring port into small crystal glasses. She was excited, happy, and inexplicably shy as she stepped out wearing what felt like very little. Dougal caught sight of her and paused, glass halfway raised. His eyes flared.

Very little indeed.

SHE WAS GOING to be the very death of him.

It would be a happy death but still. Dead on his wedding night.

Meg had taken her hair down and brushed it so that it fell over one shoulder. Her toes were bare, pink as seashells under her hem. She wore what could only be described as a veil held together with ribbons and delicate stitches he longed to tear apart with his teeth.

He forced air through his nostrils and into his lungs. She was a gentlewoman. He would be gentle, courteous. Slow.

Even if it killed him.

Something in his frozen reaction had her smiling a smile he'd never seen before. Naughty. And when she stepped closer there was a definite sauciness to the sway of her hips.

It was definitely going to kill him.

"May I have some?" she asked, when he'd stood there silent as a lump of dirt for too long. He hastened to hand her the port he had already poured for her. She took a sip, licking her lower lip. He hardened in response. His balls tingled. They actually *tingled.*

He'd been told that aristocrats did not lust after their own wives. It was considered gauche.

Fools.

"Meg." His voice was hoarse. He barely sounded like himself. He cleared his throat. "You look beautiful."

"Thank you, Your Grace."

"Don't start that, Your Grace."

She laughed a little. "I'd forgotten."

"That you were a duchess?"

"Yes." She put her glass down and turned to him, all bare skin and red ribbons. He suddenly felt hunted. Haunted by her. He would take this slow and give her the wedding night she deserved no matter the cost to his sanity. He had not courted her properly; he could at least give her this. Candles and soft caresses and gentle kisses.

"I only wanted to be your wife."

He groaned, utterly undone and he hadn't even touched her yet. That at least he could rectify. Posthaste. He reached for her, palms smoothing over her shoulders, down her arms and then back up to cradle her face. "Lady Thorncroft."

Her breath quivered as she looked up at him. He lowered his head to kiss her, brushing his lips over hers, nipping lightly at her lower lip, drawing it out so that he wouldn't grab her with his scarred hands, wouldn't maul her like a bear. He licked into her mouth until they were breathing ragged, until his cock strained painfully against his breeches.

He was so gentle she thought she might scream.

If he didn't hurry up, she might very well lose her sanity. He was holding back, touching her as if she was breakable. Heat coiled inside her, desperate for that last spark, desperate for *him*. All of him.

"Dougal," she said. "You don't have to be afraid to touch me. I thought we made that clear in the hothouse. And in your bed. The carriage."

"I'm not afraid," he said, perplexed. There was a fine sheen of sweat over his sculpted shoulders, tension in his jaw. "But you're a lady. You deserve..." he waved his hand as if he couldn't find the right words. "You know. Especially from someone like me."

She stared at him. "Is that what this is about? I thought we'd sorted that out already. You are more than good enough for me, Dougal. And hang anyone who says differently because of where you were born. You outrank most of them anyway."

"You're precious, Meg. Special."

"But I'm not delicate," she insisted. "And I don't need a duke or a pedestal. I need *you*."

She held her breath as she seemed to struggle with some internal battle.

And then he was Dougal Black. *Her* Dougal. Not a duke.

A husband.

A man finally shrugging off constraints he'd never agreed to.

And it was delicious.

He stalked towards her with single minded purpose, desire etched into every line of his face, every muscle of his chest and his thighs, until her breath hitched. And then his hands were on her and they weren't decorous or polite. They were warm and big and scarred, and he knew exactly what to do with them. He yanked her against his body, his erection pressing just above her sex, teasing, promising.

"Is this what you want, Meg?" he asked, lips tickling her ear. It sent tingles shooting everywhere. The tiny hairs on the back of her neck prickled, with desire and something more primal. "Answer me," he prodded, biting down on her earlobe.

She nodded jerkily, pleasure spearing through her and stealing her ability to speak.

"I want to hear you say it," he insisted, teeth scraping down her neck in an open-mouthed kiss. He sucked at her collarbone, and she gasped. Warmth kindled between her legs and a long liquid pull of pure lust. He pulled back, denying her. Cool air snuck between them. She made a sound of protest. A small, embarrassing sound of neediness. He looked down at her, every inch a duke, though he'd never admit it. Power and confidence emanated from him. He wrapped her long hair around his hand and tugged. "Say it."

"It's what I want." She swallowed. "Your Grace."

His voice was in her ear again, rough, silky. "Then it's exactly what you'll get."

He stalked her across the room in three steps, pushing her against the wall. She was grateful for that wall. She might have melted entirely without its support. Her knees had turned soft, her thighs hot and loose. Nervous energy prickled through her and she loved every zap. He still had his one hand in her hair, but now his other hand lowered to graze her intimately. A soft caress, a tease. She tried to get closer. He tugged on her hair again, immobilizing her. For a long moment they just looked at each other.

And then he pushed a finger deep inside her and she arched, gasping. He followed with a second finger, crooking them slightly, pulling them out just enough to have her whining, plunging them back into her heat. Again and again until her toes curled, until she gripped his arms, until he kissed her, his tongue invading her mouth with the same rhythm. Pleasure coiled, started to nip through her, started to build. She was nearly there, it would sweep her away—

And then he stopped.

Her eyes flew open.

He smirked at her.

She caught her breath. "You—"

She didn't have a chance to scold him, to beg, to chase the climax. He'd already swung her around, pushing her onto the bed. She landed with a soft bounce, and he towered over her, hot gaze raking her from toes to nose. "Dougal."

He was so handsome, bare chest gilded by fire, breeches hung low, displaying the dip of muscles, the dark hair. She wanted to sketch him with her mouth. "Dougal, please."

He moved up her body, gliding his fingers up her leg. She wanted him closer, wanted to touch him everywhere. He dipped his head to kiss the inside of her thigh, to nibble over her hip bone. He looked up at her from between her legs, blue eyes bright in the candlelight. And because he was Dougal, his voice gentled, his gaze went serious. "When you want anything to stop you only have to say so."

She nodded, affection twining with the desire flooding through her. He bit the inside of her thigh and she jerked. "Say it," he insisted, a dictatorial tone winding through his words. It did something to her. Heat tangled her tongue, hazed her brain.

"If I want you to stop, I only have to say it." She was nearly panting. He was so close, his mouth hovering above her, breath tickling her triangle of hair. "Don't stop, don't stop."

And then he was on her, feasting, licking lazily across her petals, swiping his tongue inside, teasing all around her clitoris. When she writhed nearly out of reach, his arm came down across her belly, pinning her in place. "Ah, ah," he scolded, deep voice rumbling over her mound. She twitched, full of sensation she didn't know what to do with. He finally sucked her bud into his mouth, rolling his tongue over it, lapping at it with a focused pace that did not waver, until she was moaning and gasping. He drew her with inexorable patience into the crescendo and it swept through her, so powerful as to tread the line between pain and pleasure.

When she was finally able to open her eyes, he was grinning up at her. "I will never tire of those sounds."

She blushed. Or she thought she blushed. She wasn't sure she was even capable of that. A feeling of sweet, deep peace flooded in after the waves of pleasure. He kicked off his breeches and crawled up her body and she discovered she had the energy after all.

Lots of energy, in fact.

She reached for him with her hands and her mouth and every part of her that could press against him. His breath stuttered when she closed her fingers over his shaft, stroking up and over the head. He was soft skin over hard flesh. His breathing turned harsher, and she reveled in it. She licked him from base to tip and he groaned. She licked him again and again, finally drawing him fully into her mouth. She sucked him as he had sucked at her, fluttering her tongue up the underside.

He grasped her shoulder and hauled her up. "I need to be inside of you. *Now.*"

He didn't turn her onto her back again as she'd expected, but maneuvered her so that she was kneeling, legs on either side of him. He coaxed her down and she took him inside inch by inch until she was sitting astride him. The angle brought a new level of feeling. He stroked up her rib cage to cup her breasts and she fell slightly forward. Her hair curtained them both, creating another cocoon within a cocoon. He held her up as she began to move, moaning at the intimate friction, sliding down to rub her clitoris. She hadn't known she could have two orgasms in one night, but there it was, building, building.

She rocked back and forth, taking him deeper still. He pushed up and the pressure, the angle of the thrust, his half-smile, his ragged breath, all fired through her until the orgasm stole her voice. She could only moan, head thrown back, as he thrust up again, groaning, panting and then pulled out, just as he came with a hoarse growl.

He tucked her against his side as their heartbeats slowed back down to normal. She touched the tip of her nose to his shoulder. He smelled like cedar again, and smoke. "You don't have to do that anymore, you know. Pull out I mean. We *are* married now."

He glanced at her. "Do you mind?"

"No."

"It's not that I don't want children someday," he said. "But your uncle has been starving you for years. I'd rather you had a chance to get healthy."

"It wasn't that bad," she said, through the soft glow she

thought might be emanating from her every pore.

He snorted, clearly disagreeing. Instead of saying anything else about it, he wet a towel and cleaned them both up. She was pleasantly sore, her thighs pink from the grain of his beard growing in. He brought her more tea, strong and sweet just how she liked it, as well as slices of pears and apples and fresh brown bread with butter and a hunk of honeycomb in a jar.

"You don't have to keep feeding me," she protested, though she loved it.

"Don't I?" He licked a drop of honey off of his thumb and she came very close to purring in response. The line of his throat, his shoulders, the hard planes of his stomach were more delicious than any dessert.

"You need your energy," he continued, his eyes flaring at her perusal and frank approval. "By my estimation there are many hours until morning and I intend to make good use of them."

Chapter Twenty-Seven

M EG SAT UP with a start, the sunlight streaming through the lace curtains onto the bed. Sprawled beside her, Dougal opened one eye.

"I've just had an idea," she said. She'd been dreaming about the treasure, about pirate girls running through the Abbey, spite and freedom in their veins. About angry fathers, rules and decorum. Treasure hunters with knives, rumors about gold coins, dried flowers inside the walls. Stars.

Treasure maps.

Dougal pushed up onto one elbow. "Should I be worried?"

She grinned. "I know who to ask about Dahlia." She scrambled out of the bed. "We need to get home."

He smiled softly. "I like to hear you call it home."

She kissed him quickly. "Hurry!"

Instead, he pulled her back down into the bed and covered her with his body until she was writhing and panting and moaning.

All in all, a perfectly acceptable delay.

It took no time at all to pack the carriage, and a little more time to take their leave. The duke would not hear of them leaving without luncheon, seeing as they had slept through breakfast. And most of the morning. And then there were hugs to be passed between the Cinderellas, and cubes of cheese to feed Chartreuse when he pouted.

It was early afternoon by the time they set out in the leafy carriage. Meg touched the vines. "I truly do feel like a Cinderella," she murmured. "I married my prince and I am traveling home in a pumpkin."

Dougal kissed her and pulled her against his side. It wasn't long before she drifted off, and he followed suit. They woke to the flash of the ocean on the other side of the window. "I know we should greet your family first," Meg said. "But do you mind if we stop in Perchance-By-The-Sea first?"

He nuzzled her cheek. "Are you craving a strawberry ice?" he asked. "Because I know exactly where I would like to eat one off of you."

"No, I..." she trailed off. "We're definitely coming back to that."

Dougal had the coachman detour through the town. He'd grown up there, as had his mother and his mother's mother. He knew exactly where to take them.

"It's something the constable said when that treasure hunter broke into the abbey," Meg explained. "That the old duke had such a bad temper the workmen were called in to fix the damage often enough to bear mentioning. So, it got me to thinking. Lady Marigold was away at school and there are probably only a few people still alive who remember Dahlia. But what if one of them was still in the village?"

"Such as?"

"Such as the plasterer who would have been called in to fix the hole from the duke's fit of temper, at any time, but especially on the last night Dahlia was ever home. We know they fought and that he threw things when he was angry."

He nodded slowly. "She definitely could have moved the treasure there, just to spite him. If she hadn't already."

"To show him he was not stronger, just because he was *physically* stronger." She'd have done the same to her uncle, had the opportunity arisen.

"Those treasure hunters have nothing on you," he said fondly.

"It's just a theory." She preened just a little. She couldn't help herself.

The coachman stopped in front of a small cottage off the main street of the town. "You want Old Atkins," he told them. "He lives just yonder. He's ninety if he's a day, mind."

The cottage had a cheerful green door and seashells placed in the rows into the plaster around the door and the short wall out front. A face appeared at the window. A man with a shock of white hair squinted at them. He came to the door and yanked it open before Meg could knock.

"Good evening," she said. "We're sorry to disturb you."

The old man blinked at the carriage. "You must be the new duke," he said to Dougal.

"I am. And this is my duchess."

"I always did think that carriage was ridiculous."

"Da!" A woman nudged him aside, half-amused, half-horrified. "What a thing to say to his lordship. I'm sorry, Your Grace."

Meg swallowed. Suddenly just hearing "Your Grace" made her feel warm all over now. As if Dougal was still gripping her hair, was still issuing sensual demands. He slid her a knowing glance out of the corner of his eye. She absolutely refused to meet his gaze. Duchesses probably shouldn't stand on someone's front porch squirming and giggling.

"That's quite all right," he told Atkins. "I'm not fond of the carriage myself."

"I think it's very pretty," Atkins' daughter said. "How can we help you, Your Grace?"

"We have some questions about the abbey," Meg said. "And I was told Mr. Atkins was the one to ask seeing as he'd done all the best work inside the house." A little flattery never went amiss.

Atkins puffed his chest out. "You'd be hearing right."

His daughter's smile was wry. "Won't you come in?"

"We're so sorry to intrude," Meg said again, as they followed her inside. A fire crackled in the hearth, and a cat slept in the rocking chair beside it. "We won't be long."

"Not often we have a duchess here," Atkins said, still gruff but chuffed with himself. He scooped up the cat. "Up you get,

Mittens. You're not the highest-ranking lady in the house anymore."

Meg sat because it clearly pleased him to offer her the chair. His daughter, who said her name was Alice, brought them small beer. "I'm sorry we don't have tea to offer you," she fretted. "But it's my own brew."

Dougal took a hearty sip and sighed with true enjoyment. "I can't tell you how I've been missing a good beer," he assured her.

"Now what's this about the abbey?" Atkins said. "It's not the frieze in the music room again, is it? I told them not to use that kind of glue."

"No," Meg assured him. "It's not that. We only wondered about the history of the house. Did you ever meet the Lady Dahlia, for instance?"

"Not much call for a duke's daughter to talk to a workman. Still, everyone knew she loved the ocean. The only one surprised she turned privateer was her father."

"We were told she did not get on with him."

"No one got on with that one. He was a right blighter."

Alice sighed. "*Da.*"

"Well, he was. And he's dead now, what twenty years at least? What does he care what I have to say about him? If he wanted kind words, he ought to have paid me my full wages."

"I can't argue with that," Dougal said.

Atkins gave a little triumphant "hah" in his daughter's direction.

"He kept me in work, when he bothered to pay us," Atkins allowed. "He made more holes in the walls than anyone I've met. Throwing things, throwing punches."

Something tickled the back of Meg's brain.

"Had artists going through the abbey on a regular basis to fix up the murals he'd damaged."

The tickle in Meg's brain intensified. She stood up abruptly. The treasure wasn't hidden in the ceiling or under the floor.

It was in the wall. It had to be.

Never mind that the dining room ran the length of the abbey and there were more walls than most houses.

"Mr. Atkins, would you be able to make a list of the holes you were asked to mend?"

He scratched his face. "Can't say as I could remember them all."

She refused to give into the disappointment. "I see."

He shifted on the bench, worried to have possibly upset her. He knocked over his beer, and a jar of ointment. The strong acrid smell of camphor and lavender burned their nostrils.

"Da, careful." Alice scooped up the ointment. "It's his arthritic cream," she explained apologetically. It put Meg in mind of something, but she wasn't sure what. A memory just out of reach. Someone's perfume? Maybe Lady Blackwell had a similar cream, though she'd never admit it. "Have more beer, it will mask the smell."

"Don't have arthritis," Atkins insisted, holding up his gnarled, twisted fingers. "Just proof I did good work."

"I've never seen anything like the abbey," Meg said, ignoring Dougal's snort. She tried a different tactic. "Were you the one called in after Lady Dahlia left the house for the last time?"

"In fact, I was."

Victory sparked through her, premature or not. "I hear there was a row."

"Such a one as you ever did see, if the damage was anything to go by. He was a toddler, that one."

"*Da.*"

"Bah. Never mind that, Allie. You should have seen what he did to the dining room."

Meg and Dougal exchanged a glance. "What did he do?"

"Put holes in every mural, didn't he? Took me a week just to fill them all. Except for one, which Lady Dahlia asked to fix herself. Odd that."

Meg leaned forward. Dougal put down his beer. "Do you remember which one?"

"Which one what?"

"Which hole Lady Dahlia did not want you to fix."

"Lady Dahlia," he sighed. "Now she was a hoyden."

Alice sighed too. She lowered her voice. "I'm afraid my father's memory isn't what it used to be. He wanders."

"I'm fine," he barked.

"I know, Da."

"'Twas the west wall, somewhere," he added. "She told me about green flashes over the sea."

Alice's eyes widened. "She did?"

"Aye."

Meg smiled. "Thank you, Mr. Atkins. You've been most helpful."

"He has?" Alice asked.

"I have," Atkins confirmed, though it was clear he wasn't quite sure *how* he had helped.

"We have a riddle," Meg confessed. "And it led us to the dining room but no closer. I think your father may have helped us more than I can say!" She was already on her feet. "Sorry to have disturbed your supper!" Meg tossed over her shoulder. She was halfway out the door and Dougal gave Atkins and his daughter a hasty nod and followed. A storm had blown in off the water. Rain spattered, heavy and wide as silver coins.

By the time he'd reached the carriage, Meg was already seated and urging the coachman to drive on if the duke insisted on taking such a leisurely pace. Dougal hadn't even shut the door behind him when the horses began to walk, the clip clop of their hooves loud in the quiet town. Most everyone was inside, candles burning at the windows. The sound of the sea snuck between the houses, barred from no door, no house, no carriage. The storm followed, intensifying.

Meg was vibrating like a wheel about to fly off its axel.

"I take it Atkins solved the riddle for you and if I hadn't snatched you up, you'd be marrying him instead?" Dougal asked drily.

"One of the murals is more damaged than the others. And it wasn't repaired terribly well."

"And you're not going to tell me which one it is, are you?"

"I..." She blinked slowly. "Dougal, I don't feel at all the thing."

"What's wrong...." he trailed off, reaching for her but moving slowly, as though he'd been dipped in honey. Meg swallowed. The beer had left an odd taste in the back of her throat. She wanted to ask Dougal about it but he had already slumped to the side.

She would have been concerned, but everything seemed to melt and then went black.

Chapter Twenty-Eight

T HE COACHMAN WAS loathe to disturb them and waited for three quarters of hour, despite the cold wind buffeting them and the darkness spilling like ink all around. When newlyweds did not choose to exit the carriage, every driver knew better than to poke their head in. He went into the stables for a change of clothes and a drink.

But eventually the storm crashed down harder, sputtering the torches burning along the drive and around the front door. Candles spilled warm honey light into the frozen gardens. The coachman could not feel his hands or his nose. His greatcoat dripped rivers of water when he knocked on the carriage door. "Your Grace?"

No response. Not a bark or a giggle or a hand pressed to the window. Worry gnawed at him, and he finally yanked the door open.

That was what woke Meg, the sudden onslaught of wind and cold rain. Dougal sat up abruptly, then groaned clasping his head. He squinted at the coachman, while leaning to block Meg with his body. "What the bloody hell?"

The coachman was confused. "Your Grace, we arrived some time ago but you did not respond."

He rubbed his face, then froze. He licked his lips. "There was laudanum in the beer."

Meg sat up slowly, making sure her stomach did not push up

into her throat or her eyeballs fall out of their sockets. She felt drowsy, heavy, but not ill. "Is that what that taste was?"

"She drugged us," Dougal said. "Alice Atkins." He reached for the lemonade bottle still in the picnic hamper behind them and handed it to Meg. "This should wash the taste out."

"I've never taken laudanum," she replied, sipping slowly. "I don't think I care for it. Or for her." Her eyes widened in horror. "I told her we had a riddle."

"It likely saved our lives," Dougal said. "She'd have wanted to hedge her bets." He peered carefully into her eyes. "Your pupils aren't pinpoints. You'll recover." He helped her out of the carriage. "Can you stand?"

She took a deep breath. "Yes, I think so. How do you know so much about laudanum?"

"Work in a mill can be miserable," he said. "The fibers get into your lungs." He didn't elaborate. "Has anyone come by?" he asked the coachman.

"I was in the stables, so I'm not sure, Your Grace. No carriages, at least."

"No, she wouldn't have a carriage, would she."

"The weather is too wild for her to have walked all the way here," Meg said. "She'll likely try later. We have time to find the treasure before she does."

"You should rest first."

"Not a chance."

Dougal escorted her carefully to the front door, though he was not entirely steady on his own feet. They held each other up until the rain revived the last of Meg's weary brain. She tilted her head back, letting the cold wind and water do its work.

Canterbury opened the front door. "Do you mean to drown yourself, lass?"

They ducked inside, thunder chasing them like an ill-tempered cat, sneaking around their ankles and biting at them with jagged teeth of light. "We weren't expecting you, Your Grace."

"Your Graces," Dougal corrected.

Canterbury's smile widened. "It's that happy I am to hear it.

Everyone in the servant hall has sat down to supper but I'll get them moving in no time."

"Finish your meal," Meg said. "We can wait."

"Oh, but—"

Dougal shook his head. Meg was already hastening away, pulling him along behind her. "We'll wait. But keep an eye out for housebreakers tonight."

The house was quiet, except for the rattling of the windows. The others must be taking their meals in their rooms. The painted horses and hares and countless stars escorted them down the hall. Meg had to stop herself from bouncing on her toes. She wasn't sure her stomach could handle the extra movement, but she couldn't get to the dining room fast enough.

Or at all, as it happened.

They spotted George standing just inside the door to the Gold Parlor. Dougal frowned. "George, what are—"

George turned his head, motioning them away but it was too late.

"I'd hoped the laudanum would buy me more time."

Meg froze. Tension coiled through Dougal.

Alice Atkins had beat them back to the abbey.

They stepped carefully inside the room, Dougal keeping Meg securely behind him with an outstretched arm. She felt the muscles in his arm harden before she saw the reasons why. George's left eye was red and swelling rapidly. Alice stood on the black-and-gold carpet, hand clamped savagely around Charlie's throat and pinning her wrist at a ruthless angle behind her back. Charlie looked spitting mad. Alice was eerily calm, dripping with rainwater. Her skirts were soaked, her hair plastered to her head.

"You'll want to let go of my sister," Dougal said, very evenly.

"Not until I get what I want."

Charlie hissed and pulled on her arm, only stopping when tears of pain sprang to her eyes. Dougal took another step forward. Alice tightened her hold on her throat until she squeaked. "I want the treasure, Thorncroft. It's mine. I've worked hard for it."

"You already know we don't have it," Dougal said. "But take

whatever else you want. Empty the damn house, I don't give a damn. Just let my sister go."

"Oh, I don't think I will. Not yet," she replied with a smile that could only be described as disturbing. "You might not have it, but you have Lady Dahlia's clues. So, now we're going to find it. Finally."

"That's why you drugged us? For the treasure?"

"Couldn't have you racing ahead of me, now could I? My father never mentioned the west wall before tonight. And I've been searching the dining room for weeks."

Meg's mouth dropped open. "You were the one I chased out of the window. That iron candelabra didn't fall into the wall accidentally, did it?"

"Of course not."

"And the lavender cream," Meg continued, the pieces snapping together. "You set the fire. That's why it smelled like lavender, and why we smell it on you now. It wasn't the dried flowers. It was your father's arthritic cream."

"He needs it," she spat. "And so many more medicines. You have no idea how expensive they are."

"Why burn down the music room?" Charlie squeaked.

"Because it's the furthest one from the dining room," Dougal replied. "Isn't that right? It got the household out of your way for a few hours."

"Yes. So you know I'm serious." She squeezed again and Charlie's cheeks went pale, her breath stuttering. "Now enough chatter. I'll have what I came for. Don't make me say it again."

"Stop," Meg begged, making sure the fury inside her did not touch her voice. She wanted to eviscerate her. But she knew the type. She'd get further with calm, honeyed words, however false and however they burned inside her mouth. Her uncle had trained her for this particular kind of person. "Please let her go and you and I will go to the dining room."

"We'll all go," Alice said, but she did soften her hold, however slightly. The storm lashed at the house. They could scream for help but no one in the servants' hall would hear them. They outnumbered Alice and could well attack together, but not before she could hurt Charlie, possibly fatally. She might crush her windpipe or snap her neck. Meg could see the exact moment Dougal gave into the inevitable. He was no less on guard, but he'd already moved ahead to some other plan. Alice assumed he'd given up. That she knew how dukes acted.

Not this duke.

Dougal turned, dipping his head towards Meg. *"Run,"* he whispered urgently.

"Like hell," she whispered back. She might have done it, though, if only to gain some other advantage, some way to return armed to the teeth.

"Everyone stays where I can see them," Alice demanded. "Now, move."

They filed down the hall, Charlie stifling small noises of pain.

"The west wall is still a hundred feet long," Dougal said. "Let my sister go. This will take some time."

"Then you'd best get started."

They'd reached the dining room. "Let me go in and light the candles," Meg said. She didn't know what advantage she could glean from it, but it was worth a try. Anything to keep focus on her instead of Charlie.

And then it didn't matter anymore.

Without a sound of warning, Lady Beatrice was suddenly there.

Not just there but hurling herself forward with her spear outstretched. She knocked Alice hard in the middle of her back. She gave a cry of shock and outrage and not a little pain. Her hold on Charlie slackened and Charlie threw herself to the side. Dougal grabbed her, hauling her to safety. Alice was on her knees, struggling to catch her breath. Lady Beatrice proceeded to hit her again, this time on the head with the spear. Hard.

She toppled like a felled tree. Lady Beatrice glared down her nose. "That wasn't very graceful."

Dougal hadn't let go of Charlie. "Are you all right?" he asked.

"She'll be bruised come morning," George said before she could reply, after examining her throat.

"You're already bruised," she returned, her voice raspy. She turned to Lady Beatrice. "You saved me."

"Well, of course I did," the older lady said.

"I'll call for the doctor," Dougal said.

"Bah," Lady Beatrice waved that away. "You don't need him, you just need some ice and some tea with honey. And ice and arnica for George's eye. I'll see to it."

"Dealt with a lot of strangulations, have you?" Dougal asked.

"I have a variety of interests," she shot back primly before marching away as though she hadn't just knocked a woman unconscious.

"Would you have coffee sent up? Meg and I were drugged and I admit the room is spinning a little."

"You were?" Charlie's eyes widened. "It is?"

"Laudanum. We'll be fine. We didn't drink enough of the doctored beer to harm us."

"Lady Beatrice might have killed her," George shook his head.

"Better luck next time," Meg muttered.

Charlie grinned at her and then at her brother. "You brought her home."

"I said I would, didn't I? "He grinned back. "Where's Colin?"

"In the village, chasing women, where else?"

"Thank God for that."

Charlie glared at Alice. "Who is she anyway?"

"The daughter of the workman Lady Dahlia asked to help her with a hole in the wall," Meg explained. "He remembered it was in the dining room but nothing else. He'd mended almost every inch of this room at one time or another, I think. And he is rather old now."

"She's been one of the treasure hunters this whole time?"

"One of the debutantes too, I'd wager," Meg said. "I think she was searching for some time. A new duke and then Lord Eaton's public reward for the treasure must have messed with her plans."

"Good. I'd like to mess with her face," Charlie muttered. No one mentioned manners or decorum or forgiveness.

"What should we do with her?" George asked.

"Tie her up and call the constable, I suppose," Dougal said.

"Same as with the last treasure hunter. Though I'd rather toss this one in the ocean and be done with it."

"This does seem to be a habit." Meg touched his cheek. "And you're still not a murderer. Especially of women."

"All the same, it ends now," he returned grimly. "Even if I have to take this bloody room apart piece by piece to find that bloody treasure and parade it through London."

Meg glanced inside. "It looks like you've already started." The floorboards under the window had been pried loose and left in a haphazard pile. "What on earth happened in here?"

"Dougal happened," Charlie told her. "He didn't like it when you left."

"Shut it, brat," Dougal pulled her hair lightly. "Anyway, we don't need brute force. We have Meg."

They looked at her with such confidence that a lump formed in her throat. The last vestiges of laudanum didn't help. She wondered if it made a person teary. Before she could think of what to say, footsteps thundered down the hall towards them. Canterbury was in the lead, brandishing an iron frying pan. "Where's the intruder!"

"I see Lady Beatrice reached the kitchen." Dougal stepped aside to show Alice's sprawled body. Canterbury did not lower his frying pan. "I hear she attacked Lady Charlie. Can I cosh her one more time?"

Charlie beamed. "You'd do that for me? Cosh a lady?"

He frowned at her hoarseness. "'Course I would."

"You're my favorite butler."

"Bind her and gag her," Dougal ordered, scowling down at Alice. "Send for the constable but don't leave her alone for even a second. She's devious."

"You can use my spear, as long as you bring it back," Lady Beatrice shoved her way through the crowd and placed a handkerchief of ice against George's eye with surprisingly gentle care. She nudged Charlie inside the dining room and into a chair, thrusting a cup of tea in her hands. "Drink this. Mrs. Cricket is preparing a vinegar poultice."

"I'm not drinking vinegar."

"For your bruises. But Mrs. Cricket has nine children and has seen every kind of mishap. If she tells you to drink vinegar, you'll drink it, my girl." She stroked Charlie's hair, like a grandmother would before drawing back abruptly. "I'd best see to Marigold. She doesn't care for theatrics. They don't suit her digestion."

"Will they prosecute her?" George asked dubiously as the footman lifted Alice. She moaned.

"For housebreaking, setting a fire, drugging a duke and duchess, and attempting to murder a duke's sister?" Meg said. "I should think so."

"And if they don't, she'll find herself transported soon enough," Dougal promised. "I'll see to it." He bowed to Meg, an exaggerated courtly bow that made her smile. "Your turn, my lady."

She stepped further into the dining room as Dougal lit every candle he could find. The painted stars shone above, the trees and the flowers and Pan with his naughty wink.

"Seven shells for your boat," she recited. "And seven roses for your coat. Those clues brought us into this room. Seven stars for your wrath is trickier, because this entire house is full of stars." She approached the mural she had worked on so determinedly. "But the part about wrath made me think about the old duke's temper. Atkins confirmed that he had plasterers and artists up to the house on a regular basis to the fix the damage, and himself the night Lady Dahlia ran away. Another hole in the wall might have escaped notice, at least for a little while."

"Atkins remembered the west wall, if not where exactly." She tilted her head. "When I was working on this mural, after the housebreaker, well, Alice, I suppose, meddled with it, I noticed a whole section as very badly plastered." She dragged her fingertips over the painting. "This whole section. It's still too much to smash through though." She smiled at George. "A flash of green when day turns to night. As George said, green flashes happen on the horizon in the Islands. Dahlia would have seen them regularly."

She wiped away years of soot with a handkerchief. When it wasn't enough, she used some of the vinegar water Mrs. Cricket had brought up with Charlie's poultice. Just a little, not enough to damage the paint. "I need soft bread," she said when it wasn't working quite as well as she'd like. Mrs. Cricket had already sent up coffee and baskets of bread and cheeses.

"You're washing the wall with bread?" George asked.

"It's softer than fabric and less likely to take all of the paint off."

"Damn the mural," Charlie said.

"I certainly will not."

Slowly, eventually, Meg revealed a line of green painted clumsily along the line of water. Charlie made a noise of excitement. "Just like you said!"

"And Pan is the Greek god of *panic*," Meg continued. "I'm annoyed at myself I never caught on before. Pendleton will be cross with me."

"I'd think he'd be proud seeing as you just foiled several treasure hunters and a madwoman," Dougal said, dry as toast.

"Not quite yet." Meg said. She touched Pan's eye gently and followed his imaginary line of sight. "Panic not, the treasure is in sight." It pointed to the green line and the bumpy plaster underneath. She still had no intention of bashing through such a large section of wall. There had to be another way in.

"Seven stars for your wrath." Three stars were part of the original mural, but she noticed then that their reflection cast four stars in the dark swath of blue water below. Four stars above, but only three below. See?"

All together they created a circle.

In the very center of that bumpy plaster.

Around a small rowboat, nothing like a pirate's ship. She should have known Lady Dahlia would not have been so obvious.

"X marks the spot," Dougal said softly.

"This has to be where the old duke damaged the wall while they argued."

"It has a certain poetic justice."

"I still hate to ruin this mural," Meg said even as excitement thrummed through her. "Even if Dahlia did such a poor job with the plaster."

"You'll fix it," he said. "We'll buy you an entire paint shop if we have to. And have Mr. Atkins in to supervise the plastering."

She tossed him a grateful smile as he reached for the iron fire poker.

"And you need to add poisonous flowers anyway," Charlie added.

"And a unicorn," George agreed. "With blood on his horn, naturally."

"Naturally."

Meg had never really understood what it was to have your heart feel like it might burst from joy. "And Lady Beatrice with her spear."

"Definitely," Dougal said before bringing the poker down in the circle of stars. Paint and plaster flew as the gauge became a proper opening. The ragged plaster gave way to dust and darkness.

"You found it," George said reverently. "A real historical treasure."

"Is that…." Meg lifted up a candle. "It *is*."

Dougal laughed as he gently pulled scrolls of parchment out of the hole. "Art. Your treasure is art, Your Grace."

Lord Pendleton hadn't just said that to secure her help. There really was priceless art hidden in the walls.

They unrolled the scrolls carefully, revealing late-medieval and early-Tudor illuminated letters, fanciful creatures, monks in robes, more gilded stars catching the light. There were pages and pages, along with old bibles inscribed with spider handwriting, journals, a compendium of sea monsters, Celtic knots decorating legends of the area. There were even old letters, one signed by Henry the Eighth himself. The blues were made with lapis lazuli, the rich greens with verdigris.

Meg was stunned, then disgruntled. "I'm going to have start my own museum collection."

"It looks that way."

"Pendleton will never let me live it down."

Dougal kissed the top of her head. "I still have a statue or two that he desperately wants," he murmured.

"Leverage," she sighed. "Good."

Colin poked his head into the room. He was cheerful and wind-tousled. "Have I missed dinner?" He noticed George's eye, the gaping hole in the wall, Dougal's grim hold on the poker. "Something else apparently."

"We found the treasure!" Charlie crowed.

"Really? Let's have a look—what happened to your neck?" He nearly shouted.

She shrugged. "A madwoman tried to strangle me."

Colin's face changed expression so quickly Meg wondered he didn't make himself dizzy. "*What?*"

"I'm fine now," she patted his arm. "Beatrice poked her with a spear."

"I think I need a drink."

"You already smell like a distillery."

"Well, I was told the country life of the landed gentry was a dull and tedious affair." He hugged his sister, keeping his arm protectively over her shoulders. She acted nonchalant but was clearly shaken up enough not to shove him away. "Apparently not." He glanced at the scrolls. "Not much gold."

"Thank God," Dougal muttered. "No one is likely to come steal it."

Meg wrinkled her nose. "Well…"

He groaned.

"Don't worry, we can put bars on that old medieval Lady Chapel no one uses and secure the collection inside. I've seen it done."

"I'm sure you have."

"Let's have supper in the family parlor," George suggested. "I'll let Lady Beatrice and Lady Marigold know."

As they dispersed, Dougal stayed where he was for a moment, close to Meg. "You did it," he said.

She grinned. "Did you doubt me?"

"Not for a moment."

He kissed her quickly, before she could be distracted by two-hundred-year-old art. She softened against him, and he tilted her head back, kissing her until her head was a whirl of colors and light that had nothing to do with laudanum. When he finally pulled away, it was only to drag more kisses up her throat to nip at her earlobe.

"We foiled a treasure hunter and a murderer on our first full day of being married," Dougal whispered, smiling. "What do you want to do tomorrow?"

Epilogue

Thorncroft Abbey

T HE ABBEY WAS filled with suitors.

Where debutantes had once roamed in their white dresses hunting for a duke, gentlemen now waited for Lady Charlotte Black, "Charlie" to those who earned the privilege. Three of the men in the main drawing room had been awarded such a privilege, four were hoping they might be next. There were others at the house party of course, mothers and fathers, Lady Blackwell who always wore a gown to match George's cravat—George had finally noticed—Persephone and Conall, Tamsin and Henry and Priya.

They could entertain themselves for a while longer.

Dougal had important ducal business to attend.

And anyone who said seducing one's wife was not important business would be asked to leave.

The wife in question might be one.

"Don't you dare," she said laughingly, meeting his eyes in her looking glass. "I know that look."

"I'm sure this is my most ducal expression."

"Exactly." Her thick dark hair was caught up in a simple braid coronet, the way she'd worn it when he'd first met her and wore it still. He had a fondness for it, even though it annoyed her lady's maid, Betty, who insisted on decorating it with pearl pins at every opportunity. Meg didn't mind and claimed one did not irritate one's lady's maid without severe repercussions. "We'll be late for supper."

"Canterbury will get them so drunk they won't notice." He paused, frowning. "How has my baby sister suddenly managed to fill the house with suitors?"

"I like Mr. Gracechurch."

"You like him because he donated a painting of Elizabeth the First to your collection."

She laughed. "True."

Her small art museum was beginning to garner attention, especially now that it was growing and secured behind iron bars and patrolled regularly. Alice Atkins had been charged and found guilty. She would have been hanged had Dougal not asked for transportation instead. Still, he did hope, even years later, that she was being stung by scorpions daily. Meg sent Mr. Atkins his medicines anonymously through the apothecary and had done so since the day after they found the treasure. It was just one of the many reasons he loved her.

"Betty just got me into these stays," Meg added, warningly when Dougal did not look concerned with tardiness or supper guests. "It took some effort I don't dare undo. I feel like a trussed goose."

"You look delicious," Dougal said. She had filled out once she was able to eat more than mint tea and turnips. He loved every new curve, all the softness of her.

"Betty has just gone to fetch my shoes. She'll be back any minute."

He reached back to flip the latch on the door behind him. He raised his eyebrow imperiously. A delicate shiver went through her, though she tried to hide it. "Dougal."

"Yes, love."

"We really shouldn't."

"I have to disagree." He stalked towards her, keeping her gaze in the mirror. He bent his head and kissed the top of her shoulder, her throat, finally capturing her mouth in a searing kiss. He stepped around to press her down onto the padded bench, still facing the mirror, before lowering to his knees in front of her.

The doorknob rattled. Meg stifled a giggle. There was a pause, and then retreating footsteps. "She'll know what we're doing!"

"She is unshockable," Dougal replied, tugging up the froth of her chemise skirts. "It's what I like best about her."

"But…"

He nipped at her inner thigh. "This is my favorite dimple of them all," he said, dragging his mouth towards her warm center. As hoped, it burned away Meg's half-hearted concerns. He pushed her legs open wider, suddenly, firmly. She gasped, head tilting back.

He licked at her once, twice, just enough to tease her.

There was a sound from downstairs, a shout of laughter, a clink of glasses. "Blasted suitors, already being a nuisance," he muttered.

"Don't worry, Your Grace," Meg said. "I'll find out everything we need to know about…oh, *there…* them."

He kept at his ministrations until her eyes had drifted closed and she moved against him helplessly. "How? Priya?"

"What?" She sounded dazed, muddled. Perfect.

He grinned.

She opened one eye. "You're terrible."

His fingers inched closer to her sex, stroking. "True."

"But if you hurry," she gasped. "I can still have all of their pockets picked by the time dessert is served."

"I wouldn't have it any other way." He licked at her again, deeply. "Now hush, I've ducal duties to perform."

About the Author

Alyxandra Harvey lives in an old stone house with her husband, multiple dogs, and a few resident ghosts who are allowed to stay as long as they keep company manners. She likes chai lattes, tattoos, and books. Sometimes fueled by literary rage.

Author of The Drake Chronicles, The Witches of London, Haunting Violet, Red, Love Me Love Me Not.

Twitter: AlyxandraH
Instagram: alyxandraharveyauthor